ENCORE

FAMOUS BOOK 4

EDEN FINLEY

ENCORE

CHAPTER 1
BLAKE

THE SMIRK on Jordan's lips makes me want to punch him in his goddamn beautiful face. Even across the bar, his gloating arrogance can be felt from here.

He texted me to meet him at this old-school, exclusive cigar lounge, and the minute I walk in, I feel out of place. I'm used to people staring at me—it comes with the territory of being famous —but this is different. Everyone's head turns like they're witnessing a nun walking into a porn convention. Or ... maybe the other way around. A porn convention walking into a ... convent?

It's a typical men's club, and everyone's dressed in suits.

Hey, my ripped jeans are designer—that's something, thank you very much, pretentious manly men who need men-only spaces to feel superior.

Jordan Brooks, though. He's dressed as casually as I am, but he's his relaxed, confident self. Like the environment needs to adapt to him, not the other way around. I haven't known him long, but I do know enough to acknowledge he's the complete opposite to me.

I quit music and became an actor because I like it when I can pretend to be someone else. He's an actor because, well, he loves attention.

From his insane six-four height to his deep brown hair with subtle highlights and his stubbled chin, he's undoubtedly one of the most objectively attractive men alive. His gray eyes shine in a way that's so ... Hollywood.

I sit in the plush leather seat opposite him at his low table. "Is there a reason we're meeting here and not at a club or somewhere less ..." I look around. "Uppity?"

"A gentleman's agreement should be done in a gentlemen's space." He opens his arms wide and smiles like the smartass he is.

"You're holding me to this stupid bet?"

"The bet where I told you your ex-bandmates were hooking up and you said I was crazy?"

Damn Mason and Denver for coming out on national TV last night.

"That would be the one. I actually found out a couple of weeks ago, but they gave me the impression they weren't going to come out anytime soon."

"And you weren't going to tell me?" Jordan pouts and looks ridiculous.

"Hey, I'm not going to out anyone. I might not know much about the queer community, but that's a big no-no, right?"

"Mmhmm, and I'm sure it had nothing to do with not wanting to do my movie."

Not at all. Ish.

"Are we sure this bet wasn't a hypothetical thing?" I ask. "You know, like saying 'I bet you ten million bucks that Marcus Talon won't win another Super Bowl.' Would you really make me pay you?"

"Yep. You'd deserve it for making that idiotic bet. Marcus Talon is the GOAT."

I cough in between saying, "Tom Brady."

"Should we make this bet, then? I could do with ten million

dollars. I would buy a puppy rescue and name all the puppies Blake. Blake One, Blake Two—"

"No bet. Especially when it turns out you're the type of guy who makes me pay up." Why did I make this stupid bet to begin with? Oh yeah, because I thought there was no way Denver and Mason were actually messing around considering we'd worked together for seven years, and I never once got that vibe from them.

"A bet's a bet," Jordan says. "Honor and bro-code and integrity are at stake."

"You said bro-code and integrity in the same sentence. I don't know how serious you can really be."

"I am *always* serious."

Bullllllshiiiiit.

"Why do you want me to do this movie so badly?" I ask. "I'm sure there are countless actors who could do the role—*gay* actors."

It's not that I'm against doing the role. I actually think it would be a great opportunity for me to break out from the action franchise I'm known for. It's going to be a big-budget romantic drama with two men as the leads. It has possible Oscar written all over it if they lean into the drama, though I've read the script and it feels too much like a rom-com to be considered.

Either way, it's a role I could play to break out of the typecast of action hero. Plus, I won't have to gain thirty pounds of muscle to play it. That would be a nice change.

I swear each time I wrap filming on a Coby Godspeed movie and I'm no longer rigorously working out six days a week, my muscles deflate faster than a helium balloon.

But another straight guy playing a gay character in a movie is bound to get backlash. Representation is important, and there are plenty of queer actors out there who could do the role.

"Ben won't hire another queer actor," Jordan says. "He wants a mainstream actor, someone who'll get butts in seats, and I want you. I think you have the talent to branch out from being shirtless and running after moving trains or jumping off exploding buildings."

All of which I've never actually done, thanks to stunt doubles. This is a chance to actually advance my acting career.

"What's the deal with you and Ben?" I ask.

Benjamin Randt is the director, and the entire reason I'm even up for this role is because I had a chance encounter with him and Jordan in a nightclub. That's how it works in Hollywood.

Jordan licks his lips. "We're … together." He winces.

"Mmm, sounds like true love," I say dryly.

"I'm still getting used to doing the committed thing. It's new for me."

"Because he doesn't share. That's what you said, right?" It was a passing comment Jordan made when we met—when he first tried to convince me to take on this role.

"He's a traditionalist like that. Until me, he'd never been with a guy, so he's very heteronormative in his ways."

"And you're not?"

"Fuck no." With how vehemently Jordan's against it, I get the feeling there's a story there and he might be protesting a little too hard.

"How's commitment working out for you?" I ask.

He cringes.

"That good?" I laugh.

"It's fine. Professionally, it makes sense. I think while we're making movies together, it's easier to be faithful than deal with the drama of jealousy and all that other bullshit."

"Sounds *so* romantic. I hope to find a relationship like yours one day."

"Romance is stupid."

"Says the rom-com actor."

Jordan leans back in his seat. "Okay, I'll admit romance can work when you find someone you could tolerate forever. I've seen that kind of connection. My best friend from back home and his husband are so sickeningly in love nothing could come between them. But in Hollywood? Forget it. Not possible. No way. It only took me a couple of years of living here to give up on even trying for it."

He can't be right about that, can he? I get it to a degree. I could never date a fan because I would constantly ask if they were with me for me or for my fame. The only way to find an equal in Hollywood is by being with another famous person, but to do that without conflicting schedules is next to impossible.

"You know I'm right," Jordan says.

"I may relent that it's hard to have something real in a world that's so fake."

"Wow. That's so philosophical."

"I've seen it happen, though." All my ex-bandmates are in solid relationships. With men.

By some chance, it turns out the other four guys from the once chart-topping boy band Eleven all have boyfriends, and until last night, they were all in the closet. Denver and Mason came out together while performing a duet on TV, but it's too early to tell if it was a smart decision career-wise. That's the downfall of Hollywood. To have any semblance of privacy, you need to be secretive, and when those secrets leak? There's a chance this industry could turn its back on you.

It's that easy.

It sucks, and I understand why Harley and Ryder still don't feel safe enough to step out and live their truth for everyone to see.

"You've seen it in Hollywood?" Jordan asks.

"Hey, I can name a ton of Hollywood couples who have been together for practically ever. Tom Hanks and Rita Wilson. Kevin Bacon and Kyra Sedgwick. Goldie Hawn and Kurt Russell."

"They're the exception to the rule. Hollywood relationships are lucky to last five years. Tops."

I flag down a server to order a drink. "Fine. You win. I don't even know why I'm fighting you on it when I don't exactly have firsthand proof. All my relationships for the past ten years have been ..."

"Shallow," he answers for me.

"Exactly." I'm not even sure you can call them relationships.

"You'll have to find someone on the set of our movie coming up. It helps when you have to spend time together."

"And if we have a fight and then have to still see each other every day?"

"Be professional." Jordan says this as if relationship drama is so easy to ignore.

"Do you really think you could be professional if you and Ben broke up?"

Drinks arrive, and Jordan holds his up for a toast. "That's why I said it's easier to do the monogamy thing with him while we're making movies together."

"It just sounds so ... cold and unromantic."

Jordan smiles.

"What?" I ask.

"You're perfect for this role because you're an actual romantic."

"I wouldn't go that far." How can I be a romantic when I've never experienced romance? Becoming famous at seventeen hasn't given me the opportunity to have a normal lifestyle.

"Come on, you know you want to," he taunts.

"My agent did say I should do it."

Jordan whips out a pen and scribbles something on a napkin.

"Do you carry a Sharpie around with you in case someone asks for an autograph?"

"What, you don't?"

"No." Though, thinking about it, it would make things easier. It just feels so conceited.

He slides the napkin over to me, and I huff a laugh.

"I, Blake Monroe, *solemly*—spelled incorrectly, by the way—swear I will do Jordan and Ben's gay as fuck movie. I feel like this might possibly not hold up in court?"

"Wanna kiss on it? That's legally binding."

"No, it—"

"It is when it's my lips. I'm really that good."

I sigh. "I walked right into that one, didn't I? Besides, I don't think Ben would be too pleased with that."

He holds out the pen for me. "You're right. So sign it."

"Fine." I do as he says.

Then he stands and clasps my shoulder. "I can't wait to have all the fake sex with you."

As he begins to walk off, I call after him, "Wait, there are sex scenes?"

He spins back around. "Didn't you read the whole script?"

"I skimmed!"

Jordan grins. "This is going to be so much fun."

CHAPTER 2
JORDAN

THE FIRST DAY of shooting is always the best. I'm like a kid on Christmas. I can't sleep the night before, and by the time daybreak rolls around, I'm like an excitable puppy.

"It's the first day," I sing at Ben.

He pushes me off him. "Go work out and get rid of all that excess energy. I know what you're like on a set when you don't."

"I could think of another way to wear me out …" I grind against him.

"Let me sleep. Unless you want me firing interns and production assistants all day, go away."

"Fine. The weights will do me good. I have to be nice and tight for the camera today."

Today's call sheet includes a scene where I'm half-naked for most of it. I'll be swimming and come out of the pool dripping wet, and it's supposed to be the first time Blake's character notices how hot I am.

Please, it's so unrealistic. Even straight men know how hot I am. I was a model before I was an actor. I have literally made all my money off my looks.

But I guess movies are all about the entertainment, right? Who needs realism?

Today is going to be fun.

Blake's been messaging me all week and asking for character inspiration because he's trying to get into Madden's head. I admire him for taking this role seriously, even if he's only doing it because he lost a stupid bet—a bet I totally would've let him get out of if he really wanted to, but I think deep down he knows this is a good career move for him.

I'm excited to work with him. He's been on my radar of actors I want to work with, and it has nothing to do with his acting skills. The man is hot. Blond hair, blue eyes, all-American boy. He didn't catch my eye so much when he was with the boy band Eleven, but his Coby Godspeed movies where he's being a shirtless badass …

Whew, is it hot in here? I haven't even started working out yet.

I hit the gym outside in Ben's pool house, and the plan is to work out until my excited bubble of energy has burst.

My assistant, Jojo, turns up before that happens. She enters with my morning coffee and a wide smile. "How long have you been at it this morning?"

I'm sweaty and breathless, but I still have too much excitement buzzing under my skin. I check the clock, and oops.

I lift my shirt to wipe sweat from my head. "A while." If two hours is a while. My muscles will probably cramp up later from being overworked. Either that or my adrenaline will carry me through the day, and then I won't be able to move or get up tomorrow.

"You've got fifteen minutes to shower and get dressed, or you'll be late for your first day," Jojo says. "Ben's already gone."

Okay, that's kind of annoying. He could've come to tell me. But at least if we go to the set separately, I can leave as soon as my scene is done.

Jojo hands me my coffee. "Drink that."

"Thanks." I sip it, and it's barely lukewarm. "How long have you been here?"

"Twenty minutes. I didn't realize I'd have to drag your ass out of the gym. You usually only last fifteen minutes on a good day."

"Are you attacking my stamina or my penchant for being lazy?"

"I said nothing about your stamina, Mr. Egotistical."

"Well, good. I won't have to prove it to you. You might be a woman, but I could picture Ryan Reynolds while I have sex with you."

She sighs because she's used to my shit and knows I'm one hundred percent gay and two hundred percent flirt. That makes me three hundred percent awesome.

"I'll pass. Thank you for the offer, though," she says sweetly.

"You're always so polite."

"I have to be to make up for all the times you say inappropriate things."

"Truth." I rush through my shower, and we get on the road, but from the minute I step on set, I know something's wrong.

Today's shoot is being filmed on location at a country club in LA, but where there should be lighting and camera equipment, almost nothing is set up.

There's someone crying in the corner, an intern I'm guessing, production assistants are avoiding eye contact with everyone, and then I find Ben pacing by his director's chair.

This is killing my first-day happy vibes.

I approach Ben and put my hands on his shoulders. "Hey."

He flinches.

"What's happening?" I ask.

"We're already an hour behind, the shot isn't set up, if we don't get it all together soon, the sun will disappear behind the building and the lighting will be all wrong, and—"

"Breathe." I take a deep breath and try to get him to mimic it.

He pulls out of my grasp. "Go hit wardrobe and makeup. We can't be even more late than we already are."

I don't bother arguing with him. The thing is, I've been with Ben for almost a year. He's a genius, and I admire his work, but he's the epitome of the stereotypical artist. Meaning, he's stubborn when he gets in his head, and there's no talking him down.

I stand back, let him have his rant, and then he'll get over it and pretend it never happened. An apology? I don't think he knows the meaning of the word.

"Oh, and Jordy?" Ben calls after me when I walk off.

I hate when he calls me Jordy, but that's a whole other thing. "Yeah?"

"Go check on your friend. The one you insisted I needed to cast. He's freaking out."

Aww, fuck.

Why can't anyone love the first day of filming as much as I do?

I hit wardrobe first because I already know what my outfit will consist of: me in a Speedo. That's it.

The scene today is Blake's character, Madden, meeting me for the first time after my meddling onscreen sister sets us up on a fake date. Madden's ex is getting married, and he needs a date to the wedding so he doesn't look as pathetic as the script tells him he is. It's like the gay version of *The Wedding Date* with Debra Messing and Dermot Mulroney. Just with less male prostitution.

I think Ben chose to shoot this scene first so he can play with our chemistry a bit. He originally wanted to shoot the first sex scene on the first day, but I told him doing that with a straight actor would only lead to scheduling problems when we ran overtime.

Turns out we didn't even need the love scene for that to happen.

I get in my Speedo, and they give me a robe to cover up in and slippers to wear around on set. When I get to the makeup trailer, they oil me up and then contour my abs so they look more defined on camera.

It's a rough life, but someone has to do it.

Jojo follows me like a shadow, fetching me water while I get makeup done, but when I head for Blake's trailer, I tell her to go take a break in mine.

I knock, movement sounds inside, and then a wide-eyed Blake, with his blond hair perfectly styled—and I don't mean Coby Godspeed styled where they slicked it back but teased and molded it into a high pompadour—and wearing a white button-down and chinos answers the door.

"I heard you were freaking out," I say.

"I'm not freaking out." His voice goes high-pitched. "You're freaking out. Why would I be freaking out?" Okay, now he's squeaking.

I won't admit it out loud and make him uncomfortable, but it's endearing and cute and somehow makes him hotter.

"What are you freaking out about?" I ask.

"I've never done a serious movie before. Half of my Coby Godspeed movies don't even make sense."

"If it makes you feel any better, Ben keeps playing with the script because he's not happy with it. Soon, this won't even be a serious movie. Did you hear the new title for it? *Faking It*. That's not an Oscar-winning title."

"That doesn't help. At all. I did this to get more exposure and depth and be taken seriously as an actor. I already don't get taken seriously as a musician, and with Eleven doing this reunion—"

"Whoa, Eleven is getting back together? When?"

"Shit. No one is supposed to know that. I didn't say anything, okay?" He mimes zipping his lip.

"Trust me. I'm not telling anyone."

"We're writing and recording while this film shoots, and we'll be touring afterward."

"What about acting?" I ask. Like I said, Blake has so much potential to be huge, so I don't understand why he'd go back to being a backup singer in a boy band.

"I'll still do that too. The Eleven thing is supposed to be for in between gigs. We're doing it more for fun than the money or fame."

"Doing something for … fun? And … no personal gain?" I speak in a robot voice. "Sorry. Does not compute."

"Haven't you had something you're passionate about and want to do for the sake of it? Bungee jumping? Reading? Watching old movies?"

"Sex? Does that count?"

"Uh … sure. Anyway, Eleven is like that for me. For all of us, I think. But now I've bitten off more than I can chew with this movie and the reunion, and I went from someone who would shoot back-to-back action movies with time off in between to someone who has multiple projects going on, a schedule, and, and, and—"

I step forward and rub my hands up and down his arms, consoling a second person before the day has even started. "Breathe. You've got this."

He sucks in a sharp inhale. "Yeah. I got this. I so got this."

"I'd believe you more if you weren't hyperventilating."

Blake takes one last deep breath to compose himself. "Are they ready out there?"

As he asks this, there's a knock on the door, and Jojo appears. "Set's done. Time to get this show on the road."

Blake looks like he's freaking out again.

"Breathe," I say again. "And squeeze my hand if you need it."

"You … want me to hold your hand?"

I shrug. "If anyone asks, tell them we're getting into character."

"Thank you."

"For what?" I ask.

"Trying to calm my nerves."

"Is it working?"

"Nope."

Damn.

We move to the set, and then makeup comes after me to run some more gel through my hair to give it a wet look and then spray my body with water so it looks like I just climbed out of the pool. They'll get that shot after we do the talking so I'm not all different levels of wet throughout the conversation.

Moviemaking has always fascinated me, the way scenes are chopped and shot at different times and glued together. Sometimes it feels impossible that the stories can even make sense when as the actor, you experience the scenes out of order. Watching it at the premiere for the first time is always a thrill.

When everyone's ready, Ben calls action, and I smile my character's cocky grin and say the cheesy dialogue.

"Well, well, well, what have you brought me, sis?"

Actress Lori Lacy says her line and pulls Blake forward. "This is Madden."

Blake, not Madden, looks like he's going to throw up. I can tell he's not in character.

"Madden," I say softly, softer than the script calls for, but I'm hoping to pull him into the scene.

Blake blinks at me.

"Cut," Ben says.

We all let out a collective breath.

"Blake, you're supposed to be awed by Jordan," Ben says. "Not scared of him."

"Uh. Right. Sorry."

"Go again."

We do it again. And again. And again, and again, and again.

"I give up. Take five." Ben storms off set.

My first-day happy vibes are gone now.

I lean in and ask Blake, "Does it usually take this long to settle into a scene?"

"No!" Blake yells, and everyone on set freezes at his raised tone. He lowers his head and says quieter, "And it's driving me crazy." He runs his hand over his face and then remembers the makeup. "I'm screwing the whole production."

"You're in your head. How do you usually get into Coby Godspeed's character?"

He looks around the set. "That's different. Coby is a walking meathead who's dumber than shit but can blow stuff up. It's easy to get in that mindset. Being a newly out gay guy who's nervous about going home to his family who haven't quite accepted his sexuality is …"

"A story many queer guys have faced. It's why Ben and I wanted to do this movie. We need good representation, and—"

"Which is why I didn't want to do the film to begin with because I know absolutely nothing about being gay or closeted or needing to come out."

"Your bandmates do, though. Can you draw inspiration from them?"

Denver Smith and Mason Nash recently came out, but I also happen to be on the inside Hollywood loop that they're not the only queer guys in Eleven. I'd bet my left nut that Blake has been there for behind-the-scenes conversations about staying closeted. I know he can draw from personal experience on this one, even if it's not his own.

"It will be a travesty to the gay gods everywhere if you and I don't have chemistry onscreen," I say. "We're too good-looking not to."

Blake allows a laugh, his shoulders relaxing a little, and the next take is almost perfect. After a few more, Ben is confident we have the shot.

"Let's move on." Ben levels me with his *I'm unhappy* look. "Finally."

I think I'll be staying at my place tonight.

"Blake, you're done for the day. Jordy, I still need shots of you getting out of the pool."

I swear Ben added this scene just so he could see me all wet and practically naked, and oh, look at that, with one take and one heated look from Ben, all is forgiven when he drags me to my trailer.

Best first day ever. Okay … well, best beginning and end to the first day ever. The middle kind of sucked.

Let's hope tomorrow is all smooth sailing.

CHAPTER 3
BLAKE

THE FIRST DAY of filming was shit. The second is not much better.

From only two days of working with Ben, I know he's one of those directors I was warned about when I came from the music biz to acting. He treats everyone like shit, he doesn't treat Jordan much better, and I have no idea what Jordan sees in him.

At one point, Ben threw up his hand and said, "I can't deal with this. I'm an artist!"

But … he's the director. He's in charge. So every time he tells me to stop looking constipated or scared, I do my hardest to please him. Because I have to. It's my job. I also don't want to burn my bridges with directors. That's how actors become unemployable.

Somehow, we manage to get through my scenes, and I'm sent on my merry way. I can't get out of there fast enough.

Then I remember I'm crashing with Denver and Mason because we're writing for the new Eleven album, and I can't be bothered tonight.

Yesterday, they were out late doing an interview—something they've been doing a lot of since coming out—so they weren't home when I got back and crashed out from pure mental exhaustion. Today won't be much different.

I go to my trailer and message my driver to come pick me up, and by the time I've had a quick shower and changed my clothes, he's outside waiting for me.

The drive to Malibu is long and silent, only giving me more time to dwell over how shitty my performance has been so far, and when I let myself into the house, I find Denver and Mason making out on the couch.

I try to sneak past them and not disturb them, but they pull apart when they hear me.

I wave my hand in the air. "Keep going. I'm just passing through."

"Wait," Denver says. "How is it? We didn't get to ask you yesterday."

I crash to the floor on my stomach. The answer calls for drama. "I hate you both. This is all your fault."

"That bad?" Mason asks.

"The worst."

"What's the problem?" Denver's scrunched brow in concern is all types of cute.

Denver's the youngest of us Eleven guys, and he has this baby face where he looks barely twenty. We all kind of see him as the innocent little-brother type. Ironic when he's the least innocent of us all with a drinking problem to boot.

"The director is a dick, and I suck."

"You sucked the director's dick?" Mason asks.

I flip him off. "My brain isn't gay enough."

Both of them burst out laughing.

Mason rubs his chin. "How exactly is one's brain gay?"

"Damn it, Mason. I'm being serious. I haven't lived as a gay or queer person, so it's hard for me to get into their mindset, and it really showed. The script says I turn into this lust-filled, tongue-tied adorable mess, but apparently my attempts to look like I'm attracted to a man came across as scared."

"Just to be clear, I'm not allowed to make a joke about you being scared of the D … right?"

I sigh at Mason. "Can you go back to being a depressed hermit?"

He only recently returned to Hollywood after disappearing for eighteen months. He was angry and bitter for a long time, and while I'm glad to see he's back to his old, sarcastic self, I really wish it wasn't at my expense.

"Okay, real talk," Mason says. "You're most likely over-thinking it, and mix that with first-week jitters … I'm sure it will get better soon."

I sit up. "How did you two handle being attracted to a man for the first time?"

They both look at each other and shift uncomfortably.

"That's a hard question to answer," Denver says. "I knew I had feelings for Mason for a long time, and when I acted on it … it, uh really didn't go well, and I don't think embarrassment is the kind of vibe you want your character to convey."

"I guess not."

"Maybe Ryder and Harley would be better at this kind of advice," Mason says. "My feelings for Denver were always there but not obvious, and it took being away from him to start to see him differently. We don't really have the experience to comment on instant attraction to a guy."

"Thanks anyway." I stand. "I'm going to bed early because tomorrow is another day."

"I promise it will be better," Mason says.

I go to bed, but while I lie there, I take out my phone and contemplate calling either Harley or Ryder. Then I realize it's late, Ryder has a kid, and he probably won't answer. Harley it is.

But as my finger hovers above his name, I realize I don't exactly know what to ask anyway.

How do you be gay?

I can already hear his sarcastic answer: You have sex with men.

I'll get right on that.

Fuck, I'm beginning to think that might be the answer. It's not like I hate or despise the male form. I've admired a guy's physical body or face from afar plenty of times—Jordan included in that. There's no denying he's an attractive man. I've just never had the desire to have sex with a guy. That doesn't mean I couldn't.

Ugh. I throw my phone beside me and crash out before I over-think this all over again.

Like Mason said, things will get better soon.

They don't.

From the moment I get on set the next day, it's as bad as the last two. It's a late start because the scenes we're shooting are at night, but it's well past nine before we get anything usable done, and even then, it's only snippets of the scene. It's not flowing.

Ben yells cut so many times it begins to sound like he's choking on his spit.

"He really hates me," I mutter to Jordan when a break is called. "Why did he even hire me for this role?"

Jordan averts his gaze, and a look of guilt flashes across his face.

"He didn't want me to do this movie, did he?"

Jordan's sympathetic eyes tell me everything I need to know. "Okay, so I might have convinced him to hire you. He wanted someone with more experience and diversity than an action hero, but I told him you were the right choice for what he wanted."

"Dude, you have way too much faith in me. This whole movie is doomed."

He grips my shoulders. "No, you've got this. We just need to …" His obvious struggle to come up with a solution says it all.

"Have a brain transplant?"

"Well, yeah, technically. You're acting, so you're not supposed to be yourself."

Frustration bubbles inside me. "I know that, but I think it's difficult because the only queer guys I've been around have been closeted for years. Or newly discovering."

"What about me?"

I scoff. "I have no idea what makes you tick. With this project, there's political aspects, doing the role *justice*, all the while trying not to offend a community that has so much negative shit thrown their way. It's too much to focus on and—"

"All right, I know your problem, and I have an idea." Jordan leaves and approaches Ben, who's yelling at a poor intern.

I want to yell at him to stop, but that will cause more of a scene.

When Jordan smiles at him, Ben instantly takes a deep breath, though his scowl doesn't leave his face.

I can't hear them from here, but Jordan jumps up and down and flails his arms animatedly, and a second later, he plants a kiss on Ben's cheek and comes back to me with a gleam in his eye.

"Come on. We're leaving."

"What? We didn't get the scenes done."

"And we won't unless you get out of your head and into someone else's, so let's go."

I follow him but can't help noticing how many of the staff and crew are watching as we walk off set.

"I feel like a kid cutting class," I whisper.

Jordan laughs. "Did you drive here?"

"Nah, I've got a car service."

"Give your guy the night off."

"Where are we going?"

"To get some insight."

"Hooray for vagueness being vague." But I'm willing to do anything to get this movie off the ground before I get fired, so I text my driver.

It's not too late for Ben to replace me, and while part of me hopes for that, I don't want to be known as the actor who got fired from my only serious role. That reputation follows you everywhere.

Jordan leads me to the lot, and the lights flash on … a Prius?

"This is your car?"

"The environment is important, Blake," he deadpans.

"I figured you for a Lambo or Porsche type."

"If I had my way, yeah, you're probably right. But my agent's PR person wants it to look like I care about things."

I snort. "When you don't?"

"I didn't say *that*."

Jordan Brooks is so hard to figure out. He's flirty and charismatic, but he doesn't give anything away about himself. Like, ever. Maybe he's been trained to be that way. The less he gives, the less there is to take out of context.

Ever since I've met him and we've hung out a couple of times, it's been fun but all very surface-level stuff. He doesn't exactly scream closed off, just not very deep. There's nothing wrong with that, but it might be contributing to why I can't bounce off him in scenes.

On the other hand, it's not really him I need to be connecting with—it's his *character*. If I were a good actor, I should be able to pull all that from the script, but I'm starting to think maybe my acting skills are one-note. I had criticism from playing Coby Godspeed—of course I did because opinions are like assholes: everyone has one—but the feedback was mostly positive, along with the box office numbers, so I assumed I must be a decent actor.

Apparently not.

"Are you going to tell me where we're going yet?" I ask.

Jordan doesn't answer me and drives from the studio toward Sunset. I assume he's taking me out to some hot new bar, but we've done that scene. I don't see why he'd think that would help us.

When he drives into a sketchy part of West Hollywood and pulls into a parking garage, I'm confused.

"Where we're going doesn't have valet?" I ask.

"Hell no. It's not that type of place at all."

"Are we going to get mugged?"

"You're so sheltered. It's adorable. We're not famous tonight."

"I don't know how that works for you, but for me, I can't go outside and not be recognized."

"Oh, you'll be recognized, but where I'm taking you, you'll always be treated like a human first, famous second."

"Where is this unicorn of a place?"

Jordan finds a parking space. "A gay bar."

Oh shit. My face must speak for me because Jordan doesn't miss a beat.

"You're thinking about needing to call your agent, aren't you? Are you worried about rumors of gay being contagious and you've caught it?" He's mocking me, but it's not that.

"I don't care what people think of me, but I'm picturing the headlines. With Eleven getting back together, I have to think how my actions affect the other guys."

"Are you forgetting you're playing a gay character in a movie? This is the epitome of research for your role. Tonight, when you walk through those doors, you're no longer Blake Monroe. You're Madden."

Right. I'm Madden.

I can do this.

CHAPTER 4
JORDAN

I PURPOSELY CHOSE the hole-in-the-wall bar called *Hole*, for a reason. It's old, it's run-down, but the drinks are cheap, the owners are an old married couple—the cutest old dudes in all of LA—and the clientele is the most diverse I've ever seen in this city.

There are the party guys who pregame at Hole before moving on to a twink bar later for half-naked, sweaty fun. There are the low-key regulars who meet up with their friends weekly. The bartenders are muscled, the servers are old-school campy drag queens, and the whole atmosphere of it is homey. There are Daddies, bears, twinks, lipstick lesbians, trans and non-binary people, and every other letter under the rainbow. From the stereo-types to complete opposites and everything in between, with one common theme among them all: acceptance.

Back in my modeling days, I'd come here whenever I wanted to feel like I belonged.

It's the only bar I can think of in the area where Blake can see the vast differences within the community. I think he's too in his head about playing a gay man *correctly* that he doesn't realize there is no incorrect way. All representation matters, and everyone's experiences are different. He should be playing Madden as *Madden*. Gay isn't all Madden is, and I'm hoping he'll see what I mean when we enter Hole.

As we step over the threshold, I watch for Blake's reaction.

He takes it all in but keeps a passive look on his attractive face. His square jaw is covered in the thinnest blond beard known to man, and it's so fucking sexy, but that thought makes me realize how bad an idea this might be. The guys here are going to try to eat him alive.

Eh, I'll protect him.

"Drink, *Madden*?" I ask.

He chuckles. "Sure, *Eamon*."

We walk past the small dance floor, where bodies of all shapes and sizes fill the space, and head straight to the bar where John, one of the owners, is serving. He sees me, and his face lights up.

"Superstar!"

"Ha ha, old man." I lean over the bar to give him a kiss on his cheek.

John and his husband welcomed me to this scene years ago. I'd come here after failed auditions, crappy shoots, and whenever I was feeling particularly down. They became the people who would put a smile back on my face, tell me not to give up, and encouraged me to keep going when I felt like quitting and sticking to modeling.

The model gigs were fine and paid well—at least I didn't have to shlep around as a waiter like most struggling actors—but acting has always been my dream. I went to an arts college back in Boston before moving out to LA.

"It's been too long since you've come to say hi," John says.

"I know, I know." Ben hates coming here, so I haven't been in far too long.

John's gaze catches on Blake. "Hey, you look like that guy in those action flicks."

I'm quickly learning Blake is recognized one of two ways—as

Blake Monroe, ex-boy band member, or Coby Godspeed, movie badass. And it's usually always the same demographic: women under thirty recognize him as Blake, and everyone else recognizes him as Coby.

Blake opens his mouth, but I cut him off.

"He gets that all the time. This is Madden."

Blake side-eyes me.

"What can I get you?" John asks.

"I'll grab a Coke. I'm driving." I look at Blake, who seems confused by the question. "What does *Madden* want?"

"I'll take a Macallan neat."

John gets to work preparing our drinks, and I nudge Blake.

"Liquid courage?"

"I was trying to think of what Madden would want, but I don't have a huge feel for him yet. So I went with what I wanted. Maybe we have the same tastes."

"I was half thinking you'd order a frou-frou cocktail."

"I've decided Madden shies away from stereotypes."

"Okay." I nod. "Fair enough. Though, you do know he can be stereotypical, right? There are gay men who are flamboyant, and there's nothing wrong with that."

"But when you think about representation in mainstream media, gay guys are always the flamboyant sidekick. Or the ones who aren't flamboyant, they have the tragic backstory. I read an article in *Variety* about there being a gap in the market for more diverse queer rep, so I'm trying to incorporate that."

I think we're getting to the root of his problem. "I know you're worried about not doing this role justice, but the fact you care so much means you're doing something right."

John returns with our drinks, while Blake looks contemplative.

"Do you think Madden is a dancing in a bar type?" I ask.

Blake lifts his whiskey. "After this, maybe."

I lead him to a back area with booths that are falling apart and where the music is quieter. This is where the regulars hang out.

There's a rowdy crowd of guys in their fifties and sixties in the far corner, and I push Blake down into an open booth at the front where we can still see the rest of the club. I take the same side as him and sit close. I figure we need to get used to being in each other's orbit for a while. If he can get used to casual touches and outward forms of affection from me, it will help.

He seems tense and throws his drink back, swallowing it all.

I wave over one of the drag queens to get a refill and then turn to him. "What made you want to get into acting after being in a successful boy band?"

"I thought I was supposed to be Madden?"

"Time-out on that. You've got this nervous energy pouring out of you like you do on set. So I'm trying to distract you. You said Eleven is getting back together, right?"

"We are. The others are busy writing for us while I do this movie."

"Okay, so again, why did you go into acting?"

He thinks about it longer than I thought he'd need, but I give him the time. It means he's not going to give me his rehearsed, approved PR answer.

When his new drink arrives, he sips it this time instead of guzzling it down. "When Eleven broke up, the other guys all had big plans. I had … nothing. I'm not as strong a singer as them. I started a solo album, and then one day this movie agent called me out of the blue, saying he wanted to sign me and get me some acting roles. I thought I'd do small roles here and there and see if I liked it when the studio for Coby Godspeed jumped at the chance at hiring me. And I was fucking good at it. A natural. It's why I thought this role, while challenging, would still come easy. I was wrong."

"Because you can't fathom what it's like to be queer?"

"No. Not at all. I can't relate to chasing bad guys down with guns, but there's less chance of offending people doing that than there is this."

"The pressure is getting to you. So drink up, relax, and who knows, you might even enjoy yourself. Who do you think would be Madden's type?"

He licks his sexy lips, and not for the first time since we started working together, I think about a time when those lips will be on mine. Sure, it'll be impersonal, and I'll be professional and won't slip him the tongue, but I can't wait to kiss Blake Monroe.

"According to the script, you're Madden's type."

"Does that mean you'll dance with me?"

Blake glances out at the dance floor and then back at me. "Not before I finish this." He throws back the rest of his second drink.

When Blake and I hit the dance floor, I pull him close. Our bodies meld together, a necessity in such a small space, but that tenseness about him is still there.

I lean in and say in his ear, "Come on, Madden. You're supposed to be attracted to me."

Blake's hands go to my waist, and when I'm a smartass and reach for them to move them down to my ass, he laughs.

We grind against each other to the beat, and he can probably feel my cock thicken in my jeans, but in my defense, I've been attracted to him ever since the first Coby movie came out. Teen heartthrob turned action movie star? I think he's every woman and gay man's wet dream.

Blake's confidence grows as the music goes on and the heat turns up. He relaxes in my arms, and this is the first time I've seen him embrace his role fully without overthinking. I pull back slightly to look at his face for any hint of hesitation but can't see any.

His cheeks are slightly flushed, his lips are parted, and his eyes are hooded. He's either really getting into this, or acting mode has kicked in.

I'd make a joke about my dick being that talented, but I don't want to scare him away.

Blake's gaze roams my face and then drops to my lips. Then he gets a wicked gleam in his blue eyes, and he turns, putting his ass to my front, and rubs all up on my cock.

I have to take a deep breath to calm myself, but when he crooks a finger to a random guy near us and sandwiches himself in between us, I'm taken by surprise.

He's *really* getting into this.

Mission accomplished?

CHAPTER 5
BLAKE

THIS IS ACTUALLY FUN.

When I'm not so in my head about how the public will perceive me, what it will do to my career, and worrying about offending every single one of my bandmates by misrepresenting them, I'm able to just feel and get into the head of my character.

It's freeing, almost, letting down my guard. The rumors can start about me, but like Jordan says, if I say it's for a movie role, people will believe me. That blanket of security helps me let go.

The guy in front of me works his hands all over my body, and I'm not self-conscious about it. Jordan's still behind me, his hands on my hips. I like the feel of hands on my body, but who wouldn't? I'm getting more out of this by not being Blake Monroe for five minutes.

On the outside, I might look like I have the perfect life, but like with every other member of Eleven, the media has skewed everything to the point where the real me isn't me anymore.

And when I scale everything back to "the real me," I'm … plain. Which is hard to comprehend with my lifestyle, but it's true.

I grew up with a stable mom and dad who supported me through everything. Fame was addictive, and I wanted it, but I never hit the same level of stardom as my bandmates. Even when Eleven's original label gave me the "quiet" persona, it was a little too close to home for comfort. I was always the one people forgot was in the band. "The other guy," as I got used to seeing in comments on social media—one of the reasons why I stopped looking and let a team of PR people pretend to be me.

Then I became Coby Godspeed. I'm more recognized for my acting now than Eleven, and I'm okay with that.

Jordan lowers his mouth to my ear. "You're *really* getting into this."

I lean back against his chest, moving my hips against the random guy in front of me. Turning my head, I say to Jordan, "*Madden* is getting into this."

The three of us dance and grind until my skin warms. I assume because of all the body heat radiating off both of them.

The rando in front of me moves his hands up to my shoulders. I widen my legs, and he moves his knee in between them. Apparently, my cock likes the feeling of warm bodies and intertwined limbs.

Jordan presses in behind me, the same hardness digging into my back.

My heart rate kicks up. I lick my lips because my mouth is dry, the movement catching the eye of the guy in front of me.

He watches as my tongue darts out, and he mirrors the movement before flicking his gaze up to meet mine. I can't tell if he has recognized me for who I am or not because his expression is filled with so much tension and lust it makes the room stifling.

He's a good-looking guy, shorter than my five-ten frame by a good few inches, but he's muscular, and between him and Jordan, I'm boxed in but in a secure way.

With Jordan's hot breath on my neck and this guy's intense stare, I can't help the arousal stirring in my gut. It's interesting and new, and as this guy moves his mouth closer to mine, my lips tingle in anticipation.

There's a clear moment where he pauses, just an inch away, as if he's asking permission or waiting for me to take this opportunity.

I can't think of a single reason not to. I press forward and touch my mouth to his. He weaves his hand into my hair while his tongue pushes past my lips. It's … different, but at the same time, it's not.

It doesn't last long, only enough to whet my appetite for more when he pulls away. His bright teeth blind me as he smiles, but his gaze focuses off to the side, and then his face falls.

"Damn," he says, or at least I think he does. He leans in to talk louder. "My friends are leaving. We're going to Cheap Trick a few blocks away. Come find me." He kisses me on the cheek and runs off to join his friends.

When I turn to Jordan, he's trying to contain his laughter.

He still has his arms around me. "Wow, when you go all in, you really go *all in*."

I suck on my lips, still tasting the other guy. "It was … interesting."

"It was hot."

I grind my hip against his erection. "Evidently."

Jordan pushes my hips away from him. "I'm definitely going to have to go home to Ben now to take care of that."

"Blake Monroe, giving people a reason to go have sex for over a decade." I mock salute him.

"You get enough research done? I'll drop you home on my way."

"Yeah, let's go."

Making out with a random guy kind of works, but I can't say it was some life-defining moment for me. It helped me find my groove, made me overthink less, and anytime I was unsure, I thought of that guy's mouth on mine.

For a solid two weeks of shooting, I'm not yelled at, Ben hasn't sighed the word "Cut" in a condescending manner, and coming to work has actually been fun.

But in between takes, I can tell something's up with Jordan. I admire his professionalism and envy how he can switch in and out of character in the blink of an eye.

Ever since our visit to the nightclub, though, he's been kind of distant. Hell, maybe I'm not doing better and he's just doing worse. Ben has snapped at him a couple of times, earning a scowl from Jordan, but they both get on with the job right after.

When a break is called to set up the next shot, one I haven't let myself think about until now, I corner Jordan near the craft services table.

"Hey."

He acknowledges me with a small nod.

"Are you okay?"

He smiles, but I can tell it's forced. "Are you? Ready to pucker up? Ooh, they have garlic-stuffed cheese balls. That'll make my breath nice and ripe for our next scene."

"You wouldn't ..."

"No, I wouldn't. Though I have heard of actors who do that. Like, what the fuck, man? Show your co-stars some respect."

Yep. We're at the first kissing and blowjob scene. And I'm terrified I'm going to screw it all up like I did the first few days on set. But right now, I think we have bigger problems.

"And you're sure you're okay?" I ask Jordan.

His gaze finds Ben. "Yeah, yeah. All good. Nothing to do with us."

"Nothing to do with you and Ben?"

Jordan shakes his head. "No, you and me. We're cool, right? I think we've hit our stride since we went out."

"Definitely. I'm much more comfortable in my skin ... or Madden's skin."

"That sounds a little psycho-killer."

I shove him. "I mean, you were right that I was letting the pressure get to me, and I don't know, I feel freer? If that makes sense." It probably doesn't. But being able to let my guard down with that guy in the club, it was thrilling to not care about the mundane stuff celebrities have to think about every day.

Image.

Persona.

Everyone's perceptions of us.

Jordan's distracted. He looks at Ben again, then steps forward into my space. "You know how I went straight to Ben's afterward? When I pulled up to his house, a production assistant was coming out the front door. I asked Ben about it, but he said the guy was dropping off a last-minute script change for approval."

I try not to wince because that does sound suspicious, but it could also be nothing. "Sounds legit. It seems every day they're messing with the lines and making me memorize more. My poor brain."

Jordan relents. "You're right. It makes sense. I just …"

"What's going on?"

"Well, he didn't feel like having sex. He blew me, but—uh, sorry, TMI. Ignore me. I'm being paranoid for no reason."

I can't say I've ever experienced what he's going through because all of my relationships have been temporary. Actually, you probably can't even call them relationships at all. I have no idea what it's like to not trust someone because I've never counted on anyone to pull through for me.

I do remember when Mason was cheated on by his first-ever girlfriend after we became famous, though. That wrecked him.

"He's the one who wanted exclusivity, right?" I point out. "That's what you said."

"Exactly. That's why it's stupid of me to think any different. I should stop reading into the distance he's putting between us since then too?"

"Umm, for the sake of the movie … maybe?"

"You're right. You're totally right. Okay, let's do this. Are you ready?"

"I'm ready. I think. Pretty sure."

Jordan cocks his head. "You're not overthinking again, are you?"

"I wasn't, but *now* I am."

"Bullshit. You've been thinking about kissing me *all* day. I can tell." There's the Jordan I've come to know. "Don't worry. Kissing me isn't just kissing. It's a life experience."

"Sure it is. Keep telling yourself that."

"My lips are like magic." Jordan's voice has a soft rasp to it. Tingles break out across my skin, and I think back to the club. Jordan pressed against me, the other guy's tongue in my mouth … I really should've asked for his name.

But if some random in a bar can turn my acting around, I can't help wondering what kissing Jordan could do for it.

"All the straight guys want to suck my dick after kissing me."

That's actually … pretty believable, even if it's conceited.

I look up into Jordan's eyes and swallow hard. "I have to say, if a straight guy would rather suck your dick than kiss you, I don't think your lips can be too magical."

Jordan throws back his head and laughs so hard he can barely catch his breath. "You're savage."

I bow. "I do what I can."

"I love it."

"We're ready," Ben barks across the set at us.

If I felt like I had any right to intervene in Jordan's life, I'd tell him to leave Ben because I've seen nothing but control coming from him, but that could also be that he's my boss, and the director, so I guess that's in his nature.

I keep my mouth shut, though. I don't want to be that friend— the one who thinks they know better. I just have to hope Ben's not a cheating asshole, not only for Jordan's sake, who I'm quickly coming to care about as a friend, but for the movie's sake as well.

Ben's the type of person that I've seen a million times in this industry. They're the ones who make a name for themselves and let it all go to their head.

Our management team for Eleven might have been totalitarian, but they never let fame get to our heads. Sure, Harley could sometimes be a diva, but we learned early that you don't become famous on your own. You need a team of people to help get you there, and if you treat them like shit, your time at the top will be short-lived.

It's a lesson I've always tried to remember. It's why I don't snap at assistants or make demands. I know never to become complacent in this industry.

"Today!" Ben yells.

If there's any consolation to this scene, it's that I get to kiss Jordan and watch Ben's reaction. Petty, maybe, but I *really* don't like him.

The set is arranged like a hotel room, with dim lighting beside a big queen bed.

I really wish the script called for Jordan to be getting the blowjob instead of me because I've never had to shoot a sex scene before. Not like this.

In my action movies, I get to kiss the girl at the end. One of them had me banging a chick in a bathroom, but we were both fully clothed for the scene. There were no close-ups. No shooting my fake O face.

Maybe I should've practiced in a mirror.

This is the last scene we have to shoot today, and I just want to get it done.

All I have to do is stumble into the "hotel room," let Jordan undo the buttons on my shirt, lean in, and kiss him. Get pushed down on the bed, run my hand through his hair while he moves down my body and out of shot, and then simulate the reaction to getting the best blowjob of my life. See. Easy.

I take a deep breath as we take our positions and wait for Ben to call action.

Jordan must find my nerves amusing because he won't stop

smiling at me. "You look so nervous you could puke. You're not going to, are you? I don't think I can kiss you if I'm standing six feet away so you don't vomit on me."

"Not at all."

"*Action.*"

Fuck.

The script calls for me to open the door, but Jordan must see the freak-out in my eyes because he opens the door for me and gives me a smug look that actually helps settle my nerves. Because I want to show him that kissing him doesn't affect me. I'm more worried about looking stupid on camera than anything else.

I grip the lapels of his jacket and push him inside the hotel room and kick the door behind me.

The whole set rattles with the slam of the door, and we both flinch.

"Cut!" Ben calls. "Run it again."

Great start, Blake. Good job.

This time we get as far as the bed, but Jordan steps on my toe when we try to press against each other.

I can feel the crew's frustration, but Jordan and I can't help laughing at ourselves.

"Can we be any more uncoordinated?" Jordan asks.

"I'm sure I could manage it."

Third time's a charm, though.

When Jordan's gray eyes meet mine while his hands unbutton my shirt and slip it off my shoulders, I prepare for his lips to meet mine. I try to find that free-flowing *go with it* attitude I had in the club, but it's not there.

And when he finally kisses me? It's awkward. So fucking awkward. Our lips are mashed together, I can feel everyone's eyes on us, and it's cold and impersonal.

"Cut!" Ben yells and stands, running his hands over his hair in frustration.

"Still straight?" Jordan quips.

"If it's possible, I think I'm *more* straight."

He holds his heart. "You wound me."

I chuckle.

We don't realize Ben's upon us until he's in our faces.

"I'm calling it a day. I'm done."

Here we go with the dramatic artist shit again.

"We'll get it shot," Jordan says. "It's fine."

"Maybe I should've gone with a queer actor. That was like watching two fish kiss."

"Aww, cute," Jordan says.

"That wasn't a compliment." Ben huffs. "Just … go home. Both of you. We'll reshoot tomorrow."

And I'm fucking this up again.

How long's left on the shooting schedule?

CHAPTER 6
JORDAN

I LIKE to think of myself as a pretty positive person. The life of a mid-list celebrity is cushy as fuck. But ever since seeing that production assistant leaving Ben's house, I've had a cloud of doubt hanging over me, and it's only made worse by Ben's excuses and anger toward the scenes Blake and I have been shooting.

Only, it's not Blake who's at fault this time. Yeah, the kiss yesterday was awkward, but it was our first take. Ben just gave up. Then he told me not to bother coming over to his place because he was, and I quote, "too busy regretting a casting choice."

Maybe I'm being paranoid, but I can't help thinking something else is going on, and this is exactly why I don't like relationships. All the mistrust and suspicion. Well, that, and because I always know how it's going to end—with them finding their happily ever after with someone else. It happens every damn time.

When I finally arrive on set the next day, late because of typical LA traffic, I'm expecting to get reamed about it, but it turns out I'm not the last one here. There's a flurry of talk and chatter among the crew, some hurried whispers and confused looks as I walk onto the set.

I find Blake in the clothes he was wearing for the scene yesterday, sitting on a folding chair behind the cameras and scrolling through his phone.

"Hey. Why is everyone being weird?" I ask.

His head shoots up, and his blue eyes fill with … relief? "Oh, thank God you're okay." He stands, and I'm suddenly engulfed in his arms. Which is weird. We're the kind of friends who give quick pats on the back—the straight-man hug as I like to call it. We're not *hold on for dear life* while we hug type friends.

"Am I missing something?"

Blake pulls back and gives me the once-over in an assessing way. "Oh." Then his eyes widen. "*Oh.* You don't know."

"Know *what*?"

"Uh, tabloid shit. You're dead. Apparently."

"I have a death rumor about me? That's so cool. That means I've really made it in Hollywood. Show me." I hold out my hand, but Blake refuses to hand over his phone.

"It's nothing. You don't need to see it."

My gaze narrows. "You're leaving something out." And if he's not going to tell me, then fine. I take out my phone. "I'll look it up mys—"

Benjamin Randt in Scandalous Car Crash.

"Scandalous? Car accident? Wait, wha? Is he okay?"

Blake groans. "Keep reading."

The article doesn't say much, but then I see it near the bottom.

Benjamin Randt and his passenger are being treated at Cedars-Sinai and are in critical condition, according to a source.

"Passenger?"

"We thought it was you because … well, you know …"

"I know what?"

He purses his lips. "What article are you reading? The one I saw on TMZ said witnesses told them the two in the car were, uh, in a *compromising* position."

"What?"

"Umm …" Blake's gaze darts around the place, and then he

steps forward to take my arm. "How about we go to the hospital? I'll take you."

I let him lead me, my mind caught somewhere between *Ben's in the hospital* and *compromising position*.

Blake's town car is outside the studio when we get there, and he shoves me in the back seat and climbs in after me.

My leg bounces, and he places a calming hand on my knee. "Hey, it's TMZ. What do they know? I'm sure this is all one big misunderstanding."

Except when it comes to tabloids, TMZ always seems to be closest to the truth.

Traffic to the hospital is a bitch, and I can't help thinking Ben's accident was the reason I was late to set today.

Blake's driver drops us off, where we're hit with a wall of paparazzi trying to get an update.

"Were you in the car, Jordan?"

"Are you okay?"

"If it wasn't you, who was Benjamin Randt with? Did you two break up?"

"Can you tell us anything?"

Blake wraps his arm around me and leads me inside.

We're recognized immediately by staff too, and hey, apparently celebrity status gets you some perks because they don't ask us if we're family or need permission to see Ben. They lead us straight back to his room.

Turns out the tabloids were wrong about the critical condition part, but the compromising position part? I get that answer when I pause at the threshold of his room.

It's a *shared* room.

Lying in a bed next to the window is Ben, but the first bed is taken up by none other than the production assistant I saw leaving Ben's house.

That gives me all the answers I need to know. I turn to leave.

"Jordy?" Ben croaks.

I spin back toward him and fold my arms.

The production assistant—I can't even remember his name—looks like he's scared I'm going to kill him. He wishes I cared that much about him. He's *nothing.*

"Are you going to explain?" I say when Ben doesn't immediately start groveling.

"I needed ... there was a problem with the script. Chad brought it over first thing, and we were—"

"Seen in a compromising position at the accident scene."

"I wasn't wearing my seat belt," *Chad* says. Of course his name is Chad. "I ... landed that way." He turns to Ben in a way that screams, *"Is that what I was supposed to say?"*

"Uh-huh. What way did you land exactly?"

Ben reaches his arms out toward me. "Please, come here. I can explain."

I indulge him, but for only one reason. When I reach his bed, Ben breaks out into a half-smile, like he's won, but then slowly, as I reach for his chart, he freezes.

"Something in here you don't want me to see?"

His gaze darts toward Chad and then back to me. "No, wait." Ben tries to sit up but then winces in pain and tries to curl into the fetal position before crying out more.

There's a whole bunch of stats I don't understand on the chart, but I do understand one thing.

"Oh, I see. Chad here wasn't wearing his seat belt, and when you crashed, his teeth ended up on your dick. Got it. Man, I hate when that happens."

A loud snort comes from the entryway, and when I look, Blake's trying to keep a straight face. In his defense, this whole situation is absurd. He mouths, "Sorry," to me.

I put Ben's chart back and then level him with a look. "You wanted exclusivity. *You.* Not me." Because I knew, deep down, Ben would never be mine. No one ever is.

"It's not that," Ben pleads. He's sweating now, but I don't know if it's from the pain in his dick or because he's about to lose me.

"So you're not sleeping together?"

"We are, but it means nothing."

"Give me *clichés cheating assholes say* for five hundred, Alex!"

"It's … you know … I haven't been with another man before. I feel like … like I need to …"

"Screw every man who'll let you before you can settle down? You know who would have been on board with that plan? *Me.* You've known from the beginning I'm an open-relationship kind of person, but you know what open relationships have? Trust."

"I didn't … I don't …"

I can practically hear the words he isn't saying. "You don't want me to be with anyone else, but you can't pay me the same respect. Well now, you can both go fuck yourselves. Or each other. I don't care. Let Jojo know when you're home so she can go pick up all my shit from your house. This is done."

"Jordy, wait," Ben calls after me, but I'm already gone with Blake hot on my heels.

"I'm sorry," Blake murmurs.

"I'm not." I have too much anger inside me to be sorry. Anger, disappointment, shame … it's all there. Only it's not directed at Ben. It's all on me. Because I'm suddenly twenty-two years old again, new to LA, with fame in my eyes and naivety in my heart.

I promised I wouldn't let myself get involved with someone again, that I wouldn't get invested in another relationship, and while I thought I was doing a good job of keeping Ben at arm's length, somewhere along the way, I started to care.

I thought I'd found someone who wanted me and only me. Even if I thought we had an expiration date, Ben asking for exclusivity gave me a false sense of security.

And I fell for it.

"Where are we going?" Blake asks.

"To get really, really, really, really, really, *really* drunk."

"Want to throw another *really* on there?"

"*Really.*"

Blake takes out his phone and starts tapping away. "My driver is at our service."

"More drinks!" I demand and raise my hand with my empty glass in it. Or … not so empty. Liquid splashes everywhere.

"Maybe ease up?" Blake asks and pulls my hand back down. "I probably should've suggested we do something healthier than your idea of day drinking."

"It's not like we have anywhere to be," I slur and then laugh. "Our director was getting road head and crashed his car." Okay, now that I have some liquor in me, that's hilarious.

"What do you think will happen to the movie?"

"New director would be cool, but it wouldn't surprise me if the studio halts production until he's back. Or ditch the whole production altogether."

"I'm sorry Ben's an asshole."

I shrug. "Me too. He's always kind of been that way, but this is … this is beyond assholism. This is … twat levels of twatterism."

Blake leans back in his seat. We're in a practically empty bar because it's the middle of the day, and I really hope no one tips off the paparazzi. They're going to be trying to hunt me down. We managed to escape the hospital without them noticing by using a different exit.

"Can I ask you something?" Blake licks his lips.

"Sure."

"Don't get me wrong, Ben is an asshole, but you said yourself you don't like monogamy, so, wouldn't this technically solve that problem?"

Yeah, there's a reason I don't like monogamy, but I don't want to get into it with him. Besides, it's not the point.

I lean forward, resting my elbows on the table in front of me.

"You heard him back at the hospital. He wants to sleep with other people, but he doesn't want me to. That's not how this works. There has to be open communication about it, and it has to be on an equal playing field. If he'd told me he wanted to go have sex with other guys, I would've encouraged it. I don't want to hold anyone back from discovering all aspects of their sexuality. But open relationships only work when there's trust, honesty, and compromise. Telling me to be monogamous while he isn't? Fuck that."

Blake sips his drink. "Fair enough. I understand."

"It takes a lot for me to trust someone, and ..." I sigh. "I really fucking trusted him. I don't care that it's over—I knew he wasn't my forever person ... No, wait, I don't *have* a forever person—but I'm pissed about the betrayal of trust."

Blake reaches across the table and covers my hand with his. "You're allowed to be angry."

It's a sweet, friendly gesture, and my heart warms. My mouth opens to say thank you, but a flash of commotion from the window of the bar catches my attention.

They found us.

"Oh shit." I pull away from Blake.

"What?" He turns, and his face pales. "Let's get out of here." He throws a wad of bills on the table and stands.

I stand too but wobble. Maybe Blake was right about taking it easier.

"We can't go out the front without photos being taken," he says.

A server rushes over to us. "I can let you out the back."

He follows her, and I watch them leave, and it takes longer than usual for me to register I'm supposed to go with them. Drunk reflexes are sloooow. Blake comes back and grabs my hand, dragging me with him.

"Where's a good spot I can ask my driver to pick us up?" Blake asks the waitress.

"If you go through the other side of the alley, you'll be on Bleaker. He can pick you up there."

"Thank you." He smiles at her, and she blushes.

"I'm a huge fan," she yells after us.

"Man, you must get soooo much pussy. All you have to do is flash your smile, those baby blues …"

He's texting and not paying attention to me. His driver must be nearby, because he pulls up in front of us not long later, and we jump in the car just in time for the paps to find us, but we're speeding off before they can get another shot.

"Where's your place?" Blake asks.

"They know where I live. When Ben and I went public, they camped out outside both our places for weeks."

"Take us back to Malibu," Blake says to the driver. "You can come hide out at Denver and Mason's."

"Didn't they only recently come out? How are they not bombarded every day?"

"They were for a bit, but then they went to Montana for a while. I don't know if the media has given up on trying to catch a glimpse of them or if they're unaware they're back in LA, but hey, if you're hiding out there, you'll have a distraction to throw at the paparazzi if they turn up."

"Aww, you'd throw your friends in front of a pack of wolves for me? I think this is love. Is this what real love is like?"

Blake throws his head back and laughs.

Hmm, maybe not, then.

CHAPTER 7
BLAKE

MY DRIVER DROPS us off outside Denver's home in Malibu, and Jordan stumbles his way toward the door.

I grip his shoulder. "Dude, you have to pretend to be fine. Denver's doing this whole sober living thing, and the rest of us promised to not drink in front of him."

"Wait … when did I promise that?"

"Not you and me—the rest of Eleven."

Jordan chuckles. "You were in a boy band."

"Am. I *am* in a boy band."

He throws his arm around my shoulder. "Nah. You're too …" He rubs his hand over the blond scruff on my chin. "Man-like to be in a boy band. You're in a man band!"

"Jesus H. Christ, Mason's gonna kill me. Let's try to sneak through the house and get you out to the guesthouse where you can sleep it off."

"It's not bedtime. The sun is still out."

"Do you always act like a child when you're drunk?"

"Always."

"Note to self, don't go drinking with Jordan ever again."

His phone starts ringing, and he goes to take it out of his pocket, but I stop him.

"You can't talk to anyone in your condition. Especially if it's someone from the media."

He pulls out of my grip and takes his phone out of his pocket. "It's not. It's my friends! Guess what?" Jordan yells. He has stopped now, halfway between the street and Denver's front door, holding his phone out in front of him, like he's on a video call.

"Are you okay?" the voice asks.

"I'm staying with a man band."

"Are … are you drunk?"

I lean in so the guy on the phone can see me. "Yes, he is."

Jordan's friend has dark hair over his forehead and has tattoos up the wazoo.

"Is that …" The guy squints.

"Man band." Jordan nods.

"Holy shit!"

Jordan winces. "Not so loud, Ash."

"Babe, babe … *Max*, get in here." Another guy appears on the screen. He's about three times Ash's size and also covered in tats. "It's Blake Monroe," Ash says.

I give them a wave. "I need to get Jordan inside, but I'm finding out he distracts easily when he's drunk. Do either of you know how to handle him?"

They look at each other and share a weird look I can't decipher.

"Uh, promise him sex?" Ash says.

Jordan's head darts around. "Sex? Where?"

Ash's partner mutters, "So predictable."

I try it anyway. "Umm, there's sex inside."

"Where? With who?" Hey, at least his feet are moving now.

"Thank you," I say to the two on the phone and then guide Jordan inside.

"We, uh, saw the news," Ash says.

I look around each corner to make sure Denver and Mason aren't around and try to sneak through to the back door that leads to the guesthouse.

"Ben's an ass," Jordan says solemnly. "I wish that dude bit his dick right off."

We don't make it far inside when Denver's voice comes from behind us. "What dude?"

We both freeze.

Please, for the love of everything wrong with this world, I need Jordan to act sober.

"Hey, Denver." I smile wide. "Umm, you know Jordan Brooks. I mean, of course you do. We all met in that club at the same time. This is … Jordan. Umm, yeah. I already said that."

"Is that Denver Smith?" Ash screeches from the phone.

"Who knew you were such a boy band fan," Max says.

"Man band," Jordan corrects in a very serious manner.

I ignore them. "Jordan needs a place to hide out from the paparazzi. He and Benjamin Randt just had a very public breakup."

"It included road head and a car crash." Jordan smashes his hands together and makes an explosion sound, but he's still holding his phone, so that goes flying to the floor.

I pick it up. "I might get him to call you guys back when he's sober."

Ash looks more concerned. "Look after him for us."

"Will do." I end their call, and Jordan is none the wiser. I think he forgot he was even talking to them.

"Sorry," I say to Denver. "I was trying to sneak him through unnoticed."

"It's totally fine. He can stay here as long as he needs to."

"I meant, I wouldn't have brought him here, like …" I gesture to Jordan. "This."

"Just because I'm not allowed to drink, that doesn't mean other people aren't. I'm cool with it." He says that, but he seems so blasé about the whole alcoholic thing that maybe I don't understand it completely. "Seriously," Denver says. "Drinking is a crutch for me when something bad is happening in my life, and I couldn't be happier."

Mason walks in at precisely the right moment to hear that and wraps his arms around Denver and kisses the top of his head.

It's funny to me that we all worked together for seven years when nothing was going on between them, but seeing them as a couple is the most natural thing in the world. It's as if they were this affectionate the whole time. It was weird seeing it at first, but now I can barely remember a time they weren't this close.

"Does that mean I don't have to hide from them?" Jordan whispers. Loudly.

Denver laughs. "Take a seat. Mason and I were about to have a writing sesh, but you're more than welcome to make yourself at home."

Jordan doesn't hesitate to throw himself on the couch. "Mmm, this is comfy."

"Need a hand with writing?" I ask, but I don't really know how much I can contribute. I'm not really the songwriting star out of us. Or the best singer.

I'm the least talented out of all of the Eleven guys, the one grasping on to fame any way he can. I've been lucky in that my career was able to successfully go another direction, but being back with these guys, I've definitely missed it. Jamming with them and hanging out gives me a constant hit of nostalgia that's all happy and warm.

"You can join us if you want. Or look after Jordan. It's up to you," Denver says.

Jordan's phone in my hand rings, and his assistant's name appears on the screen.

I hold it up. "Looks like I'm choosing the Jordan thing." By default. Because he's sleeping it off on the couch. It didn't take him long to pass out.

I turn my back on them and answer the phone. "Hey, Jojo, it's Blake. Jordan, uh, gave me his phone."

Her voice comes on the line. "He usually does that to me. Where are you guys?"

"Hiding at a friend's place." I don't mean to be vague or

untrusting, but being in this business for ten years, I learned the fewer people who know where you are, the less chance of a leak to a tabloid.

"The studio sent through an official announcement about the movie being put on hold. Did your agent call you?"

I run a hand through my hair. "I haven't even had a chance to look at my phone. I've been ... busy."

"Talk to your agent, but I think you've probably got the right idea. Jordan's has already called a billion times asking where he is."

"Right idea?"

"You both have a few weeks where you can hide from the spotlight until your cheating scandal is over."

"Don't you mean Ben's cheating scandal?"

"Uh, no. The photo of you and Jordan holding hands while his director boyfriend is in the hospital has rumors running rampant."

This is bad. Ben can spin the narrative and be seen as the sympathetic one.

"He cheated first," I say.

The argument that Jordan and I aren't even remotely together won't fly. The public won't believe the denial anyway. A picture is worth a thousand words. That's what we were told constantly by PR people when we hit it big. They were lenient on what we did, consumed, who we had sex with, so long as we never forgot the golden rule: don't get photographed.

"How's Jordan holding up? I never liked Ben, but it's not like I could say that to my boss."

"He's ... I don't know. How does he usually handle stress? He's passed out in the middle of the afternoon."

"That poor guy doesn't know the meaning of stress, so I'd say he's on par with expectations."

"That's something at least. I'm going to go and call my agent. Thanks for the heads-up."

"Tell Jordan to call his too so he'll stop hounding me."

"I'll get him to call as soon as he's not slurring his words."

And he's awake. "I'm not slurrying the worlds." His mumbled protest is weak.

"Good luck," Jojo sings at me.

"Thanks." I'm going to need it.

I end the call and turn back around, surprised to find Denver and Mason still there. They stare at me in that brotherly way. We always had each other's backs, but when we split, we all broke off in different directions, and I'd be lying if I said I didn't feel weird in their orbit again. It's good to be back, but weird … definitely weird. It's like no time has passed.

"What's going on?" Mason asks.

"Movie's been put on hold until Ben gets better. And …" I frown. "I think I was just outed?"

In unison, their eyebrows shoot up.

"I'm not," I protest. "In the closet, I mean. I'm not even …" I take a deep breath. "Rewind, let's start that over. Jordan and I were photographed today holding hands. The media is already running with the narrative that Ben wasn't the one who cheated, Jordan was. With me."

And even though the story is complete bullshit, that doesn't matter. This type of thing is only one of the reasons why Harley and Ryder are still closeted. Because when a secret is leaked, there's no controlling which way it will land. You can try, but once it's out there, it's unstoppable.

"Damn," Denver says. "That's a mess."

"What do I do?"

They look at each other, and it's as if I can read their minds. Who could help me in a PR crisis better than someone who has spun so many PR stories to go in his favor so his sexuality has remained a secret for an entire decade?

"I'll call Harley."

"LET ME GET THIS STRAIGHT," I say as Blake and I board a chartered plane. I'm a little hungover and a lot confused. "You tell Harley Valentine I'm having guy trouble, need a place to hide out, and that our movie has been put on hold, and his first reaction is to say 'Chuck him on a plane and we'll have a band writing retreat while we're at it'?"

"That's Harley for you. A great friend but a workaholic all the same. Seize the moment! Take every chance we get at pulling together what he's calling our Encore tour." Blake shoves a duffle bag in an overhead compartment, while I throw myself on the large leather recliner and do up my seat belt.

"Then tell me something. Why's it just you and me on the plane?"

"You mean apart from there being no room because of the billions of bags you brought? How long do you expect us to be gone?"

I might have overpacked. "I have no idea. That's why I wanted to be prepared."

"I'm giving you shit. The real answer to your question is not too long ago, the paparazzi found Mason's cabin in Montana—"

"Ooh, is this going to be a *Cabin in the Woods* type situation?

Are we all going to be in this run-down shack trying to avoid being killed?"

Blake scoffs. "Sure. Run-down shack. Uh-huh. Anyway, the others are meeting us there because all five members of Eleven in one place always brings out the reunion rumors, and we're not ready to announce anything yet. We're all taking turns in getting there to try not to arouse suspicion."

"This is like boy band ninja stuff. I like it."

"Don't you mean man band?" Blake taunts.

A flitter of an embarrassing memory tries to play back through my head. "I said that?"

"Numerous times."

"And you guys still want me around?"

"Montana's the perfect place for you right now. Mason's house is in the middle of nowhere, and it's like a winter wonderland this time of year. You can chill by the fire, stay in your room, mope, sulk ... do all the depressing things heartbroken people do."

I grunt. "Any gay bars in Montana? I need a rebound."

"You'll have to ask Mason, though I'm not sure he'd even know."

"Are Mason and Denver open?"

"I'd think you're shit outta luck, but if you want to try, that's something I'm willing to watch. Secondhand embarrassment is always fun."

"For the people it's not happening to!"

"Exactly."

"Why are we friends again?" I ask.

"Because you met me and made a stupid bet. Make stupid bets, gain stupid friends ... wait."

"I know you're trying to cheer me up, and I appreciate it, but it's not working."

Apparently, my breakup with Ben will take longer than twenty-four hours to get over. What the fuck is up with that?

I can't believe I went and got attached. To a dickhead of all people.

"You okay?" Blake asks.

I force the easygoing nature I'm known for. "Hungover."

"Try to sleep. It's a few hours before we get there."

I manage to get some sleep but not much, and as the plane lands, Blake throws me my thick jacket and stares intently.

"What?" I ask.

"Okay, this goes without saying, but whatever happens, whatever you see here, no matter what is said or done, it all stays here. Got it?"

"Are you about to tell me Eleven are secretly into orgies and I'm about to be inducted into your boy band of—" I push down my growing erection. "Okay, I can't even joke about that without getting too excited."

Blake stands and slaps my shoulder. "Get your head out of the gutter. What I'm saying is, I know you're already aware of Harley's closeted situation, and you have suspicions about Ryder, and you think they're together—"

"Cone of silence. Whatever I find out on this trip will stay between you and me."

He leads me off the plane without saying another word. I was kind of hoping for some confirmation of the popular belief that Harley and Ryder are in *loooove*.

It's a small airport, so small that when we hit the tarmac, there's an Escalade waiting for us right there.

We climb right in while the crew loads up our bags in the back, and I turn to Blake.

"Are you saying that Harley and Ryder are actually a couple?"

Our driver, a big tank of a man, starts coughing.

"You okay there, Brix?" Blake asks. "Sounds like you're choking on something that might resemble jealousy."

My gaze flicks between Blake and … *Brix*.

"Harley and Ryder are not together," Brix grumbles.

"Oh." Realization hits me. "*Oh*. Harley and his driver?"

Brix grumbles something again, but I can't make it out, and Blake laughs.

"Brix here is head of Harley's security team." He leans forward and asks Brix, "Where is Harley?"

"At the house with Denver and Mason. Ryder and Lyric will be here in a few hours."

"Lyric …" I say. "Wait, Lyric Jones? He and Ryder?"

Blake eyes me. "See what I mean by you'll learn things you need to shut up about?"

"I promise."

"Good," Brix says. "Because I wouldn't want to force someone to sign an NDA."

I swear his biceps flex.

I shift closer to Blake. "Just to clarify, that was a death threat, right?" In the rearview mirror, I see Brix's lips twitch. "I'm definitely getting *Cabin in the Woods* vibes."

That feeling doesn't last long.

When we pull up to a ski chalet type mansion, I realize I could really get used to Eleven's way of roughing it. "Yes, yes, yes. This is definitely my idea of hiding out. Are there butlers in thongs and little bow ties?"

"I'll tell Mason to get right on that," Blake deadpans.

We climb out of the car and are hit with mountain air. It was cold back at the airport but not *holy shit, my balls now live inside my body* cold.

We both hiss and grab our bags, while Brix leads us to the massive wooden front doors.

The mansion is dark wood and stone and has that warm feeling of home, even if it's large and intimidating.

Inside, Harley Valentine, Mason, and Denver are in an informal living area with papers sprawled everywhere. Mason's strumming a guitar lazily, while Denver's and Harley's heads are hunched over the coffee table.

"You all know Jordan Brooks," Blake says. "Or at least of him."

They all wave but barely lift their heads.

"Wow. They can't contain their excitement," I say.

"They usually have more manners than this, but they're in work mode."

Brix walks up behind Harley and kisses the back of his head, and only then does Harley lift his gaze. Harley welcomes his boyfriend with a soft kiss, and my chest twinges.

"Rooms?" Blake asks.

Mason puts down his guitar and stands. "I put you two in rooms next to each other. You have to share a bathroom, though. Is that okay?"

"No, this is not acceptable at all." I cross my arms. "You put me up for free, you help me hide away, and you only give me a single bedroom and a shared bathroom? What is this? The seventh circle of hell?"

Mason's deep brown eyes look at me like they're trying to assess my tone.

"Uh, I guess I should hold up a sarcasm sign? I swear I'm not one of *those* Hollywood types. I still live in a one-bedroom apartment. It's a nice apartment, but it's not ..." I wave my hand around. "Anything like this."

Mason smiles. "Follow me. Oh, and as per Harley's rules, no cell phones allowed, so you need to leave them in your rooms."

That's fine with me. My manager told me to turn mine off and only check in once a day with him.

Mason shows us to two bedrooms upstairs, and after Blake and I dump our bags and get settled in our rooms, Blake knocks on my door.

"You ready to go back down there?"

"Will you hate me if I chill up here for a bit? You guys are busy, and I don't want to be in anyone's way."

"You won't be in our way, but it's up to you."

I nod toward the wide window that overlooks a valley covered in white snow everywhere. "Have you seen this view? You might not see me for weeks."

"Come down whenever. The guys are all welcoming."

"The last time Denver and Mason saw me, I was a drunken mess—"

"If anyone understands drunken messes, it's Denver. You'll be fine."

"Okay. I'll, uh, come down soon." As soon as I can shake this melancholy.

It turns out my stomach is more impatient than my somber mood, and I drag my feet to look for food a couple of hours later. I've literally been staring out the window and doing nothing but dwelling over the scene at the hospital and the media fallout that followed.

I might have broken the rules and scrolled through some articles about Ben and me. And now, because of one insanely perfectly timed photo of Blake and me in that bar, this scandal is being turned back onto me, and it's dragging Blake into my mess.

Sex, lies, and infidelity. LA is in a frenzy, and not in a good way.

This is Kristen Stewart cheating on R Patz with her married director levels of scandal.

When I get downstairs, Harley's partner is MIA, but the others are still huddled around the coffee table. Blake lifts his head when I arrive, and just seeing him makes me feel not so alone.

This is my first real taste of drama as a famous person. I can't claim to be anywhere near as famous as anyone in this room, but it all feels like I've majorly screwed up with this Ben situation, and it's quickly piling on top of me.

Still, I smile my way through it all. Because I have to.

"Hungry?" Blake asks.

"Starving. How did you know?"

Harley doesn't look up as he says, "Blake got to hangry status about half an hour ago. Pizza is on its way."

"Pizza," I say. "Getting delivered? Do we have to hide when it turns up?"

"My mom is picking it up," Mason says. "She's a godsend when we stay here. If you need anything, just ask, and I'll send her to go get it."

I'm not really comfortable ordering around Mason's mom, and he must read my mind because he clarifies, "She's been dealing with the ugly side of fame for ten years. When we're home, she's like this protective momma bear and will do anything to keep us out of the media."

"She's amazing," Denver adds.

"All right then." I take a seat on the couch, but no sooner have I sat down Brix, Ryder Kennedy, and Lyric Jones walk through the front door.

It's obvious right away that something is wrong.

Ryder looks pale, and Lyric practically has to guide him over to us and plop him in the armchair nearby.

"What's wrong?" Harley asks.

Lyric frowns. "You guys don't know? Check your phones."

"We don't have our phones," Harley says.

I didn't see anything when I was masochistically checking out my own tabloid drama, but I also wasn't actively looking at other stories. I recall maybe seeing Ryder's face in one but didn't read the headline.

Brix takes the remote from the coffee table and turns on the TV. "News this big is gonna be all over the place."

Intrigue.

And there, on *Entertainment Tonight*, is paparazzi footage of Ryder being asked how he feels about yet another member of Eleven coming out. At first, I think they're talking about Harley, but then they show the photo I've been staring at for the last few hours, and I realize they mean Blake.

In the video, Ryder gets this irritated look on his face, right before saying, "Sexual identity needs to stop being made into an explosive issue. What do I think about Blake 'coming out'?" He uses air quotes and all. "He was supportive when I told him I'm dating Lyric Jones, so I have nothing but support for him in return." He doesn't even give the reporters time to respond before he gets in the back of a chauffeured car and it drives away.

Everyone in the room blinks rapidly with their mouths hanging open.

"Y-you came out," Harley says.

Ryder remains in his seat, staring at the screen, but it's like he's not really there. "I-it wasn't … that wasn't supposed to happen like that."

Lyric sits on the armrest of Ryder's chair and wraps his arm around Ryder's shoulder. "I'm proud of you no matter how it came out."

Ryder's bright blue eyes meet Lyric's. "I know we talked about it, but it was going to be properly. You deserve better than—"

Lyric leans in and kisses Ryder's lips softly to shut him up. "I don't care how it happened, just that it did."

Ryder still looks freaked-out.

"Where did this happen?" Harley asks.

"On our way to LAX," Lyric says. "Ryder's kind of been comatose ever since."

"Kaylee," Ryder rasps.

Lyric squeezes Ryder's shoulder. "I called Maggie on the plane, remember? She's taking Kaylee to a hotel."

"I can ask Mike Bravo to go watch them," Brix offers.

"Who's Mike Bravo?" I ask.

Everyone snickers, but no one answers me. Eh, whatever. I'm more focused on this narrative affecting Blake, and now Ryder's involved as well. I'm all about ruining lives this week.

Go me.

"I'm so sorry you've all been dragged into this," I say.

"It's not your fault." Blake's quick reflex to defend me makes me grateful.

I don't think I've ever met a more down-to-earth guy in Hollywood. Especially someone as big as him. He should be throwing diva tantrums and firing assistants. Oh wait, no, that's what Ben does.

"It isn't your fault," Ryder agrees. "I didn't have to say it to them. I just got irrationally mad at them making Blake's sexuality a big deal. They've done it to us our entire careers, and—"

"I notice you didn't tell them I'm *not* queer," Blake says.

"For all I knew, the rumors were true."

Blake tilts his head. *"Really?"*

"Hey, these two were a surprise." Ryder waves a finger between Mason and Denver. "I think straight should not be the default assumption anymore."

"Wait," Harley says. "Does this mean I'm technically the only closeted one out of all of us now? How in the fuck did that happen?"

"You do know I'm not actually *out*, right?" Blake asks. "The paparazzi saw me consoling my friend over his boyfriend cheating on him—"

I rub my chest. "Thank you so much for bringing that up."

"My point is they've all 'outed' me for the sake of a story. So maybe when I un-come out and tell everyone I'm straight, you can jump up and go *swapsies!*"

Harley's lips flatten. "You can tell everyone you're straight all you like, but I really don't think there's any way to put this behind you. People won't believe you when you deny it. Look at the Ryder-and-me rumors. We've been adamant nothing has ever happened between us, and people still don't believe us."

"Trust me," Blake says. "Once this movie comes out, there will be no questioning if I'm straight. Apparently I kiss too much like a straight dude. I didn't realize gay guys have this secret handshake they exchange before sharing saliva."

"Now there's an image." Lyric laughs.

"Ignore Ben," I tell Blake. "He doesn't know what he's talking about. Oh, and yeah, he's a *dick*."

"The director actually said you're bad at kissing?" Harley asks.

"Yep." Blake's defeated tone cuts me because he thinks he's doing a bad job when he's not.

"Technically," I point out, "he said we kiss like fish."

"And implied it was all my fault," Blake says.

"Let's see it," Harley says.

Both Blake and I look at him like he's grown two heads.

"I think we"—Harley gestures to the group—"out of anyone in this world would have valid opinions on this. It's for the good of your movie." He smiles smugly like he's setting Blake up.

"Plus, seeing Blake kiss a guy is icing on the cake," Denver adds.

Blake flips him off. "I have no issues with kissing Jordan, but apparently I kiss guys wrong."

"It was kind of stiff," I agree. "Maybe you should kiss *everyone* here and get used to kissing guys." And now everyone is staring at *me* like I've grown two heads. "I'm just trying to be resourceful. Practice makes perfect, after all."

Everyone glares at me.

What can I say? They mess with my friend, I mess with them right back.

Blake, on the other hand, thinks I'm brilliant. "So, who's gonna pucker up?"

CHAPTER 9
BLAKE

"NO TAKERS?" I taunt. There's no way any of these guys will follow through with it. They're like my brothers.

Ryder shoves Lyric forward. "Lyric will do it."

"I will?" Lyric croaks.

I pull back. "Yeah, he will? You'd be okay with my mouth on your boyfriend's mouth?"

Ryder looks panicked. "Honestly, I was trying to deflect away from it possibly being me. I didn't really think that one through."

"Good to know if there was ever a zombie apocalypse, I'd have to watch my back," Lyric says. "Love you too."

"Zombies are a totally different scenario." Ryder blows him a kiss, but Lyric's not impressed.

"You're the type of person who'd kick me in the shin so you could run faster."

Ryder opens his mouth to say something, but nothing comes.

Lyric stands. "Just for that, I'm going to kiss him. Maybe you'll learn your lesson."

"Umm, what?" I ask.

Lyric stops in front of where I'm sitting, but my gaze darts around the room, thinking he's fucking with me. My eyes bypass the scowl on Ryder's face and land on Jordan, who's obviously amused by his little setup.

All right then. I lift my chin.

Even if everyone in the room is laughing at my expense, it might actually help with the movie situation.

I stand and come toe to toe with Lyric.

He stares at me, and I stare right back, trying not to wrinkle my nose at the idea of kissing one of my best friend's boyfriends.

But as Lyric moves closer, everyone in the room holds in a collective breath. I can practically hear Ryder grinding his teeth. Lyric's long blond hair falls in his face, and his lips part.

Like on set, I tense, but it's for a whole other reason this time. This is *weird* for a multitude of reasons, not just that he's a guy.

I almost ask, *"Why are we doing this again?"* but Lyric breaks first and steps back.

"Nope, no, no. It's bad enough I already make out with a guy in a boy band on a regular basis. I *can't* make it two." Lyric moves back toward Ryder, who pulls him into his lap. And then *they* are kissing.

I'm pretty sure there's an insult in there somewhere, but also, watching the possessiveness from Ryder, I'm glad Lyric didn't kiss me. I don't want to come between a happy couple. I've already done that enough for one week. Not that Jordan and Ben were happy. Or that I actually came between them, no matter what the media thinks.

"Any other takers?" I spin in a circle.

Denver jumps up. "I'll do it."

"You'll *what*?" Mason growls.

Denver sits back down. "Or not."

"I'm starting to feel a little rejected here," I joke but knew it was going to go this way. "Is *anyone* going to kiss me?"

Jordan stands. "Okay, fine. Let's get this done. It's going to have to be me and you on film anyway."

"Wow. Sound more enthusiastic, why don't you."

Jordan slowly approaches me, and for the first time since we were at the hospital, his smile feels genuine. "Hey, if you want, we can practice as much as you need. Hell, we can even practice blowjobs. I'm a committed actor like that. And now that I'm single—"

"That's taking Method acting to a whole new level," I say. "Especially when the onscreen blowjobs are implied and not actually happening."

Jordan moves even closer now. "Did you know Leonardo DiCaprio slept in an animal carcass, withstood freezing temperatures, and ate raw bison to get into the mind of his character in *The Revenant*?"

Mason snickers. "If Leo, a vegetarian, can eat meat for a role, then surely you can eat … Jordan's meat."

I throw my arms wide. "You guys give the best support. Thank you."

"Just kiss," Harley says. "Maybe we can critique your technique."

"Jesus H. Christ, is this actually happening, or am I asleep and in a really bad dream?" I run my hand through my hair. "I'm in that dream where everyone's looking at me in my underwear, aren't I?"

"Kissing me is like the ultimate wet dream." Jordan winks. "If you gave it a proper chance, I could prove it, but you're determined to be in your head all the time." His hands find my waist, and I flinch. "See. Relax. Pretend I'm Gal Gadot."

"Only if you promise to wear a Wonder Woman costume."

Jordan's lips turn up, and I try not to think about them being on mine. I block out the disaster of a first kiss onscreen and focus on him here and now.

Like on the set, I'm conscious of everyone watching, but unlike in front of the film crew, these guys are my friends, so I'm less uptight about it. Still uptight for sure, just … not as much.

Jordan's gray eyes dance in amusement as he closes the gap and presses his tall and lean body against me.

Unlike in the movie where he's stripping me out of my clothes, he cups my face with one hand and moves in, lowering his mouth to mine and softly bringing our lips together.

My eyes close, and from the moment our lips touch, it's a completely different experience than our last kiss, but I can't put my finger on why.

It's more relaxed and charged at the same time. My instinct is to open my mouth for more, but when I do, Jordan doesn't push his tongue inside. There's a light flicker of it against my bottom lip, but he refrains like the professional he is.

It's already ten times better than our first try. There's that connection there that I felt when I was in the gay bar, like I'm truly immersing myself into the role of Madden.

Jordan's hand on my cheek moves to my hair, while his big hand on my waist wraps around my back and pulls me against him harder, but he still keeps his tongue back.

His mouth might be professional, but his lower half isn't getting the memo. He's hard against me—I can feel the stiffness of his cock against my thigh, just like I could feel it that night sandwiched between him and the other guy. I get the sudden urge to see what would happen if I kissed him properly.

It's a power trip to know I'm turning him on without even trying.

I try to compare it to the man in the club, but that kiss happened so fast, all I can really remember was liking it.

This, though. Jordan's taking his time. He moves his mouth slowly. He savors it.

Tingles shoot down my spine and land in my balls. My skin breaks out in goose bumps.

Just when I start to get into it, Jordan pulls away.

No, wait, come back.

I crack my eyes open to find Jordan smiling down at me.

"I'd say that was an improvement," he rumbles.

Understatement, but something inside me tells me not to show that.

I step away. "Gal Gadot has a very stubbly mouth." Then I lift my shirt and wipe my lips for good measure.

I think he knows I'm bluffing.

Harley clears his throat. "Uh. Yeah. Umm, that was great."

There are rounds of agreement.

"Really?" I ask. "It doesn't look like two fish kissing?"

"A couple more times and it'll be hot," Ryder says.

Jordan turns to me. "A couple more times, huh? It's a sacrifice I'll have to make. In the name of show business."

"Uh-huh. Show business." I glance down at his hard-on and then cock my brow at him, all the while praying he doesn't look at my semi and call me on it.

It's not like I'm completely hard. It's reacting to basic stimuli. But if our second kiss was ten times more explosive than our first, what will the next one be like?

Luckily, Mason's mom has perfect timing and shows up with the pizzas, breaking apart this little experiment.

After food, Jordan tries to slip away quietly, but I notice him. While everyone is focused on Ryder's coming out or our upcoming album, I haven't been able to take my eyes off Jordan.

He's his usual easygoing self, an improvement from the last twenty-four hours, but I can still see the hurt behind his eyes. It's obvious in the way he carries himself as well. His jokes seem forced, his quips lacking in the snark-to-joking ratio.

The rest of the guys and I work well into the night on the new album, and it's just like old times. Until it suddenly becomes *too much* like old times.

Mason and Harley get into an argument over lyrics, so I stand, call myself Switzerland, and tell them I'm turning in. But when I head upstairs, I bypass my room and knock on Jordan's door instead.

When he tells me to come in, I find him staring out his window. He turns to me with a smug smile.

He's shirtless, showing off every lean, tight muscle his torso has to offer. "What's up? I heard yelling. Do you need me to protect you from the other big, bad boy band members? Ooh, maybe you should change your name from Eleven to BBB… B. Big Bad Boy Band."

"Yes, because we are so threatening with our boyish good looks and these dance moves." I dramatically do a body roll and then a spin.

Jordan cracks up. "Stop before you traumatize me."

"I'll stop. I, uh, had an idea." And it's probably completely stupid and idiotic, but here I am. "About the whole Method acting … thing."

"You're here to take me up on my offer, then?"

"Offer?" I play dumb. The whole offhanded blowjob comment was a joke, I know that, but I'd be lying if I didn't consider it. Maybe for a split second. Just to see if I could get into it.

Jordan turns all the way toward me now, and as much as I tell my eyes to stay locked on his, they don't listen and sweep down and over his body, landing on the very obvious and impressive bulge in the front of his sweatpants.

Jordan chuckles, and I force my gaze back up to his face.

"Yeah, that offer." His voice has taken on a raspy quality that sounds like sex, and my dick twitches.

"I didn't say anything."

He stalks toward me. "You didn't need to. Your eyes said it all."

"Are you always this self-assured?" I'm unable to keep my gaze off his abs as he moves closer. I know he started out as an underwear model, but you could bounce quarters off them they're so hard.

"Proving my point. My face is up here." He points.

"You're such a dick." I laugh. "I'm wondering what your routine is. Your abs …"

"Uh-huh. My *routine*. Next you'll be asking if you can feel them for comparison, and before you know it, you're on your knees begging to taste my cock. It's how it always happens with the straight boys."

"Sure it is."

Something sad flashes across his eyes. "I wish I was joking."

"Wha—"

He shakes it off. "So what's this idea?"

"I was thinking of pretending to be Madden and Eamon while we're here. Kind of like living in our roles full-time until we have to go back?"

"Mmhmm, and what would this 'pretending' involve?"

"No sex," I say firmly.

"Oh, so no fun parts. Got it."

"I figure if I pretend you're my boyfriend, I'll get used to affection and stuff?" My voice cracks, and I clear my throat.

"Were you wanting to stay in character or—"

"No, I think we can still be us. I'm able to switch in and out of Madden's head well enough now, but the physical stuff, I'm still awkward and stiff." I realize how that sounds. "Uh, not *stiff*. Not, like, that …"

Jordan smirks, the fucker.

"You know what I mean," I say.

"All right then. If you think it'll help." Without warning, Jordan pulls me against him and slides his hands down my back to hold me close. His mouth is just inches away, his warm breath on my skin.

"What are you doing?" I ask.

"Are we not getting started already?"

"Oh. Umm, 'kay." Could I sound more unsure?

"You really know how to stroke a man's ego," he murmurs.

His lips part, and as he moves in, I prepare to kiss him again, but at the last second, Jordan leans his head to the side and kisses me on the cheek.

"Maybe we should start slow." He steps back, and I'm surprised by the piercing disappointment in my gut.

"Slow?"

"Well, yeah. It's not like Madden and Eamon are instant boyfriends. We'll ease you into it." Then, he unleashes the most Jordan smile I've seen yet. It's all cocky and self-assured. "You'll be changing your mind on the sex thing before you know it."

I snort. "Sure. Okay."

"Wanna sleep in here tonight? Close proximity and all that. I'll even promise to stick to my side of the bed."

It makes sense, but I hesitate.

"Already changing your mind on the sex thing? Or scared you will if you share a big, spacious bed with all this?" Jordan gestures to his body.

"You're so conceited."

"Is it conceited when I have a proven track record?"

"Of getting straight guys into bed?"

"Let's see." Jordan holds up a finger. "There was Ben, obviously."

"Ben said in an interview he's known his whole life he was gay, but he was too scared to come out until he met you."

He ignores me. "My best friend in college and I dated, but we were both pretty much smitten for the same guy. The same *straight* guy. Guess who hooked up with him first?"

"How'd that turn out?"

"You've met them. Sort of. Ash and Max. They're married now. It's kind of a thing."

"A thing?"

"Yeah. I'm a magnet for guys wanting to explore their sexuality, and it's kind of hard for me to turn down. Even though I know I should."

"Why?"

Jordan shrugs.

"Come on, you've gotta give me more than that."

"Okay, but you can't judge me."

I hold up my hands. "No judgment here. I am a safe space."

Jordan blows out a loud breath. "There's something alluring about being someone guys want to experiment with. I love first times. I love making a presumably straight man weak in the knees, and I love it when it works out and they embrace their true identity or sexuality."

"Okay, that's not as skeevy as I thought it was going to be."

"You said no judgment!"

I laugh. "Sorry. How do you even … like broach the subject? Isn't it weird hitting on straight people who have no interest?"

"That's the thing—I don't actively hit on them. You know how flirty I can be. All it takes is a few offhanded comments or innuendo, and then they come after me. And yeah, it can go bad. It *has* gone bad. A lot. I've been called every slur under the sun, kicked out of guys' apartments practically naked after they invited me there, they kissed me, they wanted me, and then suddenly realize I'm a threat to their true masculinity or what-the-fuck-ever."

"Shit. Has anyone ever hurt you?"

"Surprisingly no, but at six four, I pretty much tower over most people. If I was smaller, maybe it would've gone that way. Sometimes, the guy will have no problems being with me but then go back to their hetero life and chalk it up to their One Gay Phase, and whatever. If that's how they want to play it, then that's up to them."

I can't help feeling sorry for him. "Why do you do it, then?"

Fondness shines in his eyes. "Because when it opens up someone's mind, it's breathtaking to watch. The risk is worth the payoff."

"But I mean, if guys do go there, it's not like they're completely straight to begin with, right?"

"I have my own little theory that everyone has the potential to be fluid. All they have to do is reject the toxic ideals we're fed as kids."

"So in your mind, no one is straight."

"It's an amazing place to live. If you want to join me on this side of societal expectations, I'll welcome you with warm lips and a big di—"

And he's back.

"You're *ridiculous*," I say.

"Yet, you can't not think about it. Probably just like you can't stop thinking about that kiss earlier or the slight interest I felt below the belt."

Damn it. I was waiting for him to call me on it. "I'll admit I liked it more than I thought I would, but I wouldn't get too excited about that. I was really freaking out that it was going to be bad. When it wasn't, it was a relief."

"I could give you more … relief if that's what you want."

"If these are the types of lines you use on others, I'm surprised you have sex at all."

"Oh, I reckon I can get you to enjoy it."

"You're *that* confident?" I want to shove him away and dismiss it like I do all his jokes, but I *am* thinking about it.

His lips are plump and shiny pink, like he's wet them by running his tongue over them.

"Does it ever work out?" I ask. "Long term, I mean."

"Well, I'm single, so what does that tell you?" For a split second, something like sadness flashes in his eyes, but then it's gone. "I prefer it that way, anyway. Usually, I let them go with well-wishes and tell them to spread their wings and their legs and go fuck as many guys as possible and find their forever one."

"Charming."

He smiles. "I *am* a good-luck charm, you know."

"Oh really?"

"Yep. Basically, every baby bi guy I've hooked up with inevitably marries the next guy they're with."

"Bullshit."

"True story. It's like I'm cursed, but I'm happy for my conquests. Like I told you, relationships in Hollywood never work out. They're better off with someone who can be with them long term. I get the fun parts, and their future partner gets the relationship crap."

Why don't I believe him suddenly?

All that talk about hooking up with so-called straight guys because he likes first times felt genuine. When he first told me his and Ben's relationship was exclusive with that tiny wince, I thought it was real, but now, after getting to know him a little better, I might have misread him.

"I understand the Hollywood thing, I do, but what about the guys downstairs? They prove true love can happen in this industry," I point out.

"Wait until they've been together for forty years before you start throwing around that they have true love. True love is …" He shakes his head. "Not for me."

I want to ask him to tell me the story.

But he grunts and turns to walk toward his bed. "Stay with me if you think it'll help you with the movie. Or don't. It's up to you."

"I'll stay." I'm defiant about it now. "I'll go get ready for bed."

"I guess you'll veto a sleeping-naked rule?"

The thought of sleeping next to Jordan naked does spark some interest in my gut, but I get the impression this is his way of proving a point.

"Hey, you do you. I'm happy to wear sweats, but if you need to be naked, no skin off my nose."

Jordan drops trou. I try to remain unaffected by his dick, but it's hard. Not looking, that is. Not his dick. I'm not even going to look at it. Nope.

The second I glance down, Jordan grins triumphantly.

"It's already happening, I can tell."

"What's already happening?" *Stop looking at his junk.*

"You already like seeing me naked. Next you'll be asking if you can touch."

Not likely. Okay, maybe. "I'll take that bet," my mouth says without permission.

"Ooh, are you sure you should make another bet with me when you haven't finished paying up for the last one?"

"Hmm, true." I rub my chin. "But here you are, naked, and I'm still very much not jumping you, so what would the terms be?"

"I bet that by the time we leave to go back to LA, we will have had consensual, mind-blowing rebound-slash-friend-slash-newly-bicurious sex."

"That's a lot of sex." I swallow hard. "What do you get if you win?"

"Orgasms, duh."

I laugh. "What do I get if I win?"

Jordan pauses. "What do you want?"

What do I want? I have everything I could possibly need. I decide to go old-school mobster with my request. "A favor."

"What favor?"

"Any favor that I can cash in at any time. No questions asked."

"Mm, intrigue. I think as long as we can take murder off the possible list of favors, then I'm in."

"Fine, take away my fun. No murder."

"Are you sure you want to do this?" Jordan asks. "I've only been using half my charm, baby."

"I should've gone with ten million bucks. Easiest money I'd ever make."

"Shake on it?" Jordan holds out his hand.

I take it, and his thumb rubs against the inside of my wrist, sending a shiver right down my spine.

"Deal?" Jordan asks.

"Deal." And I already know I'm in trouble.

CHAPTER 10
JORDAN

I'M NEARLY asleep by the time Blake comes back into the room from getting ready for bed, and I picture him psyching himself up to do it. How long does it take to brush his teeth?

He lifts the blankets and climbs in next to me. "You're wearing sleep pants."

I'm facing away from him on my side, and I smile into my pillow. "You sound disappointed."

"Not at all. I'm surprised. I was sure the sleeping-naked rule was a way to use your dick in your seduction techniques."

Nope. I wanted to see what his reaction was. Other than a small flare of interest, and maybe hesitance, I can't really get a read on him. Usually, it's obvious one way or the other. Blake is confusing, and I *like* that.

I guess it's true what they say—old habits die hard. I shouldn't be encouraging this, but that doesn't stop me anyway.

"You think I have a seductive cock?" I ask sweetly. "I'll file that knowledge away for later. I need sleep. You don't get to be as pretty as I am without at least ten hours a night."

"Are you saying if you didn't get that much, you'd look like a troll? Because I'd like to see that."

"Well, there is one way you can keep me awake, but it will be the shortest bet I ever won." I roll over to face him.

"Nice try, but no way am I giving up that easily."

I don't expect him to.

If I'm honest with myself, I kind of hope he doesn't give up at all. Making the bet was a stupid, masochistic move on my part because even though every word I said to him is true—I love watching a newbie fall apart under my touch, my lips—it has burned me more times than it's worked out. I just didn't want to tell Blake that.

I don't need the sympathy.

Right before I met Ben, I'd sworn off bicurious guys altogether. The high they'd give me wasn't really worth the feeling of being used afterward.

But Ben … he was different. Or, I thought he was. There was a connection, a strong one, and the most romantic part of me—that very small, miniscule, almost nonexistent part—thought the moment I gave up the guys wanting to experiment was the one time the perfect one would land in my lap.

Okay, so Ben was grumpy and emotional a lot. He was broody and sometimes not nice, but it had to be a sign, right? He wanted *more*. He's the only one who ever wanted an actual relationship after all the sexual experimentation.

I don't hold anything against the guys who were grateful for the experience and then went and found someone they could really be with, but after a while, it really did begin to feel like I was cursed. I might have passed it off as a joke to Blake, but it holds more weight than I let on.

Which is why Ben was a breath of fresh air. Not only did he want to keep hooking up with me, he wanted to be exclusive. Finally, someone who wanted to be with me, not just use me, but those doubts from past hookups where they wanted to explore with others made me want Ben to do it while he was still with me. I could've lived with him doing that so long as he came back to me.

But they never come back to me, and I should've known that.

I should have known that's how it was going to end between us. I thought it was going to be scheduling conflicts when our run of movies together finally tapered off, but until that happened, the lines were clear.

And now … I should have bet Blake that Ben and Chad would be married within the year. That's a bet I know I'll win.

As for the stupid bet we've actually made … I don't regret it even though I have a million reasons to.

Blake is interesting and fun, but he's confusing too. He knows how to play his role, and I don't mean Madden. He's playing the part of Blake Monroe, a musician slash movie star, but that's about as deep as I've gotten.

I know from his actions that he is kind and protective. He loves the guys from Eleven. But other than that, it's like he adapts his behavior to suit his surroundings, not the other way around.

Is he in bed next to me because he really thinks it will help his acting, or is it that he's been built up into so many different personas that when stripped bare, he finds himself lost without a path to follow?

I watch him in the dark, his hardened features of an action movie star softer with his eyes closed and jaw relaxed.

"Can I ask you something?" His eyes slowly open, like he could sense me staring.

"Sure."

"Why do you really hate relationships?"

"Because they never work out isn't a good enough reason for you?"

"Nope."

"Why do you hate relationships?" I ask. "Because I know you don't have them either."

"I don't have time for them, but if I found someone I really liked, I wouldn't write it off. Isn't love all about taking chances?"

"Love is … hard. At least for me. Others make it look easy, but I'm defective. I've never said the words *I love you* to anyone."

"Not even Ben? Weren't you together for almost a year?"

I bite my lip. "Whenever he'd say it, I'd do the whole 'You too' thing and move on. It's not that I didn't love him. Maybe? I cared for him. A lot. Probably more than I ever had with anyone. But I also knew there was no future, so—"

"Which is my point. I think you don't give yourself over to love because you're always anticipating when it's going to end."

That's probably the truest statement anyone's ever made of me, but I don't want to admit it out loud.

"There has to be something you like about being in a relationship," Blake says.

I like snuggling and being pressed against someone without the pretense of it having to lead to sex like it mostly means when dating, but I don't want to tell Blake that either. It's too … not on brand for what I want people to think of me. So I do what I do all the time when it comes to this topic. I lie.

"Nah, I'm the eternal bachelor type."

"Mm, such a player." Blake's tone is too dry. Too … *knowing.* He's calling me out without actually doing it, and it makes me go on the counter-offense.

"If I didn't know any better, I'd say you were taunting me into making a move to prove myself."

"I wouldn't dream of it. If there's one thing I've learned from you, Jordan Brooks, it's that you never bluff."

That's not entirely true. Sometimes it feels like my whole life is one big bluff, but one thing I do well is cover that up. Generally with a bigger bluff.

Exhibit A: "Just wait. One day soon, you'll blink and then bam, suddenly I'll be irresistible to you."

"Can't wait."

The sad and pathetic part is, even though I know it's a bad idea to want him, I can't wait either.

There's a theory that everyone has their own fatal flaw. Mine is always going after what I shouldn't.

I wake up to an empty bed, which is probably a good thing. Somewhere in the middle of the night, I found a warmth at my side, an arm over my waist, and Blake's head buried on my shoulder.

Apparently, unconscious Blake is as snuggly as I am. I wanted to wake him and make fun of him, but instead, I went the self-preservation route. I rolled onto my side, but then we ended up spooning.

So yeah, I'm glad he's already awake and downstairs.

I'll need to go down there at some point to get some food, and I guess I need to be there so I can act like the doting boyfriend for Blake's little experiment to work.

I reach for my phone. When I power it up, notifications light up the screen for a good five minutes, and I weed out the ones I actually need to respond to. Like the one from Jojo asking if I'm okay, the couple from my agent which were bland updates saying he's hired a PR person to come up with a story she can spin to the public, but then there are the ones from Ben.

Eighteen missed calls, a couple of *I'm sorry* texts begging to explain, but nothing of substance. For a director who's good at capturing emotion onscreen, he's not great at expressing himself with words.

Maybe that's why we worked for as long as we did. He's not good at emotion, and I avoid it whenever I can.

I ignore his pleas and get out of bed to get dressed and head downstairs.

As soon as I open the door, perfect harmonies hit my ears. I don't know why boy bands get the reputation for having crappy music when being that harmonized takes a lot of talent.

They don't stop when I bypass them for the kitchen. They've

moved the coffee table out of the way and are standing in a circle as they rehearse.

Brix is at the dining table sipping from a mug and scrolling on his phone, and he mumbles, "Morning," as I pour myself some coffee.

"Morning. What are we supposed to do while they're all working?"

"You can come with me on a perimeter check if you really want. I have to make sure paparazzi haven't followed us out here. Last time, they camped outside the fence for days."

"In the snow?"

"Nah. It was warmer then."

"As fun as that sounds, I probably shouldn't in case there are cameras. No one knows where I ran off to."

"Fair enough."

I excuse myself to join the guys.

They finish their song and then take their seats around the living room, while Harley drones on about marketability and maybe speeding up the melody.

I go sit next to Blake on the couch he's sharing with Lyric. There's only a little space between them, so I wiggle my way into the gap and lean toward Blake and lay my head on his shoulder, but not before kissing him on the cheek.

He freezes, Harley's ramble dies off, and I try not to laugh into my coffee.

All eyes blink at us, awaiting an explanation.

"Method acting," Blake says.

Harley, Lyric, and Denver shout, "Yes," at the same time. The other three, including Brix at the table, scowl.

"What's going on?" Blake asks.

"If I had to *bet*"—I let the word fall from my lips with a little emphasis—"I'd say they were wagering money against us. Please, it's so rude to play silly betting games on our sex life."

Blake shoves me. "Like you aren't doing the same."

Now everyone else looks confused.

"Jordan thinks if I pretend to be his boyfriend, I'll end up wanting to sleep with him for real."

"What can I say? I'm a catch." The cocky act is second nature to me. It's at the point where I'm not sure if it's an act anymore or reflex or if I'm just that much of a douche.

"Oh, we so want in on this bet," Harley says. "We all bet that you two would hook up."

"How much?" I'm curious now.

"Twenty bucks," Harley says.

I mock gasp. "That's all we're worth to you? You guys are millionaires and you bet twenty measly dollars?" I tsk them. "You're all amateurs."

"What do you two have riding on it?" Harley asks. "Another movie role?"

Blake points at me. "Well, if he wins, he gets sex. If I win, I get to ask any favor I want. It could be anything—"

"Except murder," I interrupt.

"Except that."

Mason's sitting opposite me, and his face lights up. "Wait, so if you guys don't have sex, Blake can ask Jordan to do anything?"

Okay, now I'm nervous. "What kind of things do you think he'd ask?"

Ryder says, "I'm thinking a viral video of you in a chicken suit doing the chicken dance."

"No, it should be something big like taking over as a judge on the next season of *Fandom* so I don't have to do it," Denver says.

I lean forward in my seat. "Wait, Denver's on Blake's side now? I thought you were one of the ones who bet we would hook up?"

"I was. But if there's a chance of finding a replacement for me on that godforsaken show, I'm going to do it."

"It wasn't that bad." Mason pulls Denver close.

"Maybe you should do it, then," Denver mutters.

"If they offered it to me, I would. I liked working on the show last season."

Denver twists his head toward his boyfriend. "Wait, really? You should totally do it. You were so much better with the contestants than I was, and everyone loved you. I can make a call."

Mason grabs Denver's hand as Denver tries to get up. "Don't. It would have to fit with our tour, and—"

"They were going to do that anyway for me." Denver gets out of Mason's hold. "I'm going to go make this happen."

Harley singsongs, "Your boyfriend's your manager."

Mason stands. "Your boyfriend's your bodyguard." He follows Denver down the hall.

Harley slumps. "Touché. But we're getting off topic. Blake and Jordan. Let's get you hooked up so Jordan doesn't have to do something embarrassing."

Ryder rubs his chin. "I dunno. Having sex with Blake would be pretty embarrassing."

I burst out laughing, and Blake hits me with a couch cushion.

"I like your band," I say to Blake.

"Maybe you can take my place then because fuck all of you." Blake sulking is legit the cutest thing ever. In his Coby movies, he's this badass spy type dude who's always got a broody look on his face. The pout is adorable.

"I have it, by the way," Blake says. "The thing I'll make you do after we don't sleep together."

I swallow the lump in my throat. "Oh?"

"You have to get up onstage, with us, and sing one of our songs."

Oh, fuck. "Is now the right time to tell you that all the singing I did for that one show I was in years ago was totally not me? I'm tone-deaf."

"Even better. Wait, you were in a show where you had to sing?"

"I'm super offended you don't know my entire backlist of movies and TV shows. Don't you know who I am?" I screech.

Blake pats my shoulder. "Do you realize you're at a level of fame now where jokes like that could be taken seriously?"

"Really?" I'm way too excited about that. "That's so cool."

But also, I have to make Blake and me happen now. My career will not recover from the kind of embarrassment where I sing in public.

CHAPTER 11
BLAKE

IF I HAD KNOWN TELLING the others would result in picking sides, I probably would have kept it to myself because as I take a shower and then head back downstairs for dinner, everyone is waiting for me with suspicious and knowing looks on their faces.

"What did you guys do?" I ask.

"Nothing." Harley's sweet tone is complete bullshit. It's like he thinks I don't remember what he's like. "Dinner is set up in the formal dining room tonight. We ordered in Chinese."

"O … kay." For some reason, they all wait while I head in that direction, and then they follow me like little puppies.

When I turn the corner and see Jordan sitting at a candlelit table with flower petals spread all over the place, I don't know whether to laugh or cry.

"Oh no!" Harley says in the most overdramatic way possible. "I just remembered I already ate." He facepalms. "I'm soooo dumb."

There are murmurs of "Me too" and "Oops."

I shake my head. "Really subtle, guys. And *so* believable."

That's how I find myself eating dinner with Jordan across from me and harsh whispers behind us.

"Very atmospheric," I say dryly. "Ooh, but there's wine." I reach for the bottle to pour us some.

"Apparently Denver's not tempted by wine, so we have Mason's whole cellar to drink if we're up to it." Jordan smiles at me, and okay, I have to admit, under usual dating circumstances, this would probably be something I'd lean into given the chance.

Jordan has an easy charm about him that I don't think anyone would be immune to. If it weren't for this stupid bet, I'd probably throw myself into it fully. But there is a bet at stake, so I'm restricting this to work. A characterization exercise only.

And as nice as this could be, it would be better without the peanut gallery.

"We need to make them fuck, not fall in love," Lyric says.

"Doesn't romance lead to fucking?" Mason asks.

"You know we can hear you, right?" I call out. I turn to find their heads peeking around the corner of the doorway. "Mason, I thought you were on my side?"

"I've been known to play both. Recent revelation of mine."

Smartass.

I glare at Jordan. "Do you see what you've done?"

He throws up his hands like a busted perp. "Hey, they're helping me, so I'm not going to complain."

"Well, it's totally working. My dick loves nothing more than the feeling of being put on display and watched all the time. Quick, take me now!"

I have to admit, with all this betting business going on, Jordan seems perkier than he has since the Ben thing, so that's a bonus.

"Hey, they're feeding us and set this all up. It's only fair to give them what they want." Jordan uses chopsticks with ease, popping a wonton and rice in his mouth and smiling around the bite of food.

"I didn't realize peer pressure still happened long after being a teenager," I say.

"Do it. Do it. Do it," comes from behind us.

I eye Jordan. "You know you have absolutely no hope of

winning this bet now, don't you? Not with all them involved." I raise my voice. "They're successfully killing the mood."

There are muffled arguments about leaving us alone, and finally, I hear their retreating footsteps.

"If I'm honest, I'm not really expecting to win anyway." Jordan sips his wine. "Don't get me wrong, I really want to because I cannot sing for the life of me, and getting up onstage to sing an Eleven song might make me wet my pants in front of a sold-out arena, so yeah, there's that, but apart from anxiety-inducing performances, I'm not going to pressure someone into doing something they don't want to just for a stupid bet. I talk big game, but I'm not an asshole."

"Need I remind you about the movie? You're making me do that."

"Am I, though? Or did I encourage you to take something you wanted?"

Okay, that's true.

"Besides," he continues, "when it comes to sex, consent trumps all else. Which is why, if I were ever to win this bet, it would be because you wanted it. Ignore the guys out there and focus on us. We're supposed to be building chemistry for the movie. That's the real goal here."

I play with my napkin. "That's something I've been thinking about, actually."

"Our chemistry?"

"Yeah. We've been putting all this emphasis on the notion that the reason we don't have chemistry is because I'm straight. What if …"

"What if we don't have that spark and the movie is doomed?"

"Exactly. Onscreen chemistry isn't really something I've had to deal with because the romance aspects in action movies are practically nonexistent."

"I can think of some real-life couples who had no chemistry onscreen. Ben Affleck and Jennifer Lopez are the obvious ones that come to mind. If we don't have it, we don't have it, but we should at least work on it."

He's right.

"Also, I know we have spark," Jordan says. "At least from my side, and tell me if I'm wrong, but you enjoyed our last kiss. I know you enjoyed kissing that guy in the club. There was definite chemistry there."

A squeak comes from behind me, and I get the impression we're still not alone, but when I turn, I can't see anyone. They're probably hiding around the corner.

Instead of answering Jordan with words, I hold up my thumb and forefinger to indicate a little bit.

"I don't think it's a spark issue. All we have to do is work on making that spark obvious to everyone around us. No one would question our chemistry then," Jordan says.

"That sounds like a solid plan. Want to get started after dinner?"

"So eager to kiss me again already. This bet is all but won, baby."

"Uh-huh, so sure of yourself." Though I'd be lying if I said I didn't like that quality about him. He's somehow confident and sure without being over-the-top.

Jordan takes another sip of his wine. "I was thinking about going in the hot tub after this, so maybe we can *practice* later."

Footsteps sound behind us again, but I can't tell if they're coming toward us or away from us.

I ignore them. "Hot tub? Like … the outside hot tub? In amongst all the snow?"

"It's supposed to be therapeutic going from really hot to freezing cold. Or so I've heard."

"I've heard that's how you catch pneumonia, so yeah, totally fun. Sign me up."

"I bet you I can last longer out there than you can."

I throw my head back. "Is this going to become a thing?"

"A thing?"

"Don't play dumb."

"Do you mean are we going to place bets on all aspects of our lives? Because that sounds like fun to me."

"Until you're roped into a movie that's a disaster or have to sing in front of a large crowd …"

"Exactly."

"Being friends with you might be hazardous to my mental well-being."

Jordan wipes away a fake tear. "You say the sweetest things. Are we doing this or what?"

I wipe my mouth with my napkin. "Yeah, I'm in."

Jordan knocks on my door. "Have you gone through my bags at all?"

"Uh, no? Why?"

"My swimming trunks are missing."

I snort. "I'll give you three guesses where they are, but you're probably going to only need one when I tell you what happened to me."

"What?"

"I didn't bring trunks because even though Mason said there's a hot tub and to pack them, I didn't think I'd actually be stupid enough to go in there. Guess I was wrong about the stupid thing. Anyway, I asked to borrow some. Want to see what the guys lent me?" A Speedo, I would've expected, but this … I hold up the thong everyone insisted was the only bathing suit available.

Jordan swallows his lips like he's trying to hold back what he really wants to say. "I guess I'll be going in naked, then."

I shrug. "Up to you. I'm sure they could find you a thong to wear too if you asked."

"That thing ain't gonna cover my junk."

"Oh, the problems big-dicked people have. Are the condoms you buy too small too? Can't have anal because it won't fit? Life must be so hard for you!"

"You didn't get a good look before, did you? I'm not that big. I assure you, it will fit."

I laugh. "Oh, it *will*, will it? What's to say that if you do win this bet, that's how it will happen?"

"I don't do it any other way."

"Really?" I don't know why, but that surprises me.

"Actually, no, I take that back. I do go the other way sometimes. Especially if I'm in a relationship because I want to reciprocate—"

"But you don't do relationships. Well, apart from Ben."

"Hey, there were many 'relationships' back in the day, and I've always had the rule about it being a two-way street."

"Why does that sound so dirty in this context?" I ask.

"Because you're immature."

"Oh, and Jordan Brooks is a pillar of maturity? Is that what you're saying?"

"Are you going to let me finish my story or not? You're the one who's all interested in my sex life."

"Sorry. Continue."

"Bottom line—"

"Bottom," I snicker.

"And this conversation is done. I'll see you in the hot tub. Can't wait to see your ass in that thong."

As self-conscious as I should be about it, the way he eyes me as he walks out sets my body on fire.

I change into the ridiculous thong because no way am I getting naked with Jordan. It's a little *too* tempting, and I don't trust myself.

I want to win the bet for sure because seeing Jordan embarrass himself would make my insides happy, but at the same time, if he gets me so worked up that I couldn't resist him, I'm not going to stop it.

I'm still skeptical he can make me want him that badly. Right now, my interest is at a simmering heat with thoughts of what if …

But they're just thoughts.

I will admit I'm having fun playing this game with him, though.

Every attempt that perhaps would have once enticed me is laughable to me, but I love the attention. And maybe that's because I've always been the one to chase the girl. That's what hetero games are like. Even in the famous world. Unless we're including the fans I might have slept with back in my early Eleven days, but I don't. That was never anything more than sex for me and bragging rights for them.

I throw on a thick robe Mason keeps for guests, grab a towel from the bathroom, and make my way downstairs. I still think it's idiotic to get into a hot tub in the middle of winter, but when I bypass all the snickers in the living room and get out on the back deck, I can see the magic in it.

Especially with the candles the others have clearly set up, the overhanging lights are on, and there sits Jordan in the hot tub, his wide shoulders above the water, his hair wet, and his breaths coming out in puffs of steam.

"Is it even warm in there?" I ask.

He breaks into a smile. "Chickening out?"

"If it's fucking cold, yeah." I drop my towel on a nearby chair and strip off the robe.

"It's hot. Really hot." Jordan's eyes roam over me, from my torso to the ridiculous metallic-blue thong Mason gave me. "Mm, the water's nice too, I suppose."

"Wow." I laugh. "Seriously, I'm surprised *any* man has slept with you with lines like that."

"Please, all I have to do is flash them this broody stare." He smolders. "The clothes fall off themselves."

I climb in and sit opposite him, immediately thawing out in the hot water. My skin stings, but I welcome it.

"What are you doing all the way over there?" Jordan leans back and rests his arms on the side of the hot tub, while his foot hooks around mine. "I figure now's the perfect time to try to get into character."

"Are you actually naked, or is this another psych-out like last night?"

"You could come over here and find out."

"Incorrigible." Yet, I move anyway.

The sky out here is so clear, even with disruptive lights from the house, and as I lean back and look up at the stars, my head hits Jordan's forearm, and he moves his hand to my shoulder. I flinch and then curse myself.

"You really need to get rid of that reaction for the camera."

"I wasn't expecting it, is all. How would you like it if a creepy hand landed on your shoulder out of nowhere?"

"Since when are my hands creepy?"

"Since they wander without my knowledge!"

"Oh, I could show you wandering hands all right."

I groan. "I'm sorry I'm all … twitchy. I'm just …" *Trying desperately not to lose this bet.*

The funny thing is, though, the warmth in my gut isn't from the hot water. The edginess under my skin isn't because I'm not used to Jordan touching me. I think it's because I want more of it.

"If you want, I can tell you when I'm about to do something. Like right now, I'm going to put my arm around you and pull you against my side."

I let him. Our hips and thighs touch under the water, and I get my answer. He was not psyching me out this time. He's naked in here. And that thought lights up something inside me.

"Then," he continues, "I'm going to intertwine my feet with yours and sit here casually as if we're not touching while asking you questions to try to distract everything you've got going on up here." He taps the side of my head.

"Okay. Ask away."

"Umm, what was your childhood like?"

"Boring," I answer right away. "I come from a loving family with a mom and dad who adored me, who let me do what I want, who didn't flinch at me asking to audition for a boy band in LA, and yeah, my childhood couldn't have been more uneventful if I tried."

"Me too. Well, except being from a divorced family, but that's probably more common than parents who are together these days. And even then, my mom and dad didn't end on bad terms. Now that I'm older and out of the house, I assume they don't talk at all, but they were both very involved and civil when I was growing up."

"Ah, so your relationship issues are all on you, then. Wait, who can you blame for all your fucked-upness?"

"I think I can safely say that's on Hollywood."

"Is narcissism part of your personality? Narcissists think nothing is their fault."

Jordan's lips flatten as he thinks about it. "I think everyone is a little narcissistic, don't you?"

"Not me. I'm perfect."

"Of course you are. Blake Monroe, great-great-great-grand-nephew of Marilyn Monroe—"

"Uh, yeah, no, that's not true."

Jordan pulls back. "It's not? Are you sure? I read that about you somewhere."

"Well, if it was on the internet, it must be true."

"Duh. A few days ago I died, and now here I am. I'm basically like Jesus. Internet says so."

"Sorry to disappoint."

Jordan trails his hand down my arm, and I try not to shiver. The soft way his fingertips brush over my skin feels like his hands are all over me.

"Hmm, what else … Was the guy in the club the first guy you've ever kissed?"

"Yep."

"Had you ever thought of being with another guy before?"

"Thought about it, sure. Doesn't everyone?"

"Oh, my sweet precious baby bi, sweetie. *Honey*."

"Hooray for condescension! But I mean, we're in Hollywood. Publicly it's not very queer, but on the DL, it's like everyone and their dog is on the spectrum somewhere."

"True," Jordan relents. "Hollywood is a lot gayer than people want you to believe."

"I think it's only natural to wonder when you're surrounded by it but can't exactly ask questions, you know? I remember when I found out about both Harley and Ryder and seeing how our management team made them squash it down and basically told them to pass for straight or the whole band would suffer. We were not to speak of it or pay attention to it, and if we saw anything, it was our job to keep our mouths shut. So, yeah, I guess I've always thought about what it would be like, but maybe I've been scared into not entertaining those thoughts."

"Welcome to the town of Repression. Population: the entire queer community."

"It's a sucky place to live."

"It is. Which is why ..." Jordan moves so he's in front of me.

The water sloshes over me, and then his big hands grip my knees and push them apart while he settles in between them. He must be on his knees on the bottom of the hot tub. He's so tall, he still has his head above water.

"Why, what?" I ask.

"Why it would be a good idea for us to hook up." He lowers his head, but I reach up and cover his mouth with my wet hand.

"You just want to win the bet."

He pulls away from my hand so he can talk. "Not at all. I want you to live out any fantasy you've remotely thought about before squashing it down because you thought it was wrong."

"There's no fantasies. I haven't thought about it that hard."

"You have thought about kissing, though. And that has nothing to do with the bet." Jordan moves even closer now.

My breath becomes stilted, my cock begins to harden the

closer Jordan gets, and he's right. I have thought about kissing. Kissing him. Kissing that guy in the club. Kissing in general.

Maybe it's the repressed thing, or maybe it's that the thought of kissing a man is new and exciting, but I've never been so turned on by the idea of someone else's mouth on mine.

I nod, but it might be too subtle because Jordan doesn't close that small gap.

"I'm going to need you to say it," he whispers.

"Say what?"

"Ask for it."

Even though it's a given that if I say two little words, I'll get exactly what I want, asking a man to kiss me is nerve-racking. I don't know if it's a power trip for him or if he wants to make sure this is definitely what I want before he makes a move.

"Kiss me," I demand. He presses against me, but right before our lips touch, I smile. "And Jordan? Make it real."

He kisses me harder than he has before. Gone are the soft, tentative movements of his mouth against mine. The other times he's kissed me, he's let me lead. That is gone. Gone is any semblance of an attempt to keep his tongue away. Gone is any hesitance from his side or mine. But more importantly, gone are any inhibitions I had about doing this.

He cups the back of my hair with a wet hand, gripping tight to the short tendrils. My hair is usually kept short at the back for Coby movies, but this job required me to grow it out a little.

Jordan presses his tongue against mine and then moans into my mouth.

The hot water mixed with the frigid air on my face and shoulders makes me light-headed, or maybe it's the kiss doing that. I didn't have trouble breathing until Jordan Brooks entered my orbit.

He moves in even closer, and I can feel his hardness against my thigh under the water. I have the sudden urge to reach for it, almost like it's reflex and I've forgotten who I am or what I'm supposed to be doing. I run my hands up his chest to occupy them instead, but the hard planes under my fingers only turn me on more.

This stupid thong is already uncomfortable. The tip of my cock manages to peek out the top of the waistband, and it's a little too tight. Too restrictive.

"Fuck," I mutter against Jordan's lips and reach to pull the thong down a tiny bit to get some relief.

Jordan breaks the kiss but keeps his forehead on mine. He breathes deep and says, "I can help with that if you want."

Damn if I don't want to take him up on the offer. "Just doing some strategic rearranging." And I might give myself one hard stroke to get my dick to stop aching. "Plus, I'm not going to give it up that easy."

"My hand on your dick only counts as sex if you come."

"Is that in the gay man's rulebook?"

"I'll send you a copy."

I reach up and grab the back of his neck. "Stop ruining this with your words and use your mouth for something I actually enjoy."

"So you admit it. You do like kissing me."

And just as I thought the moment couldn't get any more ruined, Denver yells from the house, "No, Blake! Think of Jordan's embarrassment! We can take him on tour and have him as our opening act."

"Hey," Lyric complains. "That's supposed to be my job."

I cock my head at Jordan. "I thought Denver was on your side? I keep losing track."

"I think we can safely say, the only side all of them are on is the side where they get to fuck with us."

"Ignore them," Harley joins in now. "Go back to what you were doing! Here, I'll set the mood. Mase, how do you—"

Ed Sheeran's "Afterglow" wafts through the outdoor speakers mounted around on the side of the house.

Jordan, knowing he lost this round, sits back down beside me. I'm still hard, but I'm ignoring it.

"Nooo," someone yells from the house.

"You're right. I'm never going to win if they keep 'helping' me." Jordan flicks his hair and then runs his hands through it.

The light from the house bounces off his good looks, and when he smiles again, I realize something myself.

I'm never going to win this bet, period.

CHAPTER 12
JORDAN

WHEN BLAKE CLIMBS out of the hot tub, I can't help but look. After that kiss, I don't think I'll ever be able to be in a room with him without checking him out.

I was so close to touching him, to crossing lines. I was even willing to make loopholes in the bet just so I could do it.

It goes to show I never learn. I'm hiding from the world, from Ben, because he turned out to be exactly like the others, and yet here I am, making stupid bets and throwing myself at another "straight" guy.

Sure, it's a great distraction, and yes, holy shit, yes, I want to have sex with Blake Monroe, but there's a giant red flag being waved in front of my eyes, and I'm too blind to see it.

"Fucking fuck, it's freezing out here." Blake quickly towels off and then throws on a thick robe. Before it closes, I get a peek of the head of his cock trying to break free of that ridiculous—and hot—thong. It may be freezing, but his dick didn't get the memo.

It's as hard as mine, and the outline of it through the material, for the split second I saw it, makes my damn mouth water.

"I'm going to have a hot shower. Maybe you should stay in there until I come back so the shower's free when you're going to need to thaw out."

"Sounds good." Only, I don't last much longer without him in here with me. The water no longer feels hot, and anytime a part of me leaves the water, it protests about the cold. I need to make this transition as fast as possible.

So I climb out of the hot tub as quickly as I can without breaking my neck, grab the towel I brought with me, and make a run for the house, where it will be a hell of a lot warmer than out here.

My dick has the complete opposite reaction to Blake's. As soon as the cold air hits it, it's as if it tries to retreat back into my body.

I run past everyone else, who have gone back into the main living area of the house now the show is over, and head upstairs. Hopefully, Blake takes short showers, and I can jump in now.

The bathroom we're sharing is actually attached to his room, and when I reach his bedroom door, I can't hear the water running, so that's promising.

His bedroom door is ajar, so I let myself in and then head for the bathroom.

I knock. "You decent?"

There's an affirmative grunt—or, what I think is one—but when I open the door, it's very clear that I misinterpreted.

Very clear.

Blake's standing by the sink, one hand on the counter, the other wrapped around his cock. The thong sits around his thighs, like he didn't even have time to take it off.

His wet blond hair falls over his forehead; his lips are thin and pressed together.

I should turn and walk away, but then my gaze drops to his ass. The muscles contract with every thrust into his fist.

Blake Monroe jerking off is the hottest thing I have ever, ever, ever seen. And oh, look at that, my cock is no longer freezing and has come back out to play.

I almost come to my senses, but then he finally notices me.

Those blue eyes meet mine. "Fuck," he hisses.

"S-sorry." I say that, yet I can't tear my gaze away from him.

He has slowed now but still strokes his cock, moving that tight skin over the swollen and reddish head.

"I, uh, didn't hear the water running. I thought you were done, and—"

"I had to take care of this problem first." His voice is raspy, and he looks down at his cock in his hand. "Turns out jerking off is a good way to get warm too."

"I'll, uh, leave you to it and use one of the other millions of showers in this place." I turn, but I don't get far.

"Or …" he says, and I pause. "You could use this shower."

"While you're doing *that*?"

"It seemed you were enjoying watching. And if you don't touch me, it doesn't count as sex, right?"

Holy motherfucking Hemsworth brothers, I think I've died and gone to heaven.

There's something menacing and playful in Blake's eyes as he turns and leans against the vanity, showing off his muscled torso and abs and, of course, that mouthwatering cock with his hand wrapped around it.

I want to get on my knees for him. I want to swallow him whole and suck him dry. I want—

"Jordan?"

I snap out of my trance and drop my towel because no way in hell am I going to pass up the opportunity to see Blake jerk himself off until he comes.

The fancy bathroom has a glass shower, so I step in and turn the water to warm—not hot. I don't want this thing fogging up and obstructing my view. Besides, my skin is so cold, the warm water feels as if it were boiling anyway.

I itch to touch myself. My cock is hard, pointing straight up, only getting harder and more painful as I watch Blake stroke himself.

He's still leaning against the counter, putting himself on full display. One of his hands grips the vanity tight, while he picks up the pace on his dick again. His head is down, watching what he's doing, and he doesn't appear to be self-conscious about me being in here, knowing I'm not going to look away.

I do have to fold my arms, though, so I'm not tempted by my own need to get off.

As if reading my mind, he lifts his head. "You can too. If you wanted …" His gaze drops to my aching cock.

Whatever self-preservation I have left screams at me not to do it, but the thing that's inside me that has never had good self-control ignores it.

I run my hand down my body and grip my cock, giving it a few slow strokes first. Blake watches and matches my actions and speed. It feels as if he's the one doing it to me. There may be a glass wall between us, but it's as if he's in here, touching me, running his thumb over the head of my dick where precum leaks.

I imagine Blake joining me and getting on his knees to taste it while I thrust inside that virgin mouth of his until he's begging to choke on my dick.

Blake uses his free hand to cup his balls.

I want to tell him to keep going further, to reach back and play with his hole, but I hold it in. The thought of being the first and only person to touch him there drives me wild with need.

While I'm still confident I'll be able to get Blake to break, there's something to be said about anticipation, and this is edging to the fullest meaning of the word.

Hell, this is nearly downright cruel.

The thought that this is Blake playing games with me quickly gets pushed aside. Years of the same shit from bicurious guys have made me a little jaded. Because of that, if I were a smart man, I wouldn't let this go any further, and I'd take my public embarrassment like a champ.

Because singing in front of a large crowd might still hurt less than being used. Again.

It doesn't matter that I'm basically doing the same thing. I'm using Blake to distract me from Ben, but the difference is, I'm making the exact same mistake I always do.

Blake throws his head back and says my name, making all those reservations disappear. I've never heard the name Jordan said with such passion and force. Blake's thinking of me while he jerks himself. He's thinking of me as cum fills his hand. And as much as I want to be strong and protect myself, I want to come more.

All at once, Blake's muscles contract. He's not as big as he usually is in his Coby movies, but it's still impressive watching the ripples of muscle as he tenses and comes all over himself.

I unleash a moment later, shooting all over the shower glass.

There's a moment where we're both silent and breathing heavy, until Blake breaks out into a grin.

"You better wash that off and hurry up and get out. I need to shower."

"I painted it for you. You don't like my art?"

The fact he can act like his normal carefree self after that proves everything I already suspect, but I still have no desire to stop.

"Am I sleeping in your room again tonight?" Blake asks.

"Think you can do it without losing this bet?"

"After this?" He runs his finger down his chest, wiping away his cum. "Definitely."

"Damn it, why does that sound like another challenge?"

And why do I have this inability to say no even when I should?

Blake plays it cool when we go to bed, turning his back on me so he doesn't even give me a chance to try for more, which I'm thankful for, but it also sits weird in my chest. He got off, then pretended nothing happened. It leaves me with an unsettled feeling, but that melts away when I wake up in the middle of the night with him spooning me again.

It's causing a flip-flop of emotions inside me because I know what this is. But at the same time, it feels different.

Doesn't it always? That annoying little voice in the back of my mind is right.

With nearly every guy, I'd think, *this could be the one that sticks.* Each new guy is different, but then they'd go and prove they're all the same.

"I really am getting better at this affection thing," Blake rumbles against my back when he wakes up.

I've been awake for about an hour, just enjoying the feel of someone pressed against me.

His breath heats my skin as he talks. "I didn't even know I was cuddling you."

"Mmhmm. Maybe you're gay when you're asleep."

"Guess so." He rolls away and gets out of bed, stretching as he does. "I'm starving." Those abs he came all over last night are on display, and he trails his hand over them as he reaches into his waistband to adjust himself.

"We didn't even get a chance to build up your appetite," I say, unable to stop staring at the tent in his sweats.

"Still hungry. The sucky thing about not training in between Coby movies is I still have the insane desire to eat all the food. It's a constant struggle to limit myself. Coming down for breakfast?"

"Yeah. I'll be down in a minute."

He tilts his head at me.

"Just have to wait for something else to go down first."

Blake's gaze drops to where the blanket is covering my very hard dick, and I laugh.

"I told you. It's not that big. I don't think you'll be able to see it unless you have X-ray vision. I'll be down in a couple of minutes."

"What do you want for breakfast? I'll get it for you."

"Aww, that's sweet, but I'm not really a breakfast kind of guy. I'll have coffee and maybe fruit if there's any. Or eggs on toast."

"Easy peasy. Bacon, eggs, hash browns, and pancakes coming up."

"My former model self is judging you."

He smiles as he leaves the room, and I take a couple of minutes to get my dick under control. Once I have, I get dressed and head downstairs to where the others are sitting around the informal dining table near Mason's kitchen, and suddenly all eyes are on me.

There's a free seat next to Blake with a plate of eggs, a side of toast, and a coffee.

"Thanks." I sit next to him and kiss his cheek.

"You're welcome. Though, I should mention I didn't make it. Mason's mom's been here since the butt crack of dawn making sure we have everything we need."

That woman is a godsend. Kind of reminds me of my own mom back in Boston.

I dig into my food, but everyone else is still staring.

"What?" I ask.

"Are you going to tell us or not?" Denver asks.

"Tell you what?" I play dumb.

"They've already hounded me with a million questions about what we got up to last night," Blake says.

"After your hot tub shenanigans, I thought for sure one of you would be walking funny this morning," Brix mumbles.

I lean forward so I can see him better at the other end of the table. "You're in on this too?"

"We all are," Harley says. "So out with it."

"Am I Marie Antoinette?"

There are a bunch of confused stares pointed my way.

"You know, because the king had all his courtiers watch them to make sure they consummated the marriage, so it took them seven years to get any action." I point to Blake with my fork.

"King." Then point to me. "Marie Antoinette." I wave my fork around the table. "Courtiers."

"Wait," Mason says. "You guys are married now? I think you skipped a few steps. Rewind—"

Blake turns to me. "Are you sure we couldn't have hidden with your friends?"

"Want to fly to Boston tonight? It's totally doable."

"No one's going anywhere," Harley says. "We have an album to write. We'll drop the whole interest in you two and whether or not you've had sex."

I lean in closer to Blake. "Why don't I believe him?"

"Because you're smart."

When we finish up breakfast, the guys get up to work on some songs.

"We're working outside today. It's a toasty forty-two out there," Harley says.

The others groan.

Blake stands. "You want to come and watch or—"

"I think I'll help Mason's mom with the dishes, and then I'll come out."

Only, while I'm standing at the kitchen window, watching the five of them rehearse and mess around while Lyric helps and puts in his opinions, their camaraderie is palpable. Their brotherhood. Then Brix comes back from a perimeter check, and as soon as Harley sees him, he runs and jumps into his arms and kisses him senseless.

I don't have that with anyone in Hollywood. Not only the love part but also the friendship.

"I can do these if you want to go out there," Mason's mom says.

I shake my head and go back to focusing on the single plate I've been rinsing for a good few minutes now. "No, no, I'll stay and help out. My mom raised me with manners and shit." Oops, I probably shouldn't swear. "Uh, not shit. I mean …"

Mason's mom smiles. "You're fun. I like you. But I'm going to be honest here. I could have already had these dishes rinsed and in the dishwasher. I'm glad your mom raised you with manners and shit, but you're holding me back. So scoot! Get out of my kitchen."

I laugh. "Sorry. I guess I'm not much help after all."

"Put on some warm clothes and go out there and watch them. I have to admit, all those years ago, I didn't understand why Mason wanted to join a boy band of all things, but I'm glad he didn't listen to me when I told him he should get his college degree first before chasing his dream. He wouldn't have this house. He wouldn't have Denver. There's something magical about each and every one of those boys out there."

"I'm starting to see that."

"Blake would be lucky to have you."

"Oh, we're not … this is all a stupid bet, and—"

"Mmhmm, and Mason and Denver were just best friends." She guides me outside the kitchen. "Go already."

"Thanks." I run upstairs to grab a hoodie and a jacket when I pause and think about what Mason's mom said.

That Blake would be lucky to have me.

She has it all wrong. I would be lucky to have him. To actually be able to hold on to him.

But that will never happen.

I go to the side of my bed where my phone is and power it up.

More missed calls from Ben.

Messages from Jojo checking in on me while sending through selfies of her in my apartment eating Cheetos on my white couch when I don't reply to her in a timely manner.

I quickly send off a text telling her I will end her if she gets orange stains on my couch and then remind her I'm cell phone-free here. Rules of the boy band gods.

There's a voice message from my agent telling me not to panic and don't look at the news. With the mood I'm in, self-preservation kicks in, and I follow his advice.

Then I click on a message from my friend Ash, asking if I'm okay, and I realize I'm not.

I can't pinpoint why exactly either. I should be upset over Ben, but I'm not. At least, I don't think I am. Unless I'm transferring all my hurt over our breakup at Blake because Blake's the one in my bed.

Though, he's technically not at the same time.

I hit Ash's number and click the FaceTime button and then make myself comfortable in bed. There's a chance he won't answer because they're a couple of hours ahead and he'd be at work, but I need to try anyway.

Surprisingly, he answers. He's in his tattoo shop, out at the front counter by the looks of it. "Hey, what's up?"

"Are you working?"

"I am, but I'm sure my next client won't care if I'm talking to you." He turns his camera toward his husband. "He's letting me use him as practice for this wicked-cool design I want to try."

"He must love you so much."

"See, this is why you and I never worked out. You never let me ink your skin."

And I still won't. But that's because tattoos are a pain in the ass to work with. It was drilled into me when I was a model. You can lose jobs because of the wrong kind of ink or if your employer sees it and decides you aren't worth the cost of editing them out. Same thing goes for acting, really.

"You know ink isn't the reason we broke up."

Ash is a strict top, so sexually, we did not come together at all —pun intended. Like I told Blake, I don't mind bottoming, but it needs to be a give-and-take situation. I'd rather not have anal at all than bottom one hundred percent of the time. That's just me. And Ash is just him. There's nothing wrong with having preferences, but our preferences didn't align.

We love each other deeply, but we realized quickly it was more a platonic kind of love.

"Are you okay?" Ash asks.

"Are you asking because you've seen something in the media or—"

"Because you look like someone drowned a unicorn in front of you."

"Someone did, and I'm so, so sad."

"What's going on?"

I bite my lip. "What's wrong with me?"

"Where do I start?" Max yells from the background.

Once upon a time, he was kissing and grinding against me on his couch. He never did like me much, though. But again, I had an opportunity, and I took it. And then felt awful afterward because I'd always low-key known Max and Ash were in love with each other.

"Ignore him," Ash says. "What do you mean what's wrong with you?"

"Why do I always get involved with the straight ones?"

Ash's green eyes soften in sympathy. "Oh, Jord. Is the breakup with you and Ben really that bad?"

I huff. "I'm not even talking about Ben. I should be, but I'm not."

"Then who?"

"Blake."

"Blake Monroe?" he screeches.

"Shhh."

"It's okay, no one is in here but me and Max."

"Nothing has happened," I say. "Well, not really. We've been trying this whole Method acting thing, so he's kissing me and giving me affection, and ..."

"And you like it," Ash says.

"Yep. And then we made this stupid bet, and I'm regretting it now because I really want to win, but if I do, then I'm repeating past mistakes, and—"

"What bet?"

"That we'll have slept together for real by the time we leave

Montana—oh shit, no one knows where we are. Don't repeat that to anyone."

"I'm calling all the tabloids now," Max yells.

I grunt. "Can you tell your husband to go away, please?"

Ash shoves Max off camera and then comes back to me with sympathy in his eyes. "You know what you have to do, don't you?"

"What's that?"

He says the one thing I don't want him to, but I know it's the right answer. "Lose the bet. Remember all those times you'd call home heartbroken over the new baby bi who just left you? Nothing is worth going through that again."

"Not even me singing at an Eleven concert in front of the whole world? Because that's what's on the line if I lose this bet, and you know that will go viral."

"Oh damn. Maybe the heartbreak would be better."

Even as he says that, I already know it wouldn't be. Which means I only have one option.

I can't have sex with Blake Monroe.

CHAPTER 13
BLAKE

I'D THOUGHT after last night that maybe Jordan would be more relaxed, and maybe he is on the outside, but it feels like it's an act. Those few weeks of shooting helped me see the switch in him from when he's being himself to when he's acting, and the easy smile on his face as he silently watches us rehearse is definitely acting.

Why Harley is making us perform out here, where the air is so icy my lungs feel like they're freezing up, I have no idea, but I can't deny the beauty of the snow hanging around and the vast expanse of white-covered land that is technically Mason's backyard.

It's beautiful up here, and that gives me an idea. "We should shoot some scenes of us up here rehearsing to put in one of the new song's videos."

"That would look amazing," Jordan says. For the first time today, he genuinely lights up. "Though, I have to say, a stylist would go a long way." He eyes our clothes that are more for warmth than fashion. "Just sayin'."

Mason folds his arms. "I feel like we should be offended."

"Fashion is the only thing that should be offended," Jordan says. "I have some things that could work."

"Ex-model to the rescue," I say.

I watch as Jordan leaves, but when one of the guys clears his throat, I turn to find all four of them looking at me with some kind of smugness on their damn faces. I ignore that and stick to business talk. "You know it's a good idea. Think about it. We could start off here." I make a square with my hands as if looking through a lens. "Wide shot panning past us and to the snow-capped mountain in the distance, and then—"

"Spot the director in the making," Denver mumbles.

I ignore him and keep going. I explain my vision, step by step, but they don't seem convinced.

"Come on," I say to Harley. "The reason you're making us do all this choreo when we're writing the songs is so we don't have to do a boot camp before the tour."

That's how it used to work. We'd write and cut our album, announce a tour, and then go into an eight-week boot camp where we'd learn all the dance moves for the stage. We all hated it. If we're even halfway ready by the time the Encore tour is announced, it'll mean less time in boot camp.

"It's a good idea, don't get me wrong," Harley says, "but how will we know which song to put it to. Our lyrics aren't set in stone yet. The lighting is—"

"Perfect. It's all natural and bright out here today. But if it doesn't work, it doesn't work. We can come back and reshoot certain parts if we have to or even scrap it altogether." I step closer and lower my voice while looking back at the house, hoping Jordan isn't within hearing range. "At least let Jordan film us doing something. He needs a distraction. He hasn't come out and said it outright, but I think the breakup with Ben is getting to him more than he's letting on. I figure if we're out here performing anyway, why not film it? Maybe even just shots of us goofing off. I think it's too pretty out here not to take advantage."

Harley nods. "Yeah, yeah, you're right. If it doesn't work, then it doesn't, but you know I won't let an opportunity go to waste."

Jordan returns and tells us to come inside to look at clothing options, and as soon as we enter the house, I have the sudden realization as to why he brought so many suitcases. He said it was because he wasn't sure how long we'd be out here, but now I'm realizing he's a hoarding hoarder who hoards clothes.

"Are any of these going to fit us?" Ryder asks and then lowers his voice, pretending he doesn't want Jordan to hear when he says, "I don't know if you've noticed, but he's a billion feet tall."

I laugh because it's true. Denver is the tallest of us at barely six foot. He and Mason are about the same height, and the rest of us are five ten-ish.

"We can make it work," Jordan says.

Mason raises his hand. "Uh, might work for all you guys who are built like short Jordans, but no way will a model's clothes fit all this." He gestures to his body.

Jordan approaches Mason and looks him up and down. "You have these sexy wide shoulders that will look awesome in one of my coats. It'll fit you because it's a little big on me. Do you have a nice pair of dark jeans and maybe a simple gray hoodie to wear underneath?"

"He has ... jeans," Denver says. "Don't know if you could call them nice. Along with being anti-Hollywood, he's apparently also anti-designer now."

Mason flips off his boyfriend. "I have something that will work. I'll be right back."

Jordan dresses us and takes control of the impromptu video shoot.

I never noticed it while on the set of *Faking It* because Jordan never has any input, but giving him free rein of us really works for him.

He's animated and full of ideas, and it's really fucking cute. Somehow. It lights him up, and I'm thankful he looks like he's finally enjoying himself. Although I'm assuming he enjoyed himself in what I'm calling the bathroom incident too.

I've done well to pretend like that little moment wasn't a big deal to me, but it kind of was. Because even though we have this stupid bet going on, there's no doubt in my mind that I wanted to touch him last night.

I wanted to kiss him again like in the hot tub, and I wanted more. I even had to turn my back on him to go to sleep because I was sure I wouldn't have been able to refrain from touching him if I didn't.

I guess this is where I'm supposed to freak out. When Denver kissed Mason for the first time, they didn't talk for over two years. Where there's a lack of existential crisis, it's filled with wanting more of Jordan. I like his theory about everyone being fluid. Anyone having the potential to find attractiveness in someone they didn't expect. Sure, preferences would come into play a lot, and I can't deny I enjoy being with women, but if kissing Jordan a handful of times and jerking off in front of him can do it for me, I don't want to rule out any possibilities.

And I don't think I have to.

Jordan films us on his phone, so the quality is not going to be great, but it doesn't need to be. This started as a random idea, but now that it's happening, I'm in it for the distraction for Jordan.

He's a natural behind the camera.

Though, when we end a song, and he has an idea for the next shot, he's in the middle of moving the Adirondack chairs by the fire pit when he starts humming. I realize quickly why he needs to win this bet. I didn't know it was possible for someone to sound so terrible without even opening their mouth.

It's a good thing I don't plan to win anymore anyway.

We film and rehearse all day, even as the afternoon settles into dusk and the temperature drops. Instead of going inside, we light the fire pit. We sing until our lungs hurt.

It's so much fun being with the guys again, and even though

we're planning this reunion tour, I get the overwhelming sense that I need to hold on to this feeling for as long as I can.

I'm not giving up my acting career anytime soon. Harley has a new record label, and Ryder's producing for him. When Ryder's not doing that, I'm sure he'll be on the road with Lyric or at home with his family, and if Denver gets his way, Mason will be on the next season of *Fandom*, being a judge and helping new acts find their way in this industry. And the way Denver is handling all of that for Mason ... Harley jokes Denver's his manager, but it wouldn't surprise me if that ended up becoming true. We're all still on those separate paths we took three years ago when we split, so with us coming together like this, I have to expect it to be temporary. This might be our Encore tour, but it might be only that. An encore. One last song. The end.

We finally call it a day when Mason's mom comes and yells at us for being out in the cold for so long. I can't speak for the others, but I barely feel it. We're all bundled up, and the fire's warm, and the way Jordan keeps stealing glances at me, I don't know how long I'll last inside before I drag him back to his room and pounce on him.

I should at least play a little hard to get, right?

Then again, it's not like I'm expecting this to turn into anything more than sex. Jordan's already said he doesn't like relationships, he's in the middle of a nasty breakup, and the last thing either of us needs is for it to get out that we're actually hooking up. Or will be. As soon as we get through dinner.

Mason's mom brought us all homemade lasagna and salad with garlic bread and red wine, and I think I've died and gone to food heaven. I can easily see how Mason gained a few pounds while living at home, but I take an extra-big slice. I'll need my energy for later.

Jordan hardly eats. He's too busy looking at some of the footage he shot today.

A nervous ball sits in the pit of my stomach, though I'm not sure why. Maybe it's anticipation mixed with hesitation.

I don't care about the stupid bet, I don't care what it means to be with Jordan, but I do care about what it will do to us as friends.

Our whole careers, us Eleven guys have been told to watch what we do or say because all of it can be misconstrued. It's made us evaluate every situation before doing something or making a move.

Everything we've done has been calculated. This? Planning to hook up with Jordan? There's nothing calculated about it.

I want him.

End of story.

There's no way it'll get out, and even if it does, the media is painting us in this light anyway. That we went behind Ben's back, not the other way around. There's no point defending it because in the age of social media, there are people with opinions and others with even more opinions. And there's no changing them no matter how truthful and raw you are with your fans.

If Jordan was to say, "Ben cheated, and there's nothing going on between me and Blake Monroe," people would assume he's either, one, lying; two, hooked up with me for payback; or three, trying to pull sympathy from Ben's infidelity. There is no winning in this situation.

So people publicly thinking that Jordan and I have had sex isn't a big deal.

And other than that, I don't see any reason why I shouldn't hook up with him.

After dinner, we lounge by the fireplace, and I use the excuse that I'm still working on the casual-affection thing as to why I sit next to Jordan on the couch and throw my legs over his lap.

The guys bicker and fight among themselves, while my focus stays on the fireplace and the flickering flames. I need to distract myself from Jordan's hand on my thigh. He's not even moving it. It's just there, giving off enough heat to warm my entire body.

Arousal simmers in my gut, and I can't wait until that blessed moment when the others will call it a night.

When Ryder and Lyric go first, I give Jordan a nudge, but he doesn't move. He might not be tired, but he's not getting the hint that I don't actually want to go to sleep.

Out of nowhere, a cushion comes flying at my head.

"What?" I turn to where it came from.

Harley's smiling from ear to ear. "I asked if there are any more Coby movies coming up that you know of?"

"They want to do another one, but I've told them I couldn't keep doing them back-to-back like the first three. I need time for other projects. They'll probably schedule one for after the Encore tour."

"Are you okay with doing that?" Jordan asks.

"Yep. That franchise got my foot in the door. I don't want to be one of those actors who turns on the thing that made them famous."

Jordan squeezes my leg. "How did you get to be so down-to-earth?"

"Blake has always been that way," Harley says for me. "Almost like he doesn't believe his fame, even though there have been many times where a horde of a million screaming teenage girls are running after us."

"They were running after you guys more. I swear one time, this chick—she must've run track or something—she caught up to me, totally bypassed me, and tried to tackle Ryder to the ground."

Jordan snorts. "I don't think I could ever comprehend that kind of level of fame."

"You'll get there," I say. "Only instead of teenage girls, it'll be gay boys of all ages running after you."

"Mm, one could dream."

"With how hot he is, he'd probably have all the straight guys running after him too," Denver says.

Jordan's hand tenses on my thigh.

Denver doesn't know what Jordan told me, but Jordan glares at me like I've spilled all his secrets. He looks hurt. And betrayed.

I lean in and whisper in his ear, "I didn't say anything. I promise."

His frown lessens, and then he turns his attention back to Denver and Mason, who aren't giving two shits about what we're talking about over here. They're too busy arguing over Denver's sexuality.

"How you hadn't worked out you were bi before we got together is really amazing. Your denial must've been made out of Kevlar or something."

"Pretty much, but even you, Mr. Pansexuality, can admit that Jordan might not be your type, but he's fucking hot. He's got this smolder that looks just like …" Denver clicks. "You know who he looks like? If Flynn Ryder from *Tangled* was a real human." He gestures to Jordan.

Jordan turns to me. "Should I be flattered or insulted? I'm not actually sure."

"We should let them argue among themselves. I want to go to bed."

"You need me for that? I might stay up a bit longer. It's nice here. Relaxing." He's not looking at me as he talks, and I don't know what's up with that, but I lean in again so the others can't hear what I have to say.

"I wasn't thinking of going to sleep."

His cock twitches against my leg, but he doesn't respond. At least, not at first. He stares straight ahead with a passive look on his face.

I thought this would have been a simple answer for him. He's about to win this stupid bet. Again. I really should have heeded my own advice when I said to never bet against Jordan.

But right now, on the cusp of winning, there's something in the way he refuses to look me directly in the eye, the way his hand leaves my thigh, and even in the way he taps my leg for me to stand.

"We're going to bed." Could I make that sound any more like "We're going to have sex"? But surprising me, and maybe Jordan too by the way he hovers around, the guys don't say anything. Maybe they are letting up on all the sex stuff.

Or maybe I'm telling them all they need to know, like I have some sex beacon flashing or something. Ooh, is this what gaydar actually is? Queer people can detect when queer stuff is about to go down.

Fuck, don't think about anything going down.

We amble up the stairs, Jordan particularly slow, and I get the sense that maybe we're not on the same page.

I wait for him by my door, and his feet stall near his. The hallway seems long and empty between us.

"Are you okay?" I ask.

"Tired."

My gaze narrows, and I take tentative steps toward him. "You know, if you were ever going to win the bet, now's your chance."

Can I make it any clearer?

Jordan's lips twitch. "Oh, I understood that. I think everyone down there knew exactly what your plans were when we came up here. You need to work on subtlety."

"Geez, first I'm too awkward and twitchy, and now I'm too obvious? Did I skip the middle ground?"

"Seems there's only two speeds with you."

"So ... you're not interested in coming in my bedroom? Excuse the double entendre ... no, wait, don't excuse it."

Jordan throws his head back. "Blake."

"What?"

His gray eyes meet mine. "I like you. I really do. I realized when you brought me here you might be the closest thing I have to a genuine friend in Hollywood. You're someone real, which is really rare in our industry."

"And?"

The struggle in his eyes is evident.

"Oh, you actually don't want to ... with me."

"Holy fuck do I ever, but it's ... and ..." He sighs.

I step even closer and put my hand on his biceps.

Bad move. Even that is putting me on edge. Jordan's here rejecting me, but my dick isn't getting the memo.

"It's me," I say. "You can tell me anything. Just say it. No judgment, remember?"

Jordan can't even look at me as he says it. "I don't want you to be like the others."

"What others?" My face falls as hard as my hand from his arm. "Oh."

"I'm not saying …" He's quick to jump in. "Well, I *am* saying, but I don't mean you're going to be an asshole like the others were, but I'm getting over Ben, and I've been here so many times before. You have no idea how much I want to be this guy for you." Jordan pulls me against him. "You can feel it."

I sure can.

"But there comes a time I think in everyone's life where they have to choose self-preservation. And, really, I probably should've done that the second I found out Ben was cheating on me."

My heart breaks for him, which only makes me want to wrap him in my arms and console him, but I also know that this must be difficult for him. It's obvious he wants me, so I'm not questioning that, and if I push my way into his room and be there for him, it's a temptation he doesn't want.

He's asking me to back off, so I will.

I step away so I'm not tempted to change my mind. "I would never want to be like the other guys you've been with."

"I know, but—"

"No," I'm quick to say. "That wasn't me trying to persuade you to change your mind. I just wanted you to know that. You deserve so much better than Ben."

"I know that too." He smiles, but it's weak.

"I'm going to go to bed. In, uh, my room. Away from yours."

"That's probably best. I think you have all the material you need for the movie."

Right. The movie. The whole reason we landed here in the first place.

"Goodnight." I turn on my heel and head for my room, trying

to stop the disappointment from seeping in, but I think it's too late.

CHAPTER 14
JORDAN

"I'M CHOOSING SELF-PRESERVATION," I mutter as I throw clothes into my suitcase. "I'd prefer not to have sex with you because I'm a big stupid dummy." I empty my suitcase on the bed to start repacking again.

Jojo helped me on my way here, and I don't know how she made it all fit.

Ever since I made the idiotic decision to not have sex with Blake, he had no problem slipping back into friendship mode. We've slept in separate beds, the affection he was getting so good at stopped, and sometimes I catch him staring at me with sympathy in his eyes, and that makes me feel even more gross than if I'd slept with him.

I should've had sex with him.

Because today we're leaving Montana and going back to LA, where we've been called back to set to resume filming.

Which means I'm walking away from here not only having lost the bet, but I'm so sexually frustrated because even though Blake could easily switch off all the sexual tension, I'm still filled with a need for him.

The thought of making him come, being the first guy to ever see his face flushed, his blue eyes dark with lust while I suck his—

Stop!

I reach for my phone because I need the distraction. I call Ash and put it on speaker so I can keep packing while we talk.

"Don't tell me," he answers. "You slept with him."

"No, I didn't, and it's all your fault. I thought you were supposed to be my friend. You give the worst advice ever because now I'm horny and lonely and I have to fly back to LA and see Ben again."

"I'm the worst person ever. How dare I look out for your well-being!"

"Exactly. Let me be self-destructive. At least then I'd be going back to LA somewhat relaxed and not so … agitated."

"Go jerk off. That'll release endorphins or whatever it is that makes people happy."

"We're leaving in twenty and I'm not packed, and Jojo's not here to do it for me." I sound petulant and entitled, but I don't care.

Whose idea was it to starve myself of shared orgasms? That guy is a jerk.

There's a knock on my door, and I turn to see Blake standing there. "It's true," he says. "Jerking off releases the same amount of endorphins as sex with someone else. It's basic science."

Oh shit, how long has he been standing there, and how much did he hear?

"I thought I heard voices," Blake says. "I was worried you'd gotten cabin fever and went stir-crazy from not doing anything for a couple of weeks. Good to know you're not talking to yourself."

The opposite, actually. I might be sex starved and pining over someone who could never see me as more than an experimental lay, but getting away from Hollywood and pretending it doesn't exist has been exactly what I needed. Any other time I've left, it's usually been to go home to visit my parents and friends, but that's never really a vacation. I can't remember the last time I had a real vacation.

Ben took me to Cancún in between films last year, and that was pretty nice, but he was on the phone ninety percent of the time, trying to lock down his next movie.

Here, I haven't wanted to think about work because that would mean thinking about Ben, which would make me think about Chad and that car accident, and …

I grunt. "Can we stay? Do we have to go back?"

"You willing to give up the paycheck?"

"No." I throw more stuff in my luggage.

"You're never going to fit it all if you don't fold it." Blake enters the room and starts helping me.

"Sounds like you're in good hands, Jord," Ash says. "I have to go."

"Thanks for nothing," I sing.

He laughs before he ends the call.

"Were you serious?" Blake asks. "About not going back?"

"No. As much as I'd love to stay, we need to go back. This movie is already over budget and behind schedule. Everything a studio loves in a multimillion-dollar project."

"How do you feel about seeing Ben?"

"Like I'd rather put my balls in a blender than have to deal with him."

"I could make that happen if you want. It's one way to get out of doing the movie."

"You're, like, the bestest friend ever."

"I know, right? I'm so kind and considerate … Hell, I was even thinking of letting you off the hook with this whole bet thing." He continues to pack for me, taking out everything I've already put in my bags to fold it "properly" and put it back.

"Technically, I could have won. You were practically begging for it."

"Practically and actually are two different things, but the bet was that we'd have sex, and unless I'm mistaken and all those dreams I've been having about you were actually true, then—"

"You've been having sex dreams about me?"

"Every damn night." He laughs, but it sounds humorless. "I know it was smart not to go there, but it hasn't stopped me from thinking about it. Or imagining it. Or fantasizing about it."

I groan. "Blaaaaake."

"Damn, or thinking about you saying my name like that."

I pull back. "You imagine me whining during sex?"

"Is that what that sound was? It sounded more frustrated than anything. Needy."

"You're torturing me."

His smile falters. "Sorry. I'll stop messing with you."

"Is that really what it is? Just messing with me?"

Blake's lips purse as if he's trying to decide to tell me the truth or lie. "It's ... not *not* the truth, but I know where you stand. I can stop."

"Please. It's already hard enough not to randomly pounce on you."

"I'm going to go put my bags in the car. You going to be okay to pack those last few things?"

"Yup."

Blake steps closer to me and lowers his voice. "Just so you know? The pouncing thing is okay with me. The offer is there if you want to change your mind."

I'm so going to change my mind.

All I can say is, I'm thankful the flight home had some of the others on board with us because otherwise, I know I would have caved and punched my mile high club card. Mason and Denver are staying in Montana for a bit longer to be with Mason's mom, but Brix, Harley, Ryder, and Lyric were good buffers for the flight.

Still, as I get off the plane, I'm as frustrated as I was before we left Montana. If it weren't for needing to go straight to the set, I'd do something about it because I need to be strong to see Ben again.

I don't think I'm desperate enough to forgive whatever bull-shit story he wants to spew at me, but I might be desperate enough to ignore his words enough to get some release.

Blake Monroe's sex appeal is driving me to seriously low standards.

"You need to be on set today?" I ask Blake.

There are three cars waiting for us all outside the private charter terminal, and I'm guessing the last one is Blake's and mine, but then Lyric, Harley, and Ryder get into the one and wave as they drive off.

"You got called in today?" Blake asks. "I thought production didn't pick up until tomorrow."

"Ben has called me in for a meeting. I was wondering if it was a crew thing or a me thing."

"Need me to go with you?"

"What, and flex your Coby Godspeed muscles at him to scare him away? It's cute you want to defend me, but—"

"It's not defending. It's protecting. What if he wants to get back together?"

"I can handle myself. Especially against a manipulative narcis-sist like Ben."

"If you're sure."

I'm not, but I'll be fine. Probably. "I'm sure."

"Well, I'll see you tomorrow, then?"

"Tomorrow." The sooner we get this film wrapped, the sooner I can put Ben and Blake behind me.

Maybe I'll go home to Boston for a while. Find a nice Bostonian gay man who says things like "I'm wicked smaht. Let's drink some tonic and head down the cape. It'll be wicked pissa."

Aww, I miss home.

But as my driver heads toward the studio, I can't deny the hold LA has over me. This is my home too. It has been for over a decade. A break would be nice, but I don't see me settling down back in Boston anytime soon.

After dropping my bags at my apartment, the driver takes me to the studio and says he'll wait for my text to come pick me up.

I've been doing LA wrong all these years. I need to do it the boy band way because having a driver is awesome. I don't have to care about traffic. Only problem is, the less I'm focused on that, the more time I have to overthink.

And I can't help overthinking Ben and what he's going to say.

I get out of the car and text Ben that I'm here, and he replies that he's in my trailer. If this had to do with the movie, he'd at least have the pretense of meeting me on set, so I guess this will be the conversation I've been dreading but expecting.

Will he grovel and ask for forgiveness? Will he tell me it will never happen again, and it means nothing?

When I get to my trailer, nothing can prepare me for what he actually says.

"Hey."

I wait. Nothing else comes. "Hi ..."

Still waiting.

He's leaning against the small kitchen counter with his arms folded, and on the table in the eating area is a box. "All your stuff from my house is in there."

No groveling, then. Okay. Cool. It's better this way anyway.

"I sent Jojo to pick it up."

"I wanted to see you when you got it."

"*Why?*"

"To say I'm sorry."

Here we go.

"And ... I lied."

"You lied about being sorry?"

"No. I lied about ... Chad."

Huh? "You didn't have sex with Chad?"

"Yes. No. Wait." He rubs his temples. "I lied about it being nothing. He's really been there for me during recovery, you know? With me being out of action and everything"—he gestures to his crotch—"we got to know each other on a deeper level. It wasn't focused on the physical like you and me."

My breath catches because it's happening again. My throat feels tight, and tears well in my eyes, but I'm not going to let them fall. It's not Ben that I'm upset over. He and *Chad* deserve each other.

It's that I knew this would happen. I *knew* it.

"I hope we can both move on and keep this civil. For the production's sake."

Nope. Fuck civility, fuck this production, and fuck Benjamin Randt.

I blink at him. And then blink some more.

What are you supposed to say to something like that?

"Jordy?"

That snaps me out of the melancholy.

"What, you want me to congratulate you?" I snap.

"Well, no, but I thought you'd at least have some reaction."

"Why would I care?" My voice goes high-pitched, giving away that I really do care. "We were just physical, like you said. And you weren't the only one who spent the last two weeks getting to know someone better, so there's that. You're not the only one who can move on so fast."

Ben's eyes narrow. "Who?"

"Who do you think?"

And please give me a name so I can use it.

"Didn't you go away with Blake?"

I don't know who told him or if he's going off tabloid gossip, but I may as well go with it.

"Yep."

"He's straight. There's no way."

"If you remember, that's how I like 'em." Ugh, the words taste bitter as they fall out of my mouth. "Was that all? Blake is actually waiting for me back at his place. I thought this was a meeting about the movie. If I'd known it had been a pointless expedition to find whatever closure you think you needed, I wouldn't have left Blake in his warm bed to come here."

Ben eyes me as if he thinks I'm lying, and hey, he has a right. I'm lying out my ass. But without tooting my own horn, I'm a good actor, and I'm believable enough.

"We'll see you on set tomorrow for Blake's and my sex scene, and don't worry. We've been getting plenty of practice."

Motherfucker.

I take my box of belongings and leave, texting the driver to come pick me up. When we leave the studio lot, I direct him somewhere I really don't want to go.

Denver and Mason's gate unlocks with a click when I buzz and give the camera an awkward wave, and then Blake opens the front door with a wary smile.

I take a deep breath. "I need a favor."

CHAPTER 15
BLAKE

"WHAT HAPPENED WITH BEN?"

"He's a dick. What else is new?" Jordan heads for the bar area in Denver's house and then remembers it's empty. "Probably better I don't drink anyway. Apparently I do stupid things when I'm sober now too."

"What stupid thing? Come sit." I gesture for him to take the couch, and he flops down unceremoniously and slumps so his head rests against the backrest.

His long legs hang off the end, and it makes him look ten feet tall.

I want to join him, but if the last couple of weeks has taught me anything, it's that I physically need to keep my distance from Jordan so I don't break his rules. So I don't push.

Because being in his vicinity drives me crazy.

I may have been able to play it off like everything is normal, we're friends, I'm chill and whatever, but I'm really not.

I can't actually remember a time where I've wanted to kiss someone more than I do Jordan Brooks. But I'm holding back because I respect him too damn much to cross lines.

We're friends. That's all.

"You're gonna hate me," Jordan says.

"There's very few things you could do to make me hate you."

"Okay, pick the worst one, and then maybe you won't think this is that bad. Actually, times the worst by ten."

I truly think about it because I can't imagine anything he could do. "Seeing as you were reluctant to make murder a possible favor, I can't assume you've done that. But if you accidentally killed Ben and need an alibi, I'm there."

Jordan lifts his head. "Really? You'd alibi a murder for me?"

I shift from one foot to the other. "Umm, okay, I said that because I didn't think you'd actually kill someone. But if we're talking in the jokey way people do, then yes. Alibi at your service."

Jordan sinks his teeth into his bottom lip and says it all in a rush. "I-might've-told-Ben-you-and-I-are-together."

"What?"

He stands in a flourish and paces the room. "Ben is in love. Can you believe that?"

"With you?"

"No. With Chad."

"Fucking what?"

Jordan throws his hands up. "Thank you. Apparently he's all in love because while he was recovering, Chad looked after him and gave him more than just a physical connection, which is all I was to him." He lowers his voice. "It's all I ever am to them. Someone pretty to have on their arm and in their bed until they get bored of me."

"I'm so sorry, Jordan. That's shitty." And now I want to kill Ben. Maybe Jordan will need to provide me an alibi.

"So I was trying to be strong and pretend like I don't care— because I don't. I *don't*."

"You do, but you're allowed to, so go on."

"No, I really don't. I knew he wasn't going to be forever."

"But you still gave him a part of you, and he betrayed that, so you're allowed to care, and you're allowed to be mad. You don't have to be in love or have feelings for someone to hate them for the shitty thing they did."

Jordan stops pacing and blinks at me for a brief moment before he goes back to pacing. "Anyway. I told him we went away together and now we're a thing. Because I'm immature like that."

"You chose self-preservation again. Hey, you're getting good at that."

His gray eyes meet mine. "You're not mad? This could have the fans turning on you if we were to claim this publicly or if Ben tells everyone, which is a possibility."

"The media thinks we're together anyway. I don't think there's putting that back in a box."

"This could make the movie a difficult work environment."

"Ben has already achieved that, not only when it comes to you, but with me as well. He's hated me since the beginning. This is nothing new."

"Why … how …" Jordan's mouth closes.

"Why, how, what?"

"Why are you being so good about this?"

"Because I care about you and you're hurt? Because on some level, I think Ben deserves it? Because after working with him for only a couple of weeks, I know I never want to work with him again?"

"He could stop you from getting other roles. He could play the diva card and say you were terrible to work with. He could—"

I hold up my hand. "He can't touch me. At least not with the Coby movies. The studio won't fire me from them, at least."

"What about advancing your acting career? Being taken seriously."

"Do you want me to be mad? I can if you really want."

"No, I want you to really think about what could happen if you agree to this. We have an out. Tomorrow on set, you can yell at me and tell me you're done with me for everyone to hear."

"What exactly am I agreeing to? Telling Ben we're together? The crew? Coming out publicly?"

The public thing could be a problem considering my recent questioning status when it comes to my sexuality, but I'm technically already out, thanks to those photos. If I were to deny them and go back on what's already out there, I'd feel more deceptive than if I just let the cards fall where they may. It's not like Jordan and I haven't been … intimate. If we want to call jerking off together intimate. It sure as fuck isn't innocent, though, either.

"I … I don't know," Jordan admits.

"I'm happy to tell Ben and the crew whatever. Short of doing publicity tours where they ask about our sex lives, that's probably where I'd draw the line."

"I could kiss you."

"Well, I am your boyfriend, it seems." And I'm definitely not going to say no to tasting Jordan's mouth again.

He steps toward me. I lick my lips. But as he moves in, he turns his head and kisses my cheek instead. "Thank you for doing this."

"I've said it before, and I'll say it again—you deserve better, Jordan."

"Thanks." He looks down as he says it, like he doesn't actually believe me. He steps back. "I'm going to go home and unpack and get ready for being back on set tomorrow."

Is it weird I don't want him to leave? This isn't even my house, but I want to ask him to stay.

When we parted at the airport today after spending two weeks together, I should've been grateful for some space. But unlike when Harley, Ryder, and Lyric drove away and I waved them off, I didn't want to see Jordan get in that other car.

I can't put that on him, though. So instead of asking him to stay, I smile and tell him, "I'll see you tomorrow."

I stand by my decision to help Jordan even when we get to set and every pair of eyes are on our intertwined fingers as we hold hands. Jordan told me to cancel my driver and that he will drive me all over LA today, mumbling something about looking so sickeningly in love we don't want to leave each other's sides.

"I've got to get to makeup. You have to go to wardrobe," I say.

Jordan pulls on my hand and jerks me toward him. Then his arms are around me, and he's staring down at me with such … admiration. He's such a damn good actor, expressing emotions clearly with one stare. I hope to be as good as him someday. "I'll miss you." The loud tone in which he says it almost makes me laugh, because it's obvious he wants people to hear, but I take my roles seriously, so I don't break.

"You'll see me in half an hour where you get to kiss me and pretend to give me a blowjob. You'll be fine." I pat his shoulder and go to walk off when his eyes catch on something behind me.

Suddenly, Jordan grips my shirt and pulls me back to him, fusing his mouth to mine.

It's hard to think of anything else than the real kiss he gave me in Mason's hot tub because the way he claims my mouth is so forceful and desperate.

My tongue is desperate for his too. This has to seem real, after all. Yes, let's go with that excuse for why I part his lips and dive right in.

His mouth is addictive, and even when he tries to pull away, I won't let him because I'm not ready.

Then he groans, and I realize I have to stop before this turns into a porno set.

I reluctantly pull away. "Do you think that convinced them? I'm willing to keep going if you think we need it."

He lowers his forehead to mine. "If I haven't said it already. Thank you for doing this."

"Kissing you is a really terrible thing to endure, I agree."

He still looks lovingly at me when he says, "You're so mean to me."

"So, so mean, but you like it. Instead of hugs, I give insults. You should feel flattered."

"Oh, I so am."

He turns to walk away, but I call after him.

"Bye, Shnookums! I miss you already."

He spins back around and mouths, "Shnookums?"

I shrug.

We both walk in opposite directions, and I ignore all the vacant stares watching me do it. I even catch Ben's scowl before I disappear into the makeup trailer.

But now here comes the hard part. We're picking up exactly where we left off—the blowjob scene. With Jordan telling Ben we're together, I'm worried I'm going to choke again and give us away completely.

It might be true real couples don't necessarily have chemistry onscreen, but this needs to be somewhat believable. Not for the movie's sake but for Jordan's.

I do have to admit, rubbing Jordan's fake happiness in Ben's face will be fun, though. And that's what I decide to do. I'm going to have fun with it.

This production has had so many setbacks already, so many rewrites, I'm finding it hard to still give a damn.

And my new blasé attitude must work, or maybe it's that I'm more comfortable with Jordan now, but during the scene, we don't falter once.

I push Jordan inside the "hotel room," he takes off my shirt, and the whole time we're kissing, I want to kiss him for real.

Jordan lays me down on the bed softer than the script calls for, but it's intimate and sweet. He kisses my neck and moves down my chest, reaching where my pants are. They're out of frame, thank fuck, because even though there are still a million crew members watching, and this isn't exactly a romantic moment with overhead lighting, a camera mounted above us, and this is all simulated, my dick is apparently still back in Montana and is ready for real action.

I don't even have to force my turned-on face because all I have to do is imagine Jordan unzipping my pants and reaching inside to stroke me like he did to himself in that shower. I can practically feel his breath on my dick as I think about what it would be like for him to lower his head and take me in his mouth.

All that stubble that stings my lips when he kisses me, I want to feel that on my dick.

"Cut!" Ben yells, and I almost follow it up with "Nooooo."

But I manage to clear my throat and keep it tamped down.

Jordan stands and smirks at me. "Well, if no one believed it before, they do now." He stares at my crotch.

"I can't help it when I'm around you anymore. You broke me in Montana."

As we reset to do the scene again, he smiles over at me.

"Did I break you or show you what you've been missing?"

Definitely the latter.

Jordan keeps his eyes on me while he says, "I have an idea. If we really want this to be romantic, we should kiss properly. Not porno tongues but sensual tongues." He turns to Ben, who's moved in closer to us.

Ben's gaze flits from mine to Jordan's and back again. Then he nods. "If you're both comfortable with it."

"Why wouldn't we be?" I say breezily. "Jordan's tongue in my mouth is my second favorite thing."

"Oh really?" Jordan asks. "What's the first?"

"When you put it somewhere else."

Jordan looks like he's trying not to laugh, but Ben grunts and walks back to his spot behind the camera monitors.

We get through the call sheet, by some miracle, ahead of schedule. Jordan and I go to our separate trailers to shower and change to go home but meet up again to go in his car.

"Ben was … weird today," I say on the way home.

"How so?"

"He was *professional*."

"I think he might have been in shock. That whole shnookums

thing had to have thrown him. He probably spent the rest of the day trying to poke holes in our story."

Or he doesn't care, I want to say but don't. I won't hurt Jordan by pointing out Ben doesn't seem all that upset over their breakup.

I did see the flash of hurt in Jordan's eyes when Chad brought Ben some coffee and took the seat next to him to watch the scenes we were shooting.

The thing is, though, I don't actually think Jordan even likes Ben. It's the betrayal that stings, and it has been years of men doing the same thing to him over and over. They experiment with him and marry someone else.

Jordan pulls up to Denver and Mason's place and idles on the street.

I'm about to get out when I realize I don't want to say good-bye. "Got any dinner plans?"

"I've imposed on Denver and Mason too much. You should go in and have dinner with them."

"They're still in Montana for a few more days." My heart's in my throat as I say the next words, but not because of what I'm asking but what it implies. "You should come in."

Yep, I may as well have said, *"You should come inside me."*

Jordan hesitates for only a tiny second before he agrees. "Where do I park?"

CHAPTER 16
JORDAN

AFTER THE SHITSHOW that was today, I should go home to my apartment, slip under my covers, and go to sleep. Instead, I'm sitting on a stool in Denver's kitchen as Blake moves around the space confidently, like he doesn't have the same regrets I do.

As long as I can keep my hands to myself, I'll be fine. My body might be screaming at me to throw myself at him and keeps imagining how good we could make each other feel, but I'm strong enough to resist.

I think.

I fucking hope.

When Blake slides a plate over my way, I stare at it.

"I thought you said you were making your specialty? This is—"

"Grilled cheese is my specialty. You think I can cook? None of us Eleven guys can, except Ryder. I've been living out of a suitcase, mostly in hotels, for the last ten years."

"Why is that? I thought it was weird that you're crashing with Mason and Denver and don't have a place of your own."

"I was living in a hotel because I didn't know what my next moves were. I don't see the point in renting a place or buying somewhere when I'm hardly home. I used to have a house in

Montecito when Eleven were together, but I was hardly ever there. I gave it to my parents when I started the Coby movies, and I'd feel weird being all 'Okay, I'm coming home now. Get out.'"

"You could live with them."

"With my parents? I could. If I wanted to be smothered to death by their love."

"Oh no, the problem loved children have!"

Blake laughs. "Touché. They're great people, don't get me wrong. I visit them whenever I can and make sure I catch up with them, but I like my own space. When I'm home, I still feel like a child, and it's too weird. Plus, it's not exactly close. Just far enough to be a pain in the ass if I'm working in LA."

"Fair enough."

I bite into the grilled cheese and throw Blake a thumbs-up. "At least you didn't fuck up the easiest thing to cook."

"It's why it's my specialty." He joins me at the counter, pulling up another stool. "So how are you really doing after today?"

I mock gasp. "Is this a pity grilled cheese?"

"If I pitied you, I would have ordered in and gotten alcohol."

"Oh, so you don't love me enough to give me *the good stuff*?" As soon as the words are out of my mouth, I want to wince because it sounds so sexual it's not even funny.

Okay, maybe it is funny because Blake throws his head back and laughs. "I'll give you the good stuff if you want it, but I thought we agreed not to go there."

"I was talking about food and wine. Get your mind out of the gutter." But no, seriously, please stay there.

"Sure you were. Just like all those other times you'd flirt with me. Only then, you weren't actually expecting me to say yes."

We're moving into dangerously flirty territory, and he's right. When we started working on our movie, I had no doubt my flirting rolled right off his back. Now … since Montana …

He eyes me expectantly, but there's no way to respond to that.

Blake's blond hair is messy, and his blue eyes shine in amusement. "We should go for a swim."

"I don't have my trunks. Your friends stole them from me in Montana."

Blake snorts. "It didn't stop you there."

The thought of Blake all wet, naked in the pool … I can't go there, but I'm so going to. "I'm no longer hungry."

Blake stands and leads me outside, grabbing towels on the way.

It's a mistake I've made a million times over, and it's one I'll probably keep making. Because even though I'm always the one that ends up hurt, I want to watch Blake come undone again. Only, this time I want to be the one to do it.

Blake pulls his shirt over his head and drops it to the grass as he makes his way over to the pool. The outside houselights illuminate his silhouette, and as he turns his head back toward me with a coy look on his face, the blue hues coming from the pool lights give him an ethereal quality.

He could very well be the most attractive man I've ever been with.

His fingers dip into the waistband of his pants and shimmy them down his legs along with his underwear, exposing his amazing ass.

I only got a short glimpse of it when he was wearing that thong, but exposed bare … Nngh, I have to bite my knuckles before I jump him.

He dives into the pool, and I'm still completely dressed. I shuck off my shirt and undo my jeans while I toe off my shoes and socks. Blake comes up for air and watches me from the water, slowly inching toward the side closest to me.

His stare touches every inch of my skin as I remove all my clothes. My entire body heats, and when I drop my underwear to the ground and step out of them, his gaze goes right to my very hard cock.

Then the fucker smiles. "Aww, that for me?"

I reach for myself and give a soft stroke, pulling back the velvety tight skin.

There's no denying the way he reacts to me. "Shit. Maybe this wasn't such a good idea," Blake mutters.

"Why's that?"

"Because I promised I wouldn't try to have sex with you, but you're making it really hard."

"Pun intended?"

"Definitely." Blake moves toward the steps of the pool and emerges just enough for me to see his cock in a similar state.

I release mine and go to the side of the pool, lowering myself to sit on the edge and dangle my feet in the water. Blake watches me, and like the last time we were naked together, I love how his gaze wanders over me and takes me all in.

I go back to my cock, stroking slowly, and have to bite my lip to stop from noise escaping and scaring Blake off. I stare down where I'm working myself over while I lean backward and use my free hand to hold me up.

"Jord ..." Blake croaks.

My gaze flicks toward him. That hungry look in his eye, the way he can't take his attention away from what I'm doing, this is the type of shit I get high on.

Blake looks like he wants to do so many things to me, and I don't want to deny him. At all. I should, but I don't want to.

"I might need some help," I say.

He hesitates but not for long. Blake moves toward me, the water swishing around his body, and he arrives at my side. He's on the last step, covered by the water until about his nipples. With me on the side of the pool, he's just the right height, if he were to lean over—

"Are you sure?" he whispers.

"That I need help?"

"That you want it. From me."

"I don't want to want it from you, but I do. There's no changing that."

His blue eyes, only made bluer by the lights in the water, pierce through me, and I have to hold back a shudder.

"Get in the water." His voice is warm and deep, sounding very similar to the voice he uses for Coby Godspeed. It's an octave deeper than his natural voice. And even though I'm sure he purposely does it for his movies, right now I get the impression he can't help it.

"I thought you might've wanted a little taste first. I can tell you the chlorine taste isn't delightful, so now's your chance before I'm all wet."

His mouth opens, but no sound comes out. I'd mistake it for nerves if it weren't for the hungry look in his eye. "I ... uh ... wouldn't know what I'm doing."

"I can show you." I reach for the back of his head and grip his hair tight.

His tongue darts out to wet his lips, and his Adam's apple bobs.

As I gently push his mouth toward my cock, I have to hold my breath because I can't believe this is happening.

"Lick the tip."

I try to school my reaction to the first touch of his tongue on my slit, but it's near impossible to hold in the shudder.

He licks down my shaft, even though I don't tell him to, and then I don't even need to tell him the next part either. Blake instinctively moves his mouth back up, slowly, and sucks the head into his mouth.

"Fuck," I hiss.

He pulls back. "Did I do something wrong?"

"Not at all. I wasn't expecting you to ... That was ... yeah, fucking good. That mouth is ... is ..." It's going to break me.

Blake lowers his head again, and this time when he sucks me into his mouth, I let him take the lead. He tests me out, alternating between licking the head and sucking me, but he isn't game enough to go far yet, and that's fair enough. He's already done more than I thought he would.

Maybe, deep down, I'd hoped the thought of giving me a blowjob would make him rethink this and put an end to it now before it really began, but no such luck. He's not only eager for it, he's a natural.

It's difficult not to thrust into his mouth. I've had years of restraint with newbs, but with Blake … "Fuck, Blake." I grit my teeth and squeeze my ass cheeks together to try to hold myself back because I want to move in and out of his warm mouth so much I'm scared of hurting him if I let myself go. I want to fuck his face and come down his throat, but it's way, way, way, way, way too soon to put that on him.

I need him to stop before I can't help myself. "Kiss me," I say and pull him off my cock.

Blake looks up at me with confusion written all over his face.

"If you keep doing that, I won't be able to hold back," I say.

His slight frown breaks into something happier. "Maybe I don't want you to hold back."

"Whoa, slow down a bit. That's way too much pressure to put on me. We need to take this one step at a time. You don't go skiing for the first time and ask to try the diamond run first up."

He smiles. "And in this situation, your dick is the diamond run? You think highly of yourself, don't you?"

"Have you met me?"

He laughs. "True."

"Besides, we have so much more to explore tonight."

"Oh, do we?"

"Mmhmm." I pull away from him and slip into the pool. The water is heated to the perfect temperature, warming me from the inside out.

With Blake being on the last step, it brings us to basically the same height when I move toward him and wrap my arms around his back, pressing us together.

His hard cock digs into my hip, and he runs his hands over my wide shoulders and down my chest, trailing his fingers over my nipples.

I suck in a sharp breath and ask him again. "Kiss me. I've missed your lips."

"I thought maybe you might be sick of kissing me after today." Even though he's teasing, there's a seriousness to his tone I can't decipher.

"Mm, take after take of having your tongue in my mouth. I hate my job so much."

But even as I pull him closer, Blake doesn't make a move to kiss me, and that's when I realize …

"Do you want to slow down?" I ask.

He shakes his head. "I'm just worried that once we start, I won't want to stop."

CHAPTER 17
BLAKE

I WON'T WANT to stop. *Ever.* That's what I almost say, but I hold strong. While the rest of my resolve crumbles, I can still control my mouth. Or at least the words coming out of it.

When it comes to kissing Jordan, yeah, I have no control there.

Especially when he says, "We don't have to stop."

Thank fuck.

I don't think he's expecting me to practically jump him, but I do. I wrap my legs around his waist, my arms around his neck, and fuse my mouth to his.

Jordan stumbles back but grabs my ass to hold me to him as he sucks on my tongue. My hips move against him, seeking friction.

Did I think sucking a dick and grinding up on a guy could ever turn me on like this? No way. But I also never gave it much thought before.

I didn't know what truly giving myself over to someone was. Not like this. Not where I'm at Jordan's mercy, in his capable hands, and without any reservations.

Granted, there was a moment there, when Jordan said I could taste him, that a little panic set in, but not because I didn't want it. I just thought I'd be bad at it. Hell, I probably was, but the way

Jordan is with me, encouraging and supportive, and still so hard for me, I don't feel embarrassed by it.

I want to do it again and get better. I want to make him come. And with the tiny taste of precum I thought I felt on my tongue, I want the full experience of his whole load.

He feels strong as he holds me up, even though we're in water and I'm practically weightless. We kiss some more, his mouth just as firm as his arms.

I itch to do what I wanted to back in that hot tub in Montana. I want to wrap my fingers around his long shaft and stroke him until he can't control himself.

Images of him in the shower, jerking himself off while watching me do the same … Fuck. I break from his mouth. "Can I … Can …" Why can't I say it?

"What do you want?" Jordan asks. "Tell me exactly what you want."

"I want to touch you."

"I'll tell you what." Jordan carries me close to the edge until my back is pressed against the tiled lip on the side of the pool. "Wrap your hand around both of us, and while you do that, I'm going to touch you in other places."

"Other places …"

A smile takes over his face as he moves his hand and slips a finger inside my ass crack. "You can say no."

"I don't want to."

He immediately removes his hand. "Fair enough. We do this at your pace."

"No, I meant … I don't want to say no. I want you to touch me there."

"Wow, when you go all in—"

"That's what you'll be saying later."

Jordan looks stunned. "I'm a bad influence on you."

"Mmhmm." I reach between us. "You sure are." To be able to grip both of us, I have to loosen my legs around him and sink a bit further down in the water, but when I manage to do it, a ripple of pleasure shoots through me.

"Definitely all my fault," Jordan breathes. "I'll take all the credit … I mean, *blame*."

"It is all your fault." I move my hand over us, gripping tight and stroking long and hard. "It's your fault I'm this desperate for you."

Jordan makes a guttural sound at the back of his throat and kisses me again. No holding back.

It's nothing like on set earlier today. It's more heightened, it's more intense, and it surges feelings of need inside me. On set, while it did turn me on—there's no denying that—I was conscious of my mouth, my head placement, how it would look for the camera.

Here and now, there are no cameras. There's no one but Jordan and me, and I do what feels right.

My hand wrapped around us has stilled because I'm so focused on Jordan's tongue and his mouth, but when he rotates his hips, sliding his cock against mine through my fist, I remember to keep going.

Jordan breaks his lips from mine just long enough to say, "Don't stop, okay? Concentrate on what you're doing and relax for me."

I nod, and then his mouth is back on mine. I keep stroking us together, and that's when Jordan's finger presses against my hole.

I immediately do the opposite of what he told me to.

He trails his lips over my cheek and down to my neck. Where I expect him to laugh or maybe mock me for it, all he does is encourage me. "You feel so good against me. I want your body so much." More light kisses on my skin.

It's nothing I haven't been told before, but the deep timber of Jordan's voice, the way he's holding me, I can't deny there's a different allure to it.

Because Jordan's a man, because he's taking on the dominating role here, or maybe it's simply that I'm friends with Jordan and I know he's not using me for my name or because I'm famous.

Yeah, that might be the most intoxicating part of all.

With him murmuring in my ear about how much he wants me, I'm able to relax.

His finger pushes inside me, and not gonna lie, it's weird at first. It makes me squirm and not in a good way. But then Jordan's mouth distracts me, taking my lips and pushing his tongue between them.

He teases my ass, turning me inside out as he slowly fingers me. The more he plays around, the more I begin to like it, and then out of nowhere, he hits this spot inside me, and it becomes a thousand times better.

Jordan knows it too because gone are the soft words and gentle touches. He thrusts into my fist while pressing his finger against my prostate, and I almost come unglued.

My orgasm builds and builds, climbing to impossible heights. Where I expect it to crash like a rolling wave, it teeters on the edge, never falling.

"I can't wait to fuck you," he grunts.

Yes almost falls from my mouth, but he keeps going.

"Not tonight, but it will happen. If you like my finger, imagine my cock."

I'm breathing rapidly now, unable to take in enough air.

"I'll take you from behind, maybe watch you ride me. Grip your hair tight."

A moan rips from me because I want that. It's weird that I do, but it doesn't feel weird in this moment. It sounds hot and consuming, and he's right. If just his finger can turn me into this writhing, needy thing, I want to see what else Jordan can do.

"Tell me when you're close."

Close? I've been close since he first touched me.

"I want to fall apart together. Come at the same time."

"Oh, shit." My eyes roll back. "Fuck, that's … Yeah, I'm gonna—"

I don't have the time or the awareness of what's going on before I realize Jordan's finger is gone and I'm being lifted out of the pool.

My ass lands on the tiled side, and as the first spurts of cum erupt from my cock, Jordan's mouth covers the tip, and he sucks me down.

I slam my eyes shut, because the force my orgasm hits with is enough to make my entire body shake and quiver. Jordan's mouth on me only intensifies the explosion.

My breath catches, and it's all stilted, and even after I've run out of cum and Jordan pulls back and wipes his mouth, I still can't breathe right.

"I thought you said pool chemicals taste gross?" I'm proud I even got half that sentence out without needing to take a breath.

He chuckles. "They do, but that was so worth it. I didn't want you to have to taste it, especially on your first blowjob ever. You'd never give another one otherwise."

"Aww, well, thank you for looking out for me."

"You? I'm looking out for your future boyfriend. I'm a giver like that."

"He thanks you in advance," I say dryly.

I lean back, the rough surface of the cement by the pool scratchy on my back, but I don't care. "Fuck, that wrung me out."

"You and me both."

Oh, wait. I lean up on my elbows. "Did you ... Do I need to ..." I gesture toward his cock.

"I got myself there. With swallowing you down like that, it didn't take much. That was so hot. But, uh, could you maybe not mention to Denver I defiled his pool?"

"We'll throw in even more chemicals. It'll be like it never happened."

Jordan's face does something I can't really read. He's smiling, but it looks like it's taking a lot of effort. "I guess I should get out and dry off so I can go home."

"Home? You don't want to stay? Denver and Mason aren't coming home for a few days."

He eyes me. "You want me to?"

"After that? Definitely."

"Okay. I'll stay."

Getting woken up by both our phones pinging can't be a good thing.

Jordan squirms in my arms.

"Sorry." I pull back.

He laughs. "It's not the first time you've spooned me in my sleep."

"True." Only, this time I'm pretty sure it was intentional. I want to keep touching him any way I can. His body is a magnet, and I want to plaster myself to him.

"Is that your phone or mine going off?" he asks.

"Both."

"Are we in trouble?"

"Either that or we were both nominated for an Oscar when our movie isn't even out yet."

"Shit." Jordan grabs his phone on the bedside table and squints at it. "New record. Seventeen missed calls from my manager. Nine from my agent. And thirteen from Jojo."

"How did we sleep through all of that?"

"My phone is on that auto-timer thing. It switches to silent between midnight and five."

"Ugh, it's only five? We have to be on set in an hour." I reach to check my phone. "Well, I have one from my people with an added text to call them back, so maybe *you're* in trouble. Which makes sense. I'm the innocent one."

Jordan rolls toward me. "What we did last night is anything but innocent."

My ass clenches at the memory of Jordan finger fucking me in the pool. I can still feel the loss of his fingers, and I want more.

"I think we already agreed that was all your influence, though."

Jordan's smile and light attitude slip away. "We, should, uh, call everyone back. Find out what's going on."

I don't know what I said wrong, but whatever it is, I want to take it back. Last night was … eye-opening. Freeing. I'd be an idiot to screw this up when there's so much more I want to explore with Jordan.

He slips out of bed, his long body on full display with his bare ass right there. "I feel you watching me." Even the mocking tone isn't quite right.

"Did I say something wrong?" I ask.

Jordan looks at me over his shoulder. "What do you mean?"

"You kind of spaced out."

He shakes his head. "Nothing. I'm just wondering what fresh hell we've gotten ourselves into now. I'm not used to this much drama in my life."

"Okay, that is definitely my influence, but hey, it's a sign that you've truly made it. You can't say that until the media has slandered you for something they think you said, did, or took out of context."

"Fun times. The price of fame, I guess."

"It does cost a lot of your soul to reach the top, I'm sorry to say."

Jordan walks back to the bed and sits sideways on the edge so he can still look at me. "What part did you give up?"

"Practically my whole identity. All five of us Eleven guys did. Harley probably sacrificed the most. He's happy now and in a good place, but I've seen him struggle with his sexuality for the better part of a decade. It wasn't that he didn't accept himself, but he believed no one else would accept him."

"I understand that. I was warned when I first got to LA that being openly gay would typecast me, but I was adamant to do it my own way, and I guess it's kind of true. My first big role, my breakout, was me playing a gay side character on a TV drama. I was lucky to score the lead in my first rom-com movie. I only got it because the guy they wanted had a scheduling conflict. After that, I proved I can play a straight guy well, apparently."

"Do you think this role might send you backward?" I ask. "That this might be the thing that keeps you typecast as the token gay character?"

"I'm actually hoping a role like this will open the market to mainstream queer movies. I wouldn't mind being known as the gay guy who starred in all of the queer rom-coms. That's a typecast I'd be okay with. But yeah, going back to playing side characters and dying onscreen … I don't want that. It's a risk, but I think if it works out, then I could do so much good for the world of queer people. I want it to be normalized."

"It should be. Definitely."

"How do you feel about it all?"

"That I find myself suddenly bi?"

Jordan blinks. Then blinks again. "Just like that, huh? Picked a label and everything? Most people take a little longer …"

"I mean, it fits. I liked kissing you more than I thought I would. I definitely enjoyed Montana and waking up next to you. Last night was phenomenal."

Jordan bows. "You're welcome."

"It's bisexual by default, isn't it?"

"You could be fluid."

"I think Ryder identifies as that. He used to constantly tell us how sexuality is a spectrum and often changing, blah blah blah. The more labels that get tossed around, the more confused I become. It's good there are options for anyone who needs them, but for me … I can compartmentalize enough to say I've been with more than one gender. Logical conclusion: bisexual. I know some people need to go deeper than that, but I don't."

Jordan reaches for my hand. "I'm happy it's that easy for you."

"I can internalize and pretend to go through an existential crisis if you like? Wah, what is wrong with me? I don't understand why I love being fingered in the ass by a dude so much!"

"Thank you. That's better. But no, seriously, I'm glad it's not that way for you."

"Me too. I'd been around Harley and Ryder long enough to understand it from an outside perspective, but if it weren't for you, or maybe this movie, I don't think I ever would have worked it out for myself, or that it would've come so easily, so thank you."

That tight smile appears once again. "Hey, it's what I do."

CHAPTER 18
JORDAN

BLAKE'S actually ahead of schedule to break my heart.

He's saying all the usual things, the things I've heard a million times like *thank you* and *it's all because of you*.

And with Blake, it's even more confronting when he doesn't even try to deny it will happen. Like when I joked about making his first blowjob a good experience for his future boyfriend, he didn't do the expected answer of "No, this is a one-off."

How many times have I heard that one?

You're the exception. You aren't the rule. I find you attractive, but I don't see me ever being with a man long term.

Bam, they meet *the one*.

And yet, every single time, my stupid little naive heart always thinks the same. *This one could be different.*

I should be thankful Blake *is* different. Not in the sense he's promising me things I know he won't give, but because he grounds me. I make a joke about it being my fault, he agrees with me. I mention future boyfriends, and he doesn't flinch.

Hell, he's even accepted his newfound queerness probably quicker than anyone ever has in my experience. Even the ones who knew deep down something was always there. This has kind of sideswiped Blake, and he's taken it all in stride.

Times have definitely changed. Before, not identifying as the social default of straight and cis would invoke existential crises. Now, he's able to freely accept who he is with barely any questioning. It's not like that for everyone, and I'm assuming his surrounding support system has to do with that. Having people in the same situation certainly helps the process. Blake knows he's not alone.

I'd joke about having a magic dick—one taste and he's hooked—but I don't have the energy or the enthusiasm for it. I didn't lie—I am happy for him, but also a little sad, because it's usually right after the acceptance part that they walk away.

"Ready to head to set?" Blake asks as I'm finishing shaving in his bathroom with the little battery-powered electric shaver I keep in my car for situations like this.

I hate having to shave every day for a movie. If it were up to me, I'd shave once a week, if that. I don't love a full-on beard, but some scruff never hurt anyone. At least not in a bad way.

The feel of Blake's permanent stubble was heaven on my skin last night.

I splash my face with some water. "Almost. Did you call your agent back?"

"Yep. He wants a meeting with me and my manager today."

"Mine too. They're coming to set. Did yours say what it was about?"

"No, but I can guess." Blake shoves his phone in my face, and there's a photo of us kissing.

"What the fuck? How did they— Oh, wait, that's from the set yesterday. And not even the over-the-top display we put on for Ben. This was from the film."

"Someone must've had their phone on them and leaked it as a real photo instead of what it is. But this is a studio problem, isn't it? Not ours."

I whistle. "Well, whoever's problem it is, I guarantee people are getting fired today. I can see Ben doing the whole 'If someone doesn't come forward, I'll fire one person every hour until the culprit is found.' He's done it before when something like this has happened."

"So, what you're saying is today will be so much fun."

"Yep. Can't wait." Just what we need. Ben on a warpath.

"Should we go to set separately? We don't want to add fuel to the fire."

"It's probably a good idea."

Blake shifts from one foot to the other. "I'm going to head out, then. I told my manager I'd meet him in my trailer before my call time. Denver's house locks automatically when the door closes, so don't forget anything or you won't be able to get back in."

"No problem." I can't look him in the eye because suddenly it's awkward.

I want him to give me affection, but I don't want to ask for it.

He looks like he has the same reservation, but he quickly steps forward, plants his lips on my cheek, and then leaves.

I get dressed and follow him five minutes later.

As suspected, when I get to set, the crew is being yelled at, though surprisingly, it's not by Ben. A producer is laying into everyone about the NDAs every single member of the crew signs when being hired for a job.

Leaks happen. Some authorized—mostly to generate buzz about the movie—but most are unauthorized. I can't see anyone from higher up the food chain ordering this to happen.

Cheating scandals are a killer in Hollywood, and even the ones where it doesn't affect box office sales like with Brad Pitt and Angelina Jolie in *Mr. and Mrs. Smith*, they're the kind of scandals that follow actors around.

Teams will be chosen. Screenings will be boycotted. Hell, this could even affect the Eleven reunion tour. Though, that seems to have its own problems with four out of the five members now coming out, with Harley planning to take the leap next.

At least with Blake acknowledging his sexuality so fast, coming out won't be an issue for him. Unless …

I stop walking. Blake's team might be here to tell him to save his career, and to do that, they might pull some old-school Hollywood denial shit.

Taking my phone out of my pocket, I text Jojo and tell her to send my team to Blake's trailer if they're here. I leave the set, ignoring everyone who's staring at me, cross the lot to where our trailers are, and knock on Blake's door.

There are low murmurs inside, but I can't hear any actual words.

One of Blake's people answers and scowls with the fire of a thousand suns. "Good." That's all he says before he turns and goes back inside. I guess that's my invitation to join them.

As I climb the steps, all stares are turned in my direction.

"Jord, this is Tony and Anthony, my manager and agent. Or as I like to call them, Tony One and Tony Two," Blake says from the couch.

That sounds about right. They both even look the same—like a Hollywood suit. Think Ari from *Entourage* but two of them.

"Is your team here?" Anthony asks me.

"They're on their way." I make my way over to Blake and sit next to him, resisting the urge to reach for his leg and give it a reassuring squeeze.

"We were just telling Blake we want to deal with this situation quickly and without making as much noise as possible," Tony says.

Of course they do. "We could tell the truth," I say. "That the photo was a leaked still from the movie."

"That's not going to help," Blake's manager says. "It will only add to the speculation. Especially after the photo from a few weeks ago of you two holding hands in a bar. There's also low-key chatter from a tiny little blogger who's trying with all his might to go viral with a post about the night Blake Monroe kissed him in a gay bar."

Ah, fuck. "That was role research for this movie. Everything is being blown out of proportion."

"Okay, well, which narrative are you two planning to take

here?" Tony asks. "Because you're already telling conflicting stories. Whatever route we plan to go, we all need to be consistent."

I cock my head at Blake. "What have you told them?"

"That it's true that I'm not straight. That's pretty much all I had time for before you showed up."

"If that's the route you want to take this, then okay, but you need to know the risks," Tony says. "I don't think it's a good move professionally."

"Agreed," Anthony says.

Blake leans forward. "With all due respect, I disagree. I've seen what denial in this industry can do to people. If it's already out there, then I don't want to try to shove it back in."

"We're not saying you have to," Tony says, "but you at least need to deny any involvement with Jordan, who up until a few weeks ago was in a serious relationship with the director of this movie. They were talking wedding bells."

I pull back. "Fucking what? No, we weren't."

"According to the media, that's the story. Now suddenly, there are photos and stories about you two everywhere," Anthony says.

"Ben cheated. Not me," I say.

"That narrative would have worked, but when that first photo leaked of you in the bar, the media was more interested in making you two the big story instead of the truth," Tony says. "Your names would get more clicks than Ben's or his no-name conquest."

Anthony's phone rings, and he steps out to take it, but we keep going as if he's still here.

"So what are our options then?" Blake asks.

Tony leans against the counter. "If you want my honest advice, it would be to deny everything, but if you're telling me in six months' time you're going to want to go public with some same-sex relationship, with someone else and not Jordan, then the best thing you could probably do is say it's true that you're bisexual or pansexual or whatever label you want to give the public but deny the cheating rumors. They're the thing we're most worried about."

Hey, progress, I guess. He doesn't have to deny who he is.

But he can't be with me. I knew it for other reasons—that he will soon want to go exploring on his own—but hearing it from his manager's mouth … it makes it even more so.

Blake and I cannot and will not ever be together in any other way other than physical rendezvous hookups that shouldn't happen again.

It's probably best we end it now.

"We'll deny it," I say.

"Shouldn't we both get an opinion on this?" Blake asks.

There's a knock at the door, and my manager, Arianna, pops her head in, but instead of addressing me, she looks at Tony and gestures for him to follow her outside.

I slink down on the couch. "I guess they're taking it over for us, so I'm going to go with no. Our opinions don't matter."

"I don't want to deny it," Blake says.

I lift my head. "Do you know what that would mean?"

"That people think we're together? They do anyway."

"That people will think we're *cheaters*. It could affect the movie, your upcoming tour, our entire careers."

"What does it say about Hollywood that two measly photos taken out of context can ruin our whole livelihood?"

"That we live in a fucked-up world?"

"But they make it so we can't even defend ourselves. We can't complain. Our private lives might be splashed all over the internet for the world to see, but if we whine about it, we're ungrateful to all the fans who feel they have a right to our lives. Who believe they made us who we are. Instead of publicly whining, we should cry into our buckets of money and shut the hell up. It's so toxic."

"Just another cost of fame."

Blake groans. "Seriously? How did we go from friends to fake boyfriends to Romeo and Juliet in such a short span?"

I lift my hand. "I call dibs on Juliet."

"They're going to tell us we have to stop seeing each other."

"Yep." I reach for his hand and intertwine our fingers. "But hey, it was going to happen anyway."

"We don't know that."

"I do."

"I don't want it to end here. It feels like we only just got started. I was looking forward to more of last night." Blake leans in, his hot breath landing on my ear as he says, "And doing all those things you promised."

I have to squash down my growing erection, but damn it. I wanted it too.

"The only way to keep this going would be to do it in secret and take extreme measures so we don't get caught. I don't know if I want to deal with that. I've avoided it for my entire career and don't want to start now."

Blake huffs a humorless laugh. "That's kind of ironic because it feels like that's all I've ever done. Our original Eleven contracts had stipulations that if we were ever in a relationship, we had to be discreet and never confirm it publicly unless it was serious and we were getting married. We always needed to appear available to our fans."

I sigh. "Do you ever feel like it's … not worth it?"

"Many times."

"Ever thought of quitting?"

"Not once."

"Why do we do this to ourselves?"

"We're conceited and will do anything to have our egos stroked because it's addictive."

I slump. "Well, shit. I've never heard a truer statement. You know, it has never been like this for me. Before Ben, I was a mid-list to low-level celebrity that had a small fan base, and it was all so easy. If I got invited to the Golden Globes, I felt like I'd won the lottery. When Ben wanted me for his movies, I thought this is it. This is all where it's going to change. And it did. But …"

"Not how you were expecting? The more famous you are, the more problems you have."

"I'm not sure if it's worth it," I admit. I think that's the first time I've ever admitted it to myself, let alone to someone else. "I was happier when I was only kinda sorta famous."

"What do you want to do?" Blake asks, and I really wish he wouldn't put it on me.

"The guy I was ten years ago would've said fuck the system, let's do whatever the hell we want—"

"Can you be that guy, please? I don't … I'm not ready to stop."

"Neither am I."

Blake turns and throws his legs over my lap and wraps his arms around my neck. "Then we don't listen to what they have to say. We keep—"

"Blake," I whine and lower my forehead to his. "You really have to think about what you're giving up for a few weeks of sex. Don't get me wrong, it would be *superhot, holy shit the world could end and I'd die a happy man* type sex, but that's all it will be. Is risking everything for that worth it?"

Instead of answering me, Blake leans forward and presses his mouth to mine. His lips are soft, but the kiss is confident, and I guess this is my answer.

We're broken apart by the door to Blake's trailer opening and both of our teams stepping through.

It's crowded, and even though that should be a big enough sign—that it will take a team of people to cover this whole thing up—with one kiss I know we're going to defy them anyway.

"What did you all come up with?" I ask.

Arianna speaks for them all. "You two being together is career suicide."

I slowly pull myself away from Blake and gently move his legs off my lap. "Then what's the story we're running with?"

"The truth," Arianna says. "That you two are friends. Jordan, you've been helping Blake come to terms with his sexuality, but that is all. Nothing more, nothing less. You're doing this movie together, but there is absolutely nothing going on. You won't be seen out together. You won't go to any more gay bars together, and for fuck's sake, stop kissing in public."

I raise my hand. "In our defense, the photo that leaked of us kissing was us doing our job. Are you saying we have to stop doing that too?"

She scowls. "Stop showing affection in public. Better?"

Nope.

"I don't like this," Blake says. "I shouldn't have to stop seeing Jordan because the public says I have to."

He says that as if we were really, truly *dating* when we were anything but. Our whole friendship has been about one stupid bet or another. I don't want to stop either, but I think this is the right move.

To save our careers, we need to go into stealth mode.

Easy.

Totally doable.

As soon as Blake's done with me, all of this will go away anyway. I give it to the end of filming, tops.

CHAPTER 19
BLAKE

I DON'T KNOW how Jordan can be so cavalier about this, and I can't believe it's taken me this long to truly empathize with what Harley and Ryder went through for years. Apparently, I'm one of those assholes who need to experience the homophobic undertones of this industry before I can truly relate to it.

Jordan's okay with keeping us on the DL but then says it's too risky to meet up, so for days after our talk with our management teams, we show up to set, we say our lines, we get scenes done, and then we part ways as if we aren't even friends.

The crew is more confused than ever, Ben is manically grinning at us like he knows it was all an act and we were never really together, and all I can think is … I shouldn't be letting this happen.

Jordan thinks this will all be over in a few weeks, but I was too scared to ask whether he meant us, the media shitshow about it, or the movie.

I should have told Jordan that this isn't a random fling for me and that I'm having feelings I haven't experienced since I was a teenager. Maybe not even then.

When I think about Jordan, I get *butterflies*. Freaking gut-turning, nervous excitement. I'm not a butterflies kind of guy. I don't do *feelings.* Not because I'm against having them. The reason I haven't had a proper relationship isn't because I hate them. I've never met someone who's caught my attention like Jordan has.

But he's convinced it's all temporary, our management teams tell us it's career suicide, and I'm sitting back and doing as I'm told, even though it hurts inside.

It's already starting to wear me down.

I arrive to set early for another day of shooting because I left my script—updated again—in my trailer last night, and I don't know my lines, but as soon as I get to the studio, the usual stares follow me.

Considering I was part of the biggest boy band on the planet and moved on to become an action hero, it's surprising that this is the first time I've had a major scandal about me.

Sure, there had been rumors in the past—we've all had them. One of us died, one of us had a ridiculous diva rider, we were hard to work with, but they all melted away to nothing because they were nothing.

I've never had anything this big.

It's probably because the other guys in Eleven were more popular than I was, and they were always more dramatic than me. I'm the quiet, private one.

Maybe Jordan was right and mid-list fame is the sweet spot, where scandals are small and jobs are constant.

A production assistant approaches me and asks if I need anything, and I bark, "Coffee," at her like some dictator. Her face falls, and then a small line appears above her brow.

I slump and stop walking because I'm not this guy. I don't shout orders at people. I'm not Ben. "Sorry. Rough morning. Could you please bring a cup of coffee to my trailer?"

She scrambles away.

I arrive at my trailer, grab the script off the table, and then throw myself on the bed in the back and start reading through today's scenes.

Aww, fuck. It's the scene where the two characters bare their souls and admit they like each other and want to keep seeing each other, even though Madden no longer needs a fake boyfriend.

"I want this to be real," I say.

Relatability for the win. It won't be much of a stretch to get into Madden's head today.

I read over the words and let them sink in, praying they'll stick for when I need them.

There's a knock on my door, and I tell them to come in, assuming it's my coffee, but when I look up, Jordan's standing there, cup in hand and a small smile on his face.

"Word has it you yelled at a poor PA to get you this." He holds up the drink.

"I apologized right after."

"Yeah, but you don't yell. At anyone."

"I'm tired."

"Not sleeping well?"

Or at all, really. "Not so much."

"You look like you're wound tight." Jordan puts my drink down, out of reach.

"You're not going to give me that?"

"I'm going to give you something else."

I hope he meant that to sound as dirty as I heard it.

Jordan steps closer. "Do you know how many times I've gotten in my car to drive to Denver's house so I can see you?"

My stomach flips, and when Jordan reaches back and takes off his shirt, my cock tents in my sweats. "Why haven't you?"

"At first …" He reaches for my ankles and pulls me down so my legs hang off the bed. "I was trying to wait until the media circus died down. They don't seem to know where you're staying, which is good, but I have a few eager fuckheads hanging by my apartment building waiting for me to make a move."

"I'm sorry. I didn't know. Maybe you should move to a hotel for a while."

Jordan licks his lips. "Mm, maybe. But they've been a good deterrent. I've managed to stay away." He stares down at me, and even though I'm the one fully dressed, the heat in his eyes makes me feel naked.

Jordan lifts my shirt, exposing my abs. "I've been such a good boy, doing what my manager and agent told me to." His hand moves down my body and cups my cock over my sweatpants.

"I don't want you to be good. I don't want you to stay away."

"I've told myself for days that I should. That it's better for our careers. But there's one thing stopping me from being able to walk away."

"What's that?" I rasp.

"I haven't been inside this ass yet."

I quickly glance around, looking to see if there's a damn clock in here somewhere. "How much time do we have?"

"Not enough."

"Damn it."

"I had something else in mind."

"Anything." I'm already desperate for him, and he's barely even touched me.

Jordan sinks to his knees and tugs my sweats and underwear down and drops them on the floor.

My cock stands tall and ready.

"Put your feet up on the bed," he says.

I do it immediately, no questions asked, and he lowers his head. I'm craving his mouth on my cock, expecting it even. The anticipation rolls through me in a whole-body shudder. Which is why, when his tongue touches my hole, I flinch.

"Trust," he whispers, and then his mouth is back on me.

I try to relax and remember how good his finger felt moving inside me. It was weird at first, but as soon as I was able to open for him, everything changed. I want to feel that again.

Jordan places his big hand on my thigh, spreading me wider, and I adjust my feet. His other hand reaches for my cock and strokes lazily while his tongue works me open.

I want to get a better look, so I lean up on my elbows, but they're shaky at best. My body vibrates as I watch his head moving between my legs while he jerks me off with an expert hand.

"Oh, fuck." The dual sensations set my blood on fire.

Out of my control, my hips buck and writhe. How did I not know how good this could feel?

As much as I want to see everything he's doing, I can't stop my eyes from rolling back. I grip the comforter tight, and when I think I'm about to tip over the edge, suddenly, Jordan's mouth is gone.

I want to protest, but then he says, "Shh, anyone walking by could hear you, and this is exactly why I've been keeping my distance on set."

I'm confused. "I was being loud?"

"The sounds you make are sinful, and I love them, but not when we're trying to be stealthy. Do you think if I keep going, you're going to come?"

"Yes."

"Soon? We're running out of time, and it has to be quick. Want my fingers?"

"Fuck, yes."

"I'm going to use more than one this time."

"Do it."

"Okay, hang on." His hand on my cock leaves me now too, and I whine. "Seriously. You need to be quieter. Bite your pillow if you have to."

"I can be quiet." Though, can I? I didn't even know I was making any noise.

The sound of a wrapper crinkling fills my ears, and when I look, Jordan's tearing open a … condom? No, wait, that's lube. He coats two of his fingers with it.

"You carry that around with you?" I ask.

"Most days."

I frown, which only makes him smile.

"I haven't used any since Ben."

I want to play it off and say I don't care either way, but that would be a lie. A big, fat lie.

It's not normal to feel this possessive over someone, is it? Especially someone where lines have been drawn.

Jordan goes back to stroking me with one hand, but instead of his tongue on my hole, he presses a finger inside me and sucks one of my balls into his mouth.

My hips jackknife off the bed, and okay, I definitely hear my moan this time. "Fuck, how am I supposed to stay quiet?"

He hums his response, but I can't understand what he's saying. He licks and teases my balls and the base of my shaft until the point I'm so distracted, I don't really acknowledge the second finger in my ass.

Only when he's pushing them in and out of me and finding a rhythm massaging over that sweet spot inside me do I turn my attention to what he's doing. The magic of his hands and mouth working together sends me into a tailspin of euphoria, and I can't keep up.

Mouth, tongue, stroke, prostate, it's too much, but it's not enough at the same time.

Jordan lifts his head. "Come on, baby, you gonna fall apart for me?"

All I can do is nod.

"I need to swallow all of you again. One taste wasn't enough. Come in my mouth." He leans over me and covers the tip of my cock with his lips.

Apparently, that's the last thing I needed. The second the wet heat of his mouth surrounds me, I go off and forget all pretenses of being quiet. I come on a loud cry. I grit my teeth and shut my mouth to try to stop it, but it's like trying to stop a bulldozer with a rock.

Jordan's moans mix with my own, and he barely gives me time to recover before he's climbing up my body and straddling my chest.

He lowers his sweatpants and underwear to sit under his balls and then takes himself in his hand, stroking in earnest.

"Let me." My words don't come out right from trying to catch my breath. I reach for him, but Jordan shakes his head.

"I need your mouth. It'll only take a second. Watching you come undone like that ..." He grunts. "Fuck, I'm gonna—"

I quickly lift my head and suck the tip of his cock into my mouth. Where I was tempted but nervous to swallow all of him that night at the pool, this time I don't have time to think. My mouth is on him, and then he's coming, and all I can think to do is breathe through my nose and swallow.

The salty taste slides down my throat, but I barely notice. I'm too busy being distracted by Jordan's contorted face as he comes.

His cheeks are flushed, his eyes are squeezed shut, and he's biting down on his lip as if he's struggling to stay quiet while he unloads in my mouth.

Eventually, he stops and flops onto the mattress beside me.

I want to say something, but what?

Fuck our careers that we've both worked really hard for? Not likely.

Take a chance on me? Yeah, I don't really want to sound like an ABBA song.

It needs to be something profound, something that will make Jordan realize I want more than what he and our management teams have given us. It needs to be—

Jordan adjusts himself and stands. "We should get up and get out there. We have scenes to shoot."

—not that.

We don't even have time to bask in the afterglow.

"I'll go first." Jordan picks up his shirt from the floor and throws it back on. "See you on set."

I'm too numb. My dick's still exposed, and my hole is full of lube, yet I can't move. Because it all happened so fast.

One minute, I'm having one of the best sexual encounters of my life, and it feels like the next minute, he's walking out.

Before he leaves, Jordan grabs my coffee he brought me and takes a sip. "Mm, still warm. Here, drink up."

He hands it to me and heads for the door, opening it a crack and looking around before making a break for it.

Yep, I already hate sneaking around, and I don't want to do it.

CHAPTER 20
JORDAN

BLAKE LOOKS into my eyes with such sincerity it hits me in the feels. The overhead lights heat my neck, and the camera's lenses focus on only me and Blake, but that trickling sensation going down my spine has nothing to do with countless crew watching us and everything to do with the affectionate way Blake is looking at me.

It doesn't feel rehearsed. This doesn't feel like a movie set.

His blue orbs stare me down and plead with me to believe the words he's saying. "I want this. You and me. I want it to be real, and I want you to be my boyfriend, and … I love you."

I swallow hard. Fuck, why did we have to be shooting this scene today? "I …"

He presses his forehead against mine. "Please. Give us a real chance."

He's supposed to say my name there—Eamon—but he doesn't. I wait for it, and when it doesn't come, I wait for Ben to call cut.

That doesn't happen either.

What are they doing to me?

This is too real.

It's as if every single person in this room fades away, and then there's only Blake and me. There's no media, no crew, no Benjamin Randt.

"I want us to be real," I croak. "I don't think I've ever wanted anything more."

I'm not even acting.

I want more with Blake, but to get it, I risk my career, my heart, but maybe most of all, my dignity.

Because with all the other guys, even though I had hope, deep down I knew they'd all leave, and I'd accept it. With Ben, I was finally getting comfortable in the fact he wanted to stay, but I still held back and refused to give all of me. With Blake? I know how this will end, but I'm not protecting myself. And out of everyone, he might be the one I've wanted the most.

My view might be skewed because he's just the latest target of my infatuation with "straight" men, and every time that voice inside my head tells me Blake is different, another one reminds me I always think that.

How can I trust my head or my heart when neither can agree?

"We might have started with something fake," *Madden* says, "but I've fallen for you."

My chest hurts as longing stabs at it. I close my eyes and drink in the words, waiting for the one day someone would say them to me and mean it.

Not until they get sick of me. Not until they find someone else.

I want the words.

I want the promise.

And I want it to be genuine.

Permanent.

"I want a forever type person," I murmur.

Blake's eyes widen a tiny bit, and I catch myself and where I am and what I'm doing.

That wasn't part of the script, but Ben isn't calling cut.

"You can have a forever," Blake ad-libs. "With me."

Seeing as we're already off script, I kiss him hard, knowing it's all pretend but ignoring that fact for now.

I want to bask in a healthy relationship for a moment before coming back to reality and chasing the toxic situations I constantly put myself in.

I'm shallow and nice to look at. That somehow culminates into an image of someone who isn't worth getting serious over.

I'm never seen as the forever guy.

And for the first time in my life, I want to be.

I've tried not to look at Blake, tried not to pay him attention outside of our scenes together, and on other sets, the lines have been clear. It's been easy to switch in and out of character, pretend to be in love with someone I have absolutely no feelings for, but with Blake, it's so much harder to separate fiction from reality.

"Cut!" Ben finally calls.

When Blake pulls away, he's blurry through my glassy eyes. When he comes into focus, he's staring at me as if he wants to say something or ask a question I can't answer like *"Was that Eamon or you talking?"*

"Run it again with the scripted lines," Ben says. When I turn to him, he has a worried look on his face, but he nods. "Good shot, though. It might even be usable."

We run the scene again, with the correct lines, but it's not the same. It doesn't have the right tone, the right emotion. It only cements that what I just did wasn't acting. It was telling Blake I want a forever person.

We get through the rest of the shooting schedule for the day and are sent on our merry way, when Blake sidles up to me on my way to my trailer.

"I was thinking ... How do you feel about me coming over tonight?"

"Too risky."

"Come to Denver's?"

"Paparazzi know my car, and they're camped outside my apartment. I'm sure Mason and Denver wouldn't appreciate me turning up with cameras in tow. Didn't they just get back from Montana?"

Blake's shoulders slump.

"Sorry," I say.

"I thought after this morning—"

"That the paparazzi suddenly aren't a problem? This morning was a calculated risk. One I probably shouldn't have taken but did."

He grabs my arm to stop me from walking, and we come face-to-face. "Are the paparazzi the only obstacle, or are you avoiding seeing me for other reasons?"

"Just the paps," I lie.

"You have an underground parking garage in your building, don't you?"

"Yeah, why?"

Blake smiles. "Then leave it to me."

A few hours later, when he calls me to open my garage and come down to meet him, he whisks me away in his chauffeured town car with tinted windows so dark, nobody could see in.

"Where are we going? Denver's?"

"Nope. Somewhere private." At Blake's feet, I notice a duffle bag.

"Umm, so, like, the moon? Maybe a spaceship to Mars? They're the only two places I can think of that aren't keeping an eye out for us."

"Hey, I'm sure there are a bunch of perverted Martians who'd love to know what the deal between us is."

"I don't think I've ever felt this … watched before." It makes me itchy. I don't like it.

"Aliens are kinky bastards. They're probably watching right now."

I backhand his arm playfully. "I mean it. This is crazy."

"I'm sorry. This is boy band levels of normal for me."

"Except that following was mostly positive, wasn't it? I've been reading about how you came between Ben and me and that we were having an affair on set. You and I are public enemy number one."

"Dude, don't read the comments. Ever. It's been years since I've touched social media."

"I wish I had your restraint." Every time I look, I'm reminded of all the reasons why I should stay away from Blake.

Blake's driver pulls into the Angeles Hotel in downtown LA, into the underground garage, and Blake hands me a key. "Go up to room 1501, and I'll come up in five minutes. Oh ..." He reaches between his feet on the floor of the car and pulls up a wig, sunglasses, and a cowboy hat. "Unless you want the fake mustache instead of the wig." He pulls that out from his back pocket.

"You ... really came prepared for this."

"While you spent the last ten years trying to make it in this business, I've spent it doing exactly shit like this. Granted, it was a lot worse when the five of us were together than it ever was on my own, but I know how to deal with it. If you trust me."

"I do." Surprisingly.

I throw on the long, brown wig, the sunglasses, and the cowboy hat.

"You look like Cash Kingsley," Blake says.

I put up the sign of the devil. "Rock on."

I hold my breath the whole elevator ride up to the fifteenth floor. No one gets on, so I'm thankful I don't have to try to pull off some Cash impersonation.

When the elevator stops and I get off, I look for which direction to go, but there's only one door. *Penthouse Suite* is marked across it in gold.

"Going all out for me, huh, Blake?" I mutter to myself.

I use the key to let myself in, and as soon as the door's closed behind me, I rip off the stupid disguise and take in the view of downtown LA. Panoramic windows span the entire suite.

I've stayed in nice places, but this … I whistle.

A chuckle sounds behind me, and Blake steps through the door wearing that ugly fake porn stache. Even with it, he's still the hottest man on the planet. How he's never been awarded *People*'s sexiest man alive yet is beyond me.

"Admit it. You've never wanted me more." He runs his fingers over the mustache.

"Mm, maybe you should leave it on while you fuck me."

Blake stalls. No, he practically trips over his feet. "What?"

"I was joking. That thing is hideous."

"That's not the part I'm caught on. You want me to …"

"Oh. *Fuck me*?" I shrug and pretend like my body isn't already buzzing at the thought. "Why not?"

"I thought I had to give it up first. Isn't that one of your rules?"

"After today where you were practically begging me for my dick while I was fingering you, I have no doubt you'll let me in there one day. It isn't about keeping score. It's about give-and-take."

Blake still stands there unmoving.

"Seriously, take the mustache off. I can't talk sex with you when you look like that."

"Sorry, this …" He peels off the stupid-looking thing. "I wasn't expecting it."

"We don't have to—"

Blake steps forward and claims my mouth for a quick kiss. "Oh, we're going to, but this changes my plans a little."

"You had plans?"

"Mmhmm. They included room service and chilling in front of the TV. Hanging out. And then possibly later, more of what we did today."

My brow furrows. "You want a date first?"

"I did. Now, not so much."

"I'm not worth the date part now? Was my mother right? No man will buy the cow if I'm giving away the milk for free?"

Blake's mouth opens, but then he screws up his face. "That phrase has such a different meaning when referring to guys and … milk."

I gasp. "Eww, my mom is gross."

"That aside, you misunderstood me. We can do the date, but I might need to get off first, because the idea of fucking you is making my pants really uncomfortable."

"So sex first and then food and hanging out? That … actually sounds like the perfect date. No pretenses."

"So … bedroom?"

I glance around the suite, and my eyes land on the couches in the living room. One's facing the TV, but the other is facing the wide windows. "I have a better idea. Strip."

"Here?"

Instead of answering, I reach for my shirt, whipping it over my head and letting it land wherever. Blake's quick to do the same, and then it's a race to see who can get naked the fastest.

I trip over myself when I get to my socks and have to catch myself, so Blake beats me to it, and then his hands are all over my body, while I'm still trying to get my last sock off my foot.

"Hold still," he complains.

"Sock."

"Leave it on."

"Ooh, you're kinky. Sex while wearing one sock? I'm not into shaming people for what they like, but this might be too far."

"Just hurry up." Blake steps back and takes his cock in his hand, and the sock is suddenly forgotten.

"Supplies?" I ask.

"In my bag."

I scramble to find lube and condoms.

When I pull out the box, movement in the corner of my eye catches my attention.

It's Blake, shifting nervously. "I, uh, wasn't sure about those.

About whether we'd, uh, need them. Or use them. Or really, just ..."

"We should use them. I don't know how long Ben was cheating on me for, and I haven't been tested recently."

"Okay."

I stand and approach him. "You're going to bend me over this couch and look out at the view while you fuck me."

The sides of his lips turn upward. "It's cute you think I'll be looking at anything but you."

I want to tell him to stop with the sweetness, but I'm addicted to it. So instead, I shut both of us up by kissing him and hoping I don't blurt out what's going on in my head.

Blake takes control by licking into my mouth and blindly reaching for the supplies in my hand. The slight nervousness I could sense is completely gone as he presses his body to mine. He rocks his hips, grinding against me until he shudders.

"How does being with you feel this good?" he asks breathlessly.

I want to laugh, I really do, but it's a question I've heard a lot. "I'm new and shiny. That'll wear off."

"It's not that."

I can assure him it is. I try to kiss him again, but he pulls back.

"You don't make me feel like I'm famous. You don't make me want to pretend to be someone else so I get the attention I crave. It's like ..." His lips purse like he can't figure out the words.

"Like what?"

Even if I believe it to be bullshit. Even if I think his feelings are temporary—some lust-driven illusion of what something real with me would look like—I want to hear it.

"I think the shallowness of this town has made us both wary and unable to trust or give ourselves completely to someone. But with you, I can be the real Blake, and I don't have that with anyone else. Maybe on a smaller scale, I have that with the guys from Eleven, but ... I don't really fit in with them. I do, but I don't. Harley and Ryder always bonded over being queer. Mason and

Denver were best friends. We're all close, but I was mostly on my own. With you ... you feel like ... home."

That's the most romantic thing anyone has ever said to me, but I can't say that aloud. "Dude, you don't have to work so hard for it. I've already told you I'll sleep with you."

"Fine, don't believe me. I just ... wanted you to know that this means something to me. You mean something. More than what we're about to do, more than what we've already done."

My throat is thick with emotion I don't want to show, but I also know what he's saying is more likely a bond over friendship than anything physical or deeper.

"Being friends outside of this helps," I say. "It also helps that I genuinely like you."

Blake's breathtaking smile practically covers his entire face, and it feels a little too real now.

"Though, when I first met you in that club when you were with Denver and Mason, I thought you were all douchebags. It's nice to know that even the most famous of Hollywood people aren't complete assholes."

Blake shakes his head. "You're really incapable of saying something nice without a side of snark, aren't you?"

Yes. Because real emotion makes me too vulnerable, and I hate that.

"Sorry," Blake says. "I went and made this weird."

"Not weird. I just don't ... I don't talk about this stuff with anyone. I don't get serious."

He leans in and runs his nose down the side of my face and lowers his voice. "Maybe you should. It might open you up to possibilities you've never considered."

"Like what?"

"Like instead of thinking everything is temporary, maybe you'd realize some people are permanent."

I close my eyes and drink all of him in. His words. His presence. The surety with which he carries himself when he should be anything but confident in this. I knew as a teenager I was gay, but it still took years of self-reflection to make sense of it.

And Blake … it's like he discovers a part of him he didn't know existed and embraces it fully without any hesitation.

As much as I want to, I can't think of Blake as permanent. My heart won't survive it.

CHAPTER 21
BLAKE

JORDAN DOESN'T SAY ANYTHING, which I was expecting. To him, everything is temporary, and he fights even the thought of anything permanent. He hands me the supplies and backs up to move toward the couch, and when he turns and sticks his ass out, he looks at me over his shoulder and smirks.

I never thought Jordan Brooks—or any other man—naked and waiting for me to touch him could elicit this kind of need. It's warm and urgent, but also something else. It's something I've only ever heard of before or seen more recently with my bandmates.

I'm desperate for Jordan to see what this is, what we could be if he gave it a chance, but I know he won't. Or he can't. Not yet.

Jordan's long frame on display for me ... Damn. He widens his stance, bends at the waist, and folds his arms along the back side of the couch. "Are you going to stand there and look at me the whole time, or are you going to come over here and fuck me?"

"Honestly, I could stand here all night and just look at you."

Okay, so I might be experiencing my first *what the fuck* moment when it comes to having sex with Jordan.

I don't know why or how he turns me on the way he does or how I can stand back and admire his lean but tight and toned body. It doesn't freak me out, but it is hard to understand. Then again, from what I know of Jordan, he has this effect on people.

It's more than a physical thing, though, and I have to at least consider that the environment I grew up in—the Hollywood one, not my actual childhood—somehow repressed a side of me that's been there all the time. I saw firsthand what Ryder and Harley went through with label execs, and though I always wondered what it was like for them, what being attracted to men felt like, and thought about them kissing other men, I never really pictured myself doing it. I was too quick to dismiss it because of what Harley and Ryder had to endure.

Now this chance is in front of me, and my career is on the line, but there's no ignoring it this time. There's no dismissing my feelings and chalking it up to curiosity.

"As much as I love you checking me out the way you are now, I really need this." Jordan's gray eyes meet mine. "Please."

His begging cracks open my chest, and my reflex is to run to him and give him what he wants. Stepping up behind him, though, I can't help wanting to take my time. I drop the supplies by our feet as I run my hands down his back.

He rests his head on his arms and shudders as my fingertips trail all over his body. "You don't have to go slow with me," he rasps.

"I want to. I want to explore. I want to learn how to drive you crazy with need like you do to me."

"I already feel like I'm going crazy. Touch me, please." Jordan's begging does things to me, but I hold strong.

"I *am* touching you." I grip his hip.

"I need you *inside* me."

Hearing those words is like a hit of adrenaline.

I grip his taut ass cheeks and pull them apart as I drag my cock along his crack. The feel of his skin on mine makes me want to reassess the condom situation again, but Jordan's right. We should play it safe, especially with Ben being a cheating twatface, but I make a mental note to bring it up with Jordan again later.

Maybe that will be too *exclusive* for him. I just want to know what it would feel like to be inside him with nothing between us.

As I bend to get the lube, I can't help myself. I kiss one ass cheek and then the other.

Jordan pushes backward, and I want to make him feel as good as I did this morning when he used his tongue on me. In me. Before I can hesitate, I take my chance and run my tongue over his hole.

"Fuck," he hisses.

I pull back to ask if this is okay, but he reaches behind him and grips my head to keep me there. I dive back in and love the urgent grunts that come out of his mouth.

I blindly search for the lube and cover my fingers with it, but with the way Jordan desperately rocks his hips to get my tongue deeper, I hold back. The way he's trembling and moaning keeps me here, teasing and licking him.

He whispers harsh curses and then uses his free hand to grip his cock. "I'm close to coming and you're not even inside me yet."

I replace my tongue with my finger. "Let's fix that." I press against his hole, and he pushes back, taking it easily.

"More. I can take it."

I use two fingers this time and move in and out of him. He bears down on me, his ass gripping onto my digits so tight, I have no idea how that's going to feel on my dick.

I'm so hard that I'm getting impatient. My cock leaks.

Jordan chants, "Oh fuck, oh fuck, oh fuck. *Blake* ... I'm gonna—"

I pull out of him and stand. "Not yet."

Jordan groans loud and low while his body trembles.

"So, so needy," I taunt while I grab the condom and cover myself.

"I am. I'm so ready for it."

Slowly, I take a deep breath and press against his hole. His body is open and ready and accepts me easily.

Being inside him, inside his tight heat, it unleashes something inside me, and I can't hold back. It starts out slow, but it doesn't take long for me to lose myself. Over and over again, I move in and out of him. I chase that high, the ultimate relief.

Jordan gasps, pushing back to meet my every thrust. I press my hand down in the middle of his back for leverage as I continue to push inside him.

It doesn't take long for him to start trembling in my arms, for his breath to become stilted.

I throw my head back and moan. "I want to keep doing this all night, but there's no way my body will let me. You feel too good. I never …" I fuse my eyes shut. It's never been this good, has it?

Sex is sex. Get in, get off, get out.

My thighs ache. Sweat drips down my skin.

"Blake," Jordan breathes. "I need more. I need to touch myself."

"Do it," I encourage.

"Keep going," he says. "Don't slow down."

Like that's even a possibility at this point.

He reaches between him and the couch, gripping his cock and stroking hurriedly. The fast movement of his hand, the sight of my cock disappearing between his ass cheeks … I know this image is going to be spank bank material for years to come. His long torso and wide shoulders, every contour of his muscular back … it's a new kind of sexy to me.

Every single muscle in Jordan's body tightens, and his ass grips my cock so hard I see stars.

The power of my release knocks me off-kilter, slamming into me and unfurling everything inside me until there's nothing left.

Jordan continues to stroke himself, but I know he's close.

I empty into the condom but don't stop moving inside him until I know I push him over the edge. I stay inside him, pressed all the way in so he's full of all of me while I reach around him and take over jerking him off.

He comes all over my hand, while I slump against Jordan's back with my sweaty forehead resting in the middle of his shoulder blades. It's impossible to catch my breath or move or do anything. My limbs feel like jelly, and I wait for my legs to fall out from beneath me.

"That was …" There are no words to describe that.

"You think that was good, wait until it's flipped the other way." Jordan's voice is teasing, but my cock twitches inside him.

I should really pull out and get rid of the condom. "Date now. Flip later. I need to recover from that first." I step away, and Jordan stands upright.

"You're younger than me. By a lot. Your refractory period should be ready to go."

I deal with the condom and then turn to Jordan. "How old are you?"

He grins. "I'll never tell."

"You don't look a day over thirty."

He gasps. "I'm twenty-nine."

My face falls—no, wait. "You said you've been out here, what? Fifteen years? If you were twenty-nine, you would've gotten here when you were … fourteen? That doesn't add up."

"Ooh, look, someone can do math. I came out here as soon as I graduated college."

"You're thirty-seven?" I screech. "Not even."

"No. I've only been out here …" Jordan's face scrunches as he counts. "Eleven years."

"So there's only five-ish years between us. That's nothing. So your refractory period should be ready to go, fuckyouverymuch."

"Just say the word." He strokes his cock, which is already getting hard again.

"I don't know if I'm going to be able to keep up with you."

"I can't wait to see you try."

My dick makes a valiant effort to get hard again but fails. "Food first."

We order room service, which they leave outside the door for us so we're not seen by staff. I've booked the room under a fake name and done all the cloak-and-dagger shit our management team used to do with Eleven.

I wrap a hotel robe around me while we eat, and Jordan lounges around in his boxer briefs.

We're watching some movie I'm not familiar with, but Jordan seems to know it well. He laughs before things are funny and tells me to watch certain parts that are coming up.

When I'm done with eating, I lie back and put my feet in his lap, letting out a content sigh when he mindlessly rubs them. "I wish we had tomorrow off. I can't be assed to finish this movie. I've never felt like this on set before."

Jordan's hand on my foot freezes. "Wow. I'll take that as a huge compliment. Thank you so much for saying doing a movie with me is practically torture."

"It has nothing to do with you. I love working with you, obviously. It's Ben. It feels like the whole thing is moving away from its original direction, and while I thought that would be a good idea in the beginning, I'm not feeling the script anymore."

Jordan's lips flatten. "I might hate the guy, but when it comes to films, he knows what he's doing. I think he's trying to make it more serious for the potential to get Oscar noms."

"I think it's the wrong direction, personally, but what do I know? I'm too mainstream and know nothing about what the Academy deems Oscar-worthy."

Jordan's fingers dig into my foot. "We only have a few weeks left of shooting."

"Yeah, then when it releases next year, it'll be press junkets and—"

"Mm, you get to spend more time with me, answering the same questions over and over again."

"The spending time with you part won't be so horrible. Though knowing our management teams, they'll probably want to split us up for the press tour."

His lips try to turn up in a smile, but they don't quite get there. "Your future boyfriend will probably want that too."

My gut twists like it always does when he says stuff like that. I've been playing it off, but after what we just did, I don't want him to keep saying it. "I think I know what I want."

"Want?"

"Yeah. For my favor that I still have to cash."

He shifts positions on the couch to turn to me. "Say what now? I won that bet."

"Hmm, did you, though?"

"Yes. You offered yourself to me, and I turned you down. Ergo, I win."

I tap my chin. "Technically, the bet was that we would have had sex by the time we left Montana, and we didn't."

"Oh, so we're loopholing it now? Let me guess, you want me to get up onstage with you and sing a duet so it can go viral, and I will never work in this town again."

"It's not that, I promise."

Jordan looks horrified. "It's going to be *worse* than that? Actually, I can't think of anything worse."

I fidget with the rope that ties the robe together because once I say this, I'm thinking he will find it worse than embarrassing himself in front of millions of people. "I want you to give us a real chance. I know you hate commitment, and the last time you tried it, it didn't end well—"

"*Every time* I've tried it, it didn't end well."

"I also know it will be hard for you to trust me when I say I am different to Ben, different to everyone else, but I am. This isn't about sex or exploring or whatever. I don't think it ever was."

"Can we go back to the singing in public thing?" Jordan whines.

"This isn't even about being boyfriends because I know that term makes you cringe. It's about trying. You've already written me off and think I'll end up with another guy."

"That's because it always happens. I'm cursed."

"Maybe it happens because you expect it to and don't really try. When you crack jokes about future boyfriends all the time, you know what it makes me think? That you're not interested in anything more. So, yeah, maybe it never works out because of you. Not them."

"And Ben? I gave him a chance. Ended the same way."

"Did you really, though? When we first met, you called your-self his toy. When I asked about you two, you winced when you said you were in a relationship. You had one foot out the door already."

His hand on my foot leaves me, and I immediately miss his touch. "So you're saying it's my fault he cheated?"

"Not at all. That's his fault. If he had a problem with you, he should've come to you first instead of turning to someone else, but what I'm saying is, maybe you would have more success in relationships if you weren't constantly expecting it to end."

"Why do I feel like I'm in a therapist's office?"

"Dr. Blake, at your service."

Jordan finally breaks into a smile. A small one, but it counts. "You're the most unprofessional therapist ever. Fucking your client? That violates all kinds of laws."

I throw my feet off his lap and then crawl toward him because I can tell if I let him get away with snarky comments, he'll move on, and this conversation is not done.

Jordan's eyes narrow as I get close.

"Give us a real chance to grow something here." I lean in and kiss his cheek and then nuzzle my way down to his neck. "We have fun together. We respect each other. We—"

"Only have a few weeks until our schedules will take us in different directions."

Okay, he still needs some convincing.

I straddle his lap. I never thought of myself as one of those guys who connected sex with emotion, and maybe Jordan's hard cock under me is merely a physical response to me being close to him, but considering we're talking about giving us a real shot and his dick is on board, I have to assume he really does want it. It's his heart and his head that are letting him down.

I want to convince him we could have something amazing, but I fear he may never be open enough to accept it.

I don't know what I can do to show him, but I'm going to try everything I can to make him see. He might not be ready for the emotional stuff, but he's definitely ready for the physical.

I grind against him. "Ready to fuck me now?"

Jordan's eyes darken. "I've been ready since Montana."

"Good."

CHAPTER 22
JORDAN

BLAKE LEANS BACK and slowly opens his robe, slipping it off his broad shoulders. His blond hair falls in his face as he looks down between us, his hard cock pressing against mine behind my boxer briefs.

I'm sure the sight is hot, but I can't tear my gaze away from Blake's face. He's so goddamn beautiful it hurts.

I used to think of myself as an optimistic kind of guy, and to a point, I am, but if anything the last eleven years have taught me, it's that I've turned bitter somewhere along the way.

I thought I was above it all, that I didn't care I wasn't relationship material, but it turns out it cuts deeper than I care to admit.

Blake's saying all the right things; he's offering himself to me, and as much as I crave to jump all in, there's the voice in the back of my head screaming at me that Blake doesn't know what he wants.

He wants me now, but what will he want in a few months? What will he do when our schedules have us apart for months at a time and he gets lonely?

"Jordan." Blake's voice brings me back to here and now. His tone begs me to focus.

I reach between us and grip his cock, loving when Blake's eyes roll back and his kissable lips part.

Leaning forward, I kiss along his insanely square jawline that earns him the big bucks on film. My hand travels down his spine and dips into the crease of his ass. "You want to do this right here?" I ask. "Want to ride me?"

"Yes." He sits back. "But lube."

It's on the floor, a little out of reach, but that doesn't stop Blake from leaning over the side to try to get it without leaving my lap.

I can't help it—I grab a handful of ass cheek as he does it. Fuck, I can't wait to be inside him. I take advantage of his position and shuffle to take off my underwear, at least down to my thighs.

Like him, I don't want to stop touching him while we get ready.

He comes back with both the lube and a condom, dropping the lube on my stomach as he opens the foil wrapper and starts rolling the condom down my dick.

His hands on me send a shiver down my spine.

I know I shouldn't compare him to others—that's exactly what he's asking me not to do—but it's hard not to when Blake's exactly the same yet somehow different than what I'm used to in these situations.

Sex with previously presumed straight guys is usually me doing all the work, advancing to the next stage. At least the first couple of times.

Blake has no issues with taking charge. When he's finished with the condom, he takes the lube again and dribbles it down my cock and then coats his fingers.

He reaches behind him, and I can see in his face the moment his finger breaches his tight ring of muscle. He closes his eyes, and a shuddery breath falls from his lips.

I want to offer to do that myself, but watching him do it is one of the hottest things I've ever seen, so instead, I stroke his cock and keep watching.

After a couple of minutes, he starts thrusting into my hand, rocking his hips. He rides his fingers until precum leaks from his tip, and I can't take it anymore.

"Are you ready?" I croak.

"I … I think so."

"Go slow." I grab the base of my cock while Blake positions himself on top of me.

The head of my dick presses against his hole, and it takes all of my strength not to thrust inside him.

He lets out a long, slow breath, and when I meet his gaze, his focus is intense. A line appears above his brow, making him look like his stubborn and determined Coby character.

Instead of encouraging him with words, I use my lips. I cup the back of his head to bring his mouth to meet mine and move my tongue against his, silently waiting for him to relax while trying not to explode inside him.

He eases down on me while I kiss him. It's supposed to be a distraction for him, but it's for me as well. The more of me he takes, the more pleasure that surges through me. He's cautious, stretching himself properly on my cock.

When Blake's fully seated, he breaks the kiss and leans back, locking his eyes on mine. For a moment, we stay like that, getting lost in each other's gaze while I'm buried deep inside him.

Our connection is more than naked bodies coming together.

He braces his hands on my shoulders and tests out rotating his hips before moving up and down over my cock. The whole time, he never takes his eyes off mine. It's as intense as it is hot. I'm not going to come like this, but that makes it better because it's drawing it out. Warmth builds in my gut, my balls tighten, but I never reach the edge.

The stirring in my gut, the need I have for more … it doesn't take long for me to thrust upward. I can only take so much.

I only do it once and then check for Blake's reaction.

He trembles. "Do that again."

So I do. It gives the added friction I need and the action on his prostate to get him over the finishing line.

He takes me easily now, only demanding I go faster. I grip his hips hard, pulling him down to meet my body as I thrust into him over and over again.

His fingers tighten around my shoulders, and for a split second, I think he's going to come untouched, but that might be a bit much to ask for his first time. His face contorts in frustration, like he's riding the line and needs that little bit extra.

"I need … I need …" He can't speak. It looks like he can barely breathe.

"Touch yourself," I say. "It'll get you there, and I want you to come for me while I hold you close."

It only takes a few strokes for him to come all over my chest. His ass clamps down on my cock, and I fall apart too.

Blake's face as he comes could win awards, and I almost want to joke that if the Hollywood thing didn't work out, Blake would have a future in porn, but the thought of Blake having sex with someone else is enough to sour me on the idea.

He's getting into my head and my heart, even though I'm trying to fight it.

Blake falls against my sweaty chest, and I run a hand down his damp back.

We're both sated, and I know without a doubt what I'm about to say could be the stupidest thing I've ever done, but it needs to be said, and I need to at least try to be happy for once in my life.

"Okay," I breathe. "We can do this."

Blake sits up and stares into my eyes. "For real?"

I swallow hard and nod. "For real."

CHAPTER 23
BLAKE

I DON'T END up checking out of the hotel. And every night since, Jordan finds his way to my room and my bed. Mainly because my driver practically kidnaps him for me. Though, is it actually kidnapping when Jordan is one hundred percent all in?

To avoid being caught together, we go separately, but we always use my driver. It's a nondescript town car, so it doesn't draw attention, and the company I use has a lot of different celebrity clients, so it's not suspicious.

I love waking up to him. Sleeping next to him feels right, and when we're wrapped around each other, the warmth that engulfs me is a fixture I need in my life.

Jordan's slowly coming around to the idea of us together, or at least, he's less vocal with his protests. That has to mean something, right? I hope he's not too in his head about it because I'm not.

I want Jordan Brooks. Plain and simple. Do I know what the future holds? Nope, but neither does anyone.

Having to continue to hide isn't my first choice, but baby steps. Jordan agreed to give me a real chance, but bringing the media into it can fuck that up so easily. Plus, our management teams have been working overtime trying to keep us out of the spotlight and off the tabloid pages, especially together. We've denied it publicly; to come out now would be admitting we lied. I don't think that's more or less forgivable than the cheating scandal.

It's not that I want to shout it from the rooftops, but going out in public would be nice. I've never had that before with anyone. I've never seriously considered being with someone enough to want to go on a date at an actual restaurant. Even when I was dating women, this whole keeping it under wraps thing was the norm for me, so I don't know why Jordan's different, but I'm hoping it means we're both different for each other. I don't want to be like his past lovers.

His alarm goes off early one morning. I have a rare day off on the schedule because Jordan needs to shoot some family scenes that my character isn't a part of.

Jordan tries to slip out of bed, but my arm tightens around him, and he laughs. "I don't want to get up either, but I have to."

"Call in sick."

"Yeah, I'm sure that will go down really well."

"Just think, as soon as the movie is over, we can spend actual time together."

"We're practically spending twenty-four hours a day together now."

"Mm, not enough. Especially when I can't do this on set." I kiss the back of his neck, and he turns his head so I can bring my lips to his.

I roll on top of him, and he groans.

"Blake, I really don't have time." As if proving his point, his phone goes off again.

I slump and fall onto my back.

Jordan jumps out of bed and pulls on a fresh pair of underwear and jeans from a bag he brought last night.

The minute I saw it, I booked the suite for another week. At this rate, we'll be staying here indefinitely. Or at least until the movie is done.

"What are you doing with your day off?" Jordan zips up his pants, and I'm so mesmerized by the move, wishing it was doing the reverse, that I miss his question.

"Huh?"

"Day off. Got any plans?"

I shake out of my stupor. "Yeah. Harley somehow got a hold of my schedule, so we have a band meeting. All our songs are pretty much written. We just need to find time to get into a studio to record them. Harley wants us to do it together instead of individually—he's adamant it sounds better when we harmonize off each other instead of manufacturing it together afterward, but I think it's going to a lot of trouble for minimal reward. Depending on if we go over schedule, they might need to add my part in at another time. Or have one of the other guys record it. I can sing my part live when I have to."

"You don't care if someone else sings your part?"

"I love the guys, and I love being in Eleven, but I'm not doing this reunion for the love of the music. I'm doing it for them and the fans. It's a totally selfish act, though, because I was genuinely happy when I was with Eleven."

"You need to find something that makes you happy in the mess that is Hollywood," Jordan says.

"Don't get me wrong, I love acting too, but it's a different kind of happiness. I want to keep doing both."

Jordan puts on a T-shirt and then leans over the bed and kisses me softly. "You should do both."

"I plan on it."

He pulls away and stands upright. "Maybe in between my movies, I can meet up with you on tour somewhere. Europe sounds nice. I've never been."

"Not even for movie releases?" I ask. "Cannes Film Festival?"

"Nah, the one big movie I did was still really only promoted in the US."

"Do you think *Faking It* is going to be good enough to go

international?" I ask. He says Ben knows what he's doing, but I'm not sold yet. Maybe because Ben's a dickhead.

"I can never really tell until I see the cut and edited product."

"True. It's the same with my Coby movies. I just really want it to do well."

"It will."

I want to believe him. "How do you know?"

Jordan shrugs. "Someone smart once told me if you go into something thinking it will fail, it probably will."

"That person sounds like a genius. A hot one."

Jordan laughs and then leans down to kiss me once more. "Have fun with the guys."

"See you tonight? I can tell my driver to bring you back here."

"Why do you think I packed the bag?"

Yes.

"He's alive!" Mason says as soon as I step inside Denver's house.

"Ha, ha," I say dryly and flop down next to Ryder on the couch.

All the guys are already here, and yeah, I'm a little late because I went back to sleep after Jordan left and then had to shower so I didn't smell like sex when I got here.

After a nice long nap, I finally feel like I'm catching up on some sleep. I could've kept sleeping had Harley not messaged me reminding me about the meeting.

Jordan and I have been making each other come in various ways every night. His whole give-and-take philosophy has me on my knees, on all fours, standing, sitting, using every which position we can come up with. It's hard to keep up, and I don't think I've had this much sex in my life. Any guy who has said they've gotten bored of Jordan Brooks clearly didn't have the same experience I've had.

But it's not only the sex I love. I love hanging out with my friend, who's funny, and snarky, and supportive. He knows that this Eleven tour and our schedules might clash with seeing each other, but he still told me to go for it because it's what I want.

I just hope it's because he's secure enough to know I wouldn't fuck around on him and not his way of pushing me away again. Only time will tell on that one.

"What's with you?" Harley asks.

It takes a second to realize he's talking to me. "What?" When I look around the room, everyone is staring.

Mason assesses me, looking me up and down. "There's something about you that's …"

Denver gasps. "You had sex."

I try to keep my face neutral, but I don't think I pull it off. "I … uh … Huh?"

"Did you finally lose the bet to Jordan?" Ryder asks.

"Please, they so did it in Montana," Denver says.

"No, we didn't. And no, it's … not that." I'm supposed to be an actor. I lie for a living. But I'm totally unconvincing.

Mason snorts. "Still comfortable in your heterosexuality, then?"

I flip him off. "Fine. I was wrong, and you all were right. Jordan's …"

"Hot," Ryder and Harley say together.

"That's a given. He was a model," I point out. "But there's something about him that's …" Wordless. "Is there a word for someone who's both charismatic and broken but somehow still likable? He acts shallow, but he's so much deeper than he lets people see. He's a phenomenal actor and can summon all this emotional shit onscreen, but then off it, he tries to act like nothing can get to him and nothing bothers him, but I can tell that it's only because he doesn't let himself feel those things. It's like he's numb to everything in real life and saves it all for the camera."

Four pairs of eyes blink at me.

"What? Why are you all staring at me like that?"

"A-are you falling for him?" Mason asks.

Is it that obvious? "No?" Why did my voice pitch at the end like I was asking a question?

"Who knew Ryder was right all this time?" Denver says.

"Thank you! Of course I am." Ryder cocks his head. "But, uh, about what?"

Denver smiles. "Sexuality being on an ever-moving spectrum. When I started having feelings for Mason, I thought I was, like, mostly straight? That I was maybe a one on the Kinsey scale, but I never really allowed myself to look at other men. It's only been since being with Mason that I can look at other guys and freely find them attractive, so now I'd consider myself a two or a three."

"I'm still a one," Mason says and kisses Denver's cheek. "You're the only one for me."

"For now," Denver says.

"No, forever." Mason glances around the room. "I, uh, wasn't going to do this here, or in front of these losers, but come to think of it, I can't think of a more fitting way. We fell in love while touring with these guys. It only makes sense for them to be here for this." Mason slinks off the couch and onto his knees. "Denny ... My Denny."

Denver's mouth drops, but no noise comes out.

Mason reaches into his pocket and pulls out a platinum ring. "I lived without you once, and I never want to do that again. No matter what we do, where our careers take us, what happens in the future, I don't want to do it without you."

Denver squeaks, and I try to hold back a chuckle.

"Marry me?" Mason asks.

"But you ... and ... I ..." Denver's mouth slams shut, and he stares at the ring. "You said you never wanted to be engaged ever again."

Mason doesn't miss a beat. "That was before I knew what true love is really like."

"Shit, yes, I'll marry you," Denver says. "Fuck, when we retell this story, we'll leave the swearing out."

"I love you," Mason says.

"I love you too." Denver launches himself at Mason, and they kiss and practically dry hump each other on the floor.

"That's something I don't need to see," Harley says.

"Agreed." I stand. "Let's, uh, let them celebrate."

They wave us off without breaking apart.

Harley, Ryder, and I go into Denver's formal dining room and sit around the white glass table that looks like a bubble. The chairs are uncomfortable but not more uncomfortable than watching your bandmates fuck. An electric chair would be more comfortable than seeing that.

And yes, I'm being dramatic.

Probably because while I'm happy for Mason and Denver, I can't help acknowledging the jealousy growing inside me.

It's hard to tell which part I'm jealous of. The marriage? I've never contemplated it. Like Jordan, that's one thing I've never considered while being in Hollywood. But maybe, just maybe, I see the other guys of Eleven settling down and I'm beginning to want it for myself.

I want to know what it feels like to have that someone you share everything with.

"So, you and Jordan, huh?" Harley says. "At least you've already got a jump start on the coming out part."

With the proposal and everything, I'm starting to feel stupid about my fling with Jordan. He says he's giving us a real shot, and the comments have stopped, but is he? What if I'm putting myself out there for someone who actually doesn't see me as a long-term option. Not because he thinks I'll walk away, but that maybe he will?

I need to change the subject before I blurt all my insecurities over these guys. "Are we really going to talk about me and Jordan when that"—I point to the living room next door—"is going on?"

Harley shrugs. "Walls are thick. I can't hear them. In my mind, they've stopped kissing and are playing a game of chess. Because they're like brothers to me, and if they're brothers, then that's all kinds of messed up."

"Brocest," Ryder says. "That's hot."

Harley and I screw up our noses at him.

Ryder merely turns to me. "So, you and Jordan."

I throw my head back. "It's … nothing. Well, it's not nothing. I want it to be more than just sex, but we have to hide it because we denied anything was going on between us. If we were to say we're in a relationship now, everything will blow up in our faces. I think career-wise I'll be all right because I still have Coby Godspeed and Eleven. Jordan, on the other hand … he's spent the past decade trying to make it in this business, and he's finally been given his big break. This could undo all of that."

"Hiding isn't as bad as you might think," Harley says. "Brix and I do it, and we've never been happier."

"Yeah, but he's your head of security. You guys have excuses to be around each other. Same with Ryder and Lyric—they were producer and artist. Jordan and I have the excuse at the moment of being co-stars, but when the movie wraps, we can't be seen together. Already as it is, our management teams don't want us together at all. We've been staying in a hotel so we're not caught."

Ryder sighs in sympathy. "Relationships in Hollywood are never easy."

"Then why do you do it?"

"Because finding the one person who not only complements you but encourages you, loves you, and supports you is worth it," Harley says.

I can see that between Harley and Brix.

"And because when you dedicate your life to the fans and other people, it's okay to take something selfish every once in a while," Ryder adds. "Lyric taught me that."

"You really like him, don't you?" Harley asks me.

"I do. I've always liked him. We clicked as soon as we met. But

I think that's just Jordan. He's easy to get along with. The sex stuff … that's been a surprise."

Harley blocks his ears. "Again. Brotherly. Talk to this perv about the sex stuff." He nods in Ryder's direction.

"If you have any questions, I'll be happy to answer."

"Not about sex. Jordan's got that covered. *Really well.*"

"Lalalalalala," Harley sings.

I laugh. "Okay, what songs do I have to learn?"

Harley keeps going until I reach over and pull his hands from his ears.

"What new songs have you got for me?"

"Oh! That, I can talk about."

Good. I need anything to get me out of my head.

CHAPTER 24
JORDAN

I SENSE BEN WATCHING ME. Which is ridiculous because of course he is. He's the director. But this isn't like every other day or any other scene. It's entirely possible I'm reading into it because it's the first scene in a while where Blake hasn't been involved.

Either way, I'm eager to get out of here as soon as we're done for the day. Since we've started staying at the hotel, it's become a bit of a routine. Blake's driver picks me up and takes me to the basement, and then I take the elevator up to Blake's room, where he's always waiting for me.

Sometimes naked, sometimes already with room service as he stuffs his face because he was too hungry to wait while his driver comes back to the studio to collect me.

The way we fall into the pattern is so easy, and it's nothing like how Ben and I started our relationship. That almost felt contractual. He told me what he expects, how our relationship would play out publicly, and basically gave me a terms and conditions. That should've been my first red flag, but I actually found his honesty refreshing. I somehow thought it meant we would each know where we stood the whole time.

With Blake, even though my insecurities try to convince me

it's a bad thing, I'm enjoying not knowing what the future holds. I'm also enjoying not thinking about how this will end, when it will end, or convincing myself that it's inevitable. It's hard to turn those doubts off, but by keeping it to myself when those thoughts occur, it's like I'm not giving it a voice. I'm not letting it get away from me and turn into this big thing I'm certain will happen.

And when Ben finally lets us wrap for the day, and I use Blake's driver to take me straight to our hotel room, I walk through the door to the suite and find Blake sitting at the dining table. He lifts his head and gives me this amazing smile that makes me feel like I'm the only person in the world. Stuff like that makes all those worries fade away to nothing.

When I'm with him, I believe everything he's saying. When we're apart, my brain tries to convince me I'm holding on to a dream that could never be real.

If we are going to make it long term, I need to deal with those abandonment issues, because there will be times where we're apart. It's unavoidable in this industry.

Blake tilts his head at me. "What's up? You're staring."

"You look …" *Like home.* "Really good."

"The guys said something like that too. Said I was glowing or some shit. Apparently, it's all because of you."

"All because of me?"

"Apparently you're a big deal or whatever," he says dryly. "How was today?" He stands and approaches, kissing me on the cheek in greeting, and for some reason, it reminds me of a housewife in the fifties welcoming her husband home. And for some other weird reason, I like it.

I pull him against me and wrap my arms around him so I can kiss him hard.

Blake laughs against my lips. "Miss me that much?"

"The set is different without you. The vibe is weird."

"I guess we'll have to make all our future movies together, then."

"Oh, our agents will love that." I nod toward the script on the table. "More changes?"

"Nope. It's actually a script for another Coby movie."

"Is it any good?"

"It's a Coby Godspeed movie. What do you think?"

"Brainless action and no real substance? Sounds awesome."

He picks the script up off the table. "You know, if you do want to do another movie together, I get a cool new hacker sidekick in this one."

"Really?"

"I can put your name up for it, if you want?"

Stepping out of the rom-com drama box could be good for me. "When is it shooting?" I ask.

"Not until next year. I have to get through the Eleven tour first, but it will be the next thing I shoot."

"I'll probably need work in between. If we can get our schedules to line up, I think it could be great for my career."

"And you get to spend time with me." Blake pouts.

"That's a given. Do you think I could pull off a nerdy hacker type?"

"Why do hackers need to be nerdy?"

"Because instead of having social lives, they spent all their youth on their computers learning how to be hackers?"

"Oh. Right. That. Maybe you had no friends in high school because you were too hot."

"Sure, because that's how high school works." I take the script from his hands and place it back on the table. "Are you ready for our scene tomorrow?"

Blake's hands snake around my shoulders. "Ahh, the dreaded actual sex-sex scene. Not really. I'm used to having my hands and mouth all over you now, but I swear I'm going to get too into it, and everyone will be watching, and have you seen what we have to wear for it?"

"Yeah, those flesh-colored socks really don't accommodate for hard-ons."

"I'm kind of hoping I'll be so nervous about embarrassing myself in front of the entire crew that my dick won't cooperate."

"That's how it usually is with sex scenes. It's so awkward it's impossible to actually be turned on by them."

"I didn't have that problem with our last one." Blake presses his hardening cock against me. "Hell, just being near you turns me on. I know what it's like to have your tongue lick up and down my shaft. I can practically feel your mouth suck on the tip of my cock just thinking about it."

My eyes narrow. "Are you trying to tease me?"

"Is it really teasing when I'll follow through?"

I cannot get enough of this man. I turn us and push him so he's resting on the edge of the dining table.

He grips the edge and leans back, widening his legs.

I don't hesitate to drop to my knees. I want to take my time and unwrap him like a present, but like anytime I'm with him, I lose myself. As soon as I have his jeans undone and his cock freed, it's fast, needy, and messy all at once. Drool drips down my chin, slurps echo through the suite, and then Blake comes on a loud cry while I drink up every drop.

As he comes back down, he runs a hand through my hair. "I don't think I've ever come so hard or fast in my life."

I wipe my mouth. "I usually like to take my time but can get by in a pinch."

Blake pulls me up and slams his mouth against mine, drinking me in and no doubt tasting any remnants of himself on my tongue. "Take me to bed," he whispers.

"Mm, you ready to go again already?"

"Nope, but after that, you deserve to take whatever you want from me, and I have no doubt if you peg my prostate hard enough with your fat cock that I'll be able to come again."

I'd have to not come in my pants to do that, and I'm dangerously close with all this sex talk.

Blake coming out of his shell makes me weak, and when he leads me to the bedroom, strips naked, and gets on his hands and knees with that delectable ass in the air, I prep him as fast as I can until I can sink inside his body and make him mine.

I manage to hold myself back from coming until Blake's writhing and stroking himself in earnest to get himself off again, but the second he screams my name, I no longer have control or any way to stop my orgasm from slamming into me.

I have no idea if I get Blake off or not, but as I slam inside him, I'm too distracted to try to figure it out. Only when I collapse on top of him do I have the mind to ask if he finished.

"I don't think I'll be able to get it up again anytime soon," he says.

"Maybe that's how we should play this sex scene." I roll onto my back. "Let's make each other come until it's impossible for us to get turned on tomorrow."

"Good plan."

The plan doesn't work. At least, not for me. As Blake and I wait on set in our robes, wearing practically nothing except our nude illusion socks over our junk, I can't help but find his squirming adorably hot.

I don't know what that says about me, but whatever.

"I'm getting a glimpse into what drag queens go through, and I have to say, I'm not a fan." He tries to adjust himself.

"You're not supposed to be tucking anything down there."

"I'm not. It's just … tight. Feels weird."

I lean in and lower my voice. "You usually like tight things wrapped around your dick."

Blake groans. "Can you maybe not do that right now?"

I grip his shoulder, but he steps away.

"Or touch me. I can't get a hard-on."

"I'm going to have to touch you during the scene. You know that, right?"

"I should've asked for a stunt double or CGI sex in my contract."

"I'm trying really hard not to be offended." I'm lying. This is the awkward part I think all actors hate doing, and it's the first time he's ever done this type of scene. The blowjob one was different. He was only shirtless in that, and it was a close-up. This will have his ass showing, side shots of Blake on top of me. It's all choreographed and led by an intimacy expert—that's an actual job.

"It's a closed set," I say. "It'll be fine."

"It'll be awkward as fuck."

"Well, yeah. That too."

Blake shoves me. "You're not helping."

"Hey." I squeeze his hand. "It's just me out there. If you get overwhelmed or need a break, need me to take the lead or whatever, I'll be there."

He takes a deep breath. "Thank you."

Ben walks on set with a storm cloud above him. "All right, let's get this shitshow started." Ben in a crappy mood. Just what we need to make this more fun.

"Ignore him," I say to Blake. "Focus on me. Are you ready?"

He shakes his head.

"Too late." I drop my robe and take my spot on the bed while Blake stands at the foot of it, biting his lip in that sexy way he does when he's nervous. I don't think it's supposed to be sexy, but it is.

The lights, the noises, and the bustling set make it difficult to really channel my character, but when Ben calls action and Blake crawls on top of me, I do what I told him and only focus on him.

His skin on mine, his breath on my cheek, the way he kisses me … he's not even grinding against me, but it feels as though he is. Suddenly, it's easy to bring emotion to the scene. It might be simulating sex, but the point of it is intimacy.

Ben calls, "Cut."

Apparently, we're blocking a camera.

So we rearrange position and try it again, but then our body makeup is all wrong, and it's another twenty minutes before we run it again while we get touched up.

The intimacy specialist gives us tips to incorporate, like try making sound and communication with nonverbal cues.

This time he really is pressed against me, and even though we made each other come countless times last night, it's easy to get carried away when it comes to Blake.

The moan they wanted isn't even forced. It happens naturally.

That's when Ben calls cut again. "This is a cinematic masterpiece, not porn. Do it again."

Blake mumbles something I can't hear, but I'm pretty sure it's "Cinematic masterpiece my ass."

With each take, Blake's confidence grows, and we do eventually get the shot after about twelve hours of constant breaks, touch-ups, and sex lessons from their "expert." It's tempting to tell them all it would be quicker if we could just fuck on camera because Blake and I have that down pat, but real sex and movie sex are completely different.

When we're done, our sweat has mixed with the oil and makeup on our bodies. Blake stands and quickly wraps his robe around him while the crew work to unpack the set around us.

He steps forward and lowers his voice so they can't hear. "You were right. That was the least sexy thing we've ever done."

"Ironic, isn't it?"

"I've always been kind of proud of my ass—"

"It is a fine ass."

"But yeah, after having it on display for twelve hours, I'm a little over it."

"I can admire it for the both of us, then. I'm gonna grab a shower in my trailer. See you back at the hotel?"

"As long as you want to do anything but have sex."

I burst out laughing. "Deal." I really want to kiss him goodbye, but we still have to keep this thing quiet.

We go our separate ways, but I almost trip on my feet when I find Ben watching us. I thought he was out of here as soon as he said we were wrapped for the day.

I ignore his look of derision and push past him. He's forgotten by the time I get to my trailer.

It feels good to get all the sticky makeup off my body, but I rush through my shower. I don't think I've ever been excited to hang out with someone and not have sex before. Today was exhausting, but I can't think of any better way to order food, watch TV, and then go to bed where Blake will spoon me.

Only, when I step out of the shower and wrap my towel around me, I'm not expecting to find Ben waiting on my couch.

In my trailer.

Like he owns the place.

"Get out," I say easily.

He ignores me. "You're *actually* fucking around with him, aren't you?"

"I have no idea what you're talking about." Shit, are my cheeks heating? I don't blush.

"Yes, you do. It's obvious."

"Why do you care? You're with *Chad*."

"It would be a shame to kiss your entire career goodbye for a fling with someone who's probably going to go back to being straight after this movie wraps."

"You don't know anything about Blake Monroe. You never gave him a chance. To you he's a brainless guy who does nonserious movies."

Ben stands. "You don't want more rumors of you cheating to get out, do you? No one will hire you because the public will turn on you. Think about everything you've worked for to get here."

"Why does that sound like a threat?"

He puts his hands up like a busted perp. "No threat here. I

don't need to threaten you. The leaked photos are doing it for me."

Suspicion prickles my skin. "Y-you … you leaked the set photo."

It makes sense. Normally he's the one to handle those types of scandals, but he had a producer do it for him because he didn't care.

"Now why would I do such a thing?" Ben's smarmy voice gives it away.

"Holy shit, you did. You did it to cover up *your* mess. You did it to protect your own ass and throw me under the bus."

"Who would believe that? You're the one who's now dating the guy you cheated with."

I grunt in frustration. "You're an even bigger asshole than I thought you were."

"I'm here for a simple reason. End it with Blake, or your fans will make your career crash and burn."

"Why do you want to ruin me?"

He pretends to think. "How about that you used me to get ahead in your career, and now you owe me?"

"Oh, I *used* you? We all know it was the other way around. I was your ticket to owning who you are, but you didn't care about me. You wanted me on your arm, and you hate that I'm not pining for you."

"Whatever you want to tell yourself to feel better about sleeping your way to the … middle. Don't fuck your career before it really has time to take off."

"I still don't know why you're here or why you're pretending to care about my career, but it's not needed. I know the risks. My management team has been shoving them down my throat since Blake and I were first photographed together."

"One wrong move in this industry could ruin you forever. You know that."

Even though I'm learning this the hard way, I'm learning faster that I don't care. I was happier when I was lesser known. I wasn't as scrutinized.

Is losing all of it worth the risk of what I want to have with Blake?

There's no question: absolutely.

"I'll be fine. Now excuse me, I need to get dressed and go meet my *boyfriend*."

Wow. Boyfriend. There's a label I didn't know I'd be using again.

Ben pauses at the door. "Don't say I didn't warn you."

As I dress and wait for Blake's driver to come pick me up, I toss the boyfriend label around in my head a couple more times. It doesn't make me wince or recoil like it did when I was with Ben. Instead, it sends butterflies swarming through my gut and brings a smile to my face.

And when I arrive at the hotel and climb into bed next to an exhausted Blake, I know it feels *right*.

CHAPTER 25
BLAKE

MY PHONE BLARES at *get fucked o'clock*, but I don't remember setting my alarm. Then I wake properly and realize it's my ringtone, not an alarm.

I roll away from where I've plastered myself to Jordan's back, and he mumbles a complaint, even though he's still sleeping.

Anthony's name flashes on the screen. Why's my agent calling me this early? I slip out of bed and wander into the living room to answer it, but I get the feeling I don't want to know.

"I really hope you're calling because someone wants to offer me fifty million dollars to do their next movie and you couldn't wait for a reasonable hour to tell me." I hold my breath.

"I wish. Who did you piss off at Plymouth Studios?"

"Umm, no one? I don't think."

"You had to have pissed someone off. Check out the news in Variety about the next Coby Godspeed movie."

"Huh?" I put him on speaker while I open the site on my phone. There it is in black and white. "They recast me?" I screech.

"So, I reiterate, who did you piss off? We were in the middle of negotiating your next paycheck. We were almost ready to sign. Now they have this no-name new hotshot actor taking your place."

"I … I don't understand."

"Apparently, they've been looking at this guy for a while in case our negotiations went sideways, but now they undercut you and cast you out, and I need to know why so we can fix whatever damage you've done."

"I've done nothing! Let me call the director. He likes me."

"You didn't read the whole article, did you? He walked when he found out you weren't going to be involved. You lost the franchise."

"They James Bonded me," I mutter.

"I can't help thinking this all has to do with you coming out, but that doesn't make sense because they were still negotiating up until yesterday."

A raspy voice comes from behind me. "I think I might have an idea." Jordan's face is forlorn with worry and regret, and I have no idea what he's going to say, but just like I knew this phone call wouldn't be good news, I'm not holding on to any hope here.

"Is that Jordan?" Anthony asks. "I thought you promised there wouldn't be any more between you two?"

"Well, we lied," I say.

"There's the problem. It's leaked or there was another photo or cheating accusation—"

"It was Ben," Jordan says.

"Ben?" I ask.

"Last night, he cornered me in my trailer and warned me against ruining my career by being with you. It felt like a threat, but I shrugged him off and basically said I'll do what I want. I didn't think …" He runs his hand through his hair. "I didn't think he'd come after you. I would've—"

"What? Ended it with me? I wouldn't have allowed it."

"I'm so sorry. I'll fix it," Jordan says. "I don't know how, but I will. I'll get you the role back. Somehow."

"It's too late for that," Anthony says. "The contracts were signed last night."

Jordan shakes his head. "I didn't know. I didn't know what he was implying. He was talking about *my* career, about *my* future. He told me to stop seeing you, and—"

I smile. I can't help it. "You chose me over your career?"

"I … I wasn't thinking. I didn't know he'd do this. And now you've lost Coby, and it's all my fault, and—"

"Hey, breathe." I step toward him. "Anthony, I'll call you back."

"Let me see what I can find out. If Benjamin Randt thinks he can get away with this shit, he's sorely mistaken." Anthony ends the call, and I throw my phone on the couch.

"Jordan," I say cautiously. He looks like a wounded animal that might run away at any second. "It's okay." I try to rest a reassuring hand on his upper arm, but he pulls away.

"It's not okay. It's really not. You *are* Coby Godspeed."

"I'm also Madden. Blake Monroe from Eleven. A quiet straight guy. I'm all those things and none of them. They're roles I have played to try to find the real me, and the only time in the last ten years where I have felt I've been my genuine self is when I'm with you."

His gray eyes soften, but then he steps back. "You can't."

"I can't what?"

"Tank your career for me."

"So, when you thought Ben was threatening your career, it was okay to ignore it?"

"That was a threat. A vague one at that. I didn't know he was actually going to do anything, and if I'd known he was going to do it to you instead of me … I would've just ended it between us."

I'm hurt by that but not surprised. Jordan's been used so many times, he can't see what he brings to a relationship other than sex. And under normal circumstances, I'd agree with him. Sex isn't worth risking a career for.

But sex with Jordan? Nights of hanging out with that one person who understands more than any other person you've ever met? The guy who's supportive of you to the point of self-destruction?

That person is worth risking a career for.

"It would be a mistake," I say. "To end us."

"Not if it saved your franchise."

"It's too late for that, and even if it wasn't, if I had to choose between you and Coby Godspeed, I'd choose you. Did I want to do the next Coby movie? Of course I did. They're fun to work on. But is it my entire life? No. I still have this Eleven tour coming up, and that's going to take a lot of my time, and then after that, I have a choice of anything I want to do. That's actually exciting. Roles come and go. What we have … it could be so much more."

Jordan still doesn't look convinced. "What if Ben comes after me next?"

Okay, I suddenly see where he's coming from. If the roles were reversed, I wouldn't want Jordan to risk his future for me, but not because I don't think we won't work out. I wouldn't want him to miss out on opportunities simply because he chose me as his partner.

"Then, I guess that's something you need to weigh up. It's easy to walk away from a hypothetical. Is it as easy to walk away now you know the threat is real?"

Jordan blinks at me with his lips slightly parted.

He doesn't have an answer, and neither do I.

"How did you want to play this?" I ask, even though I'm terrified of the answer.

Jordan refuses to look at me. "I don't know yet."

I can't deny the little pang in my heart that he has to think about this longer than I do, but it's unfair of me to feel that way. Jordan's not in the same position that I am. He's worked hard to get where he is. He hasn't been handed everything on a silver platter because he was a teenage pop star.

"Okay, you need some time," I say. "That's totally doable. Until you come to a conclusion on how this is going to unfold, we should probably go back to either keeping our distance or trying to hide it better."

"I ... uh, yeah. You're right. I think I'll stay at my place tonight."

"We'll go separately to the set?"

"I think that's best."

Just because I agree with him doesn't mean it doesn't hurt.

I keep the hotel room for a couple more nights out of pure optimism, but after days on set where Jordan is the most professional he's ever been since I met him, I check out of the place that has so many hot memories as well as emotional ones.

I didn't think it would hurt this much, but the more I think about it, the more it makes sense. I think back to when Eleven got their first big break. If someone had asked me to pick between the group and them back then, it would've been an easy decision. Bye-bye, love, hello, fame. And that was after landing my first ever audition. I can't imagine what it would be like for Jordan, who's been out here for over a decade trying to make it.

After another god-awful day on set where Ben's surly, Jordan's distant, and my mood bounces off both of them, I head for Harley's studio in West Hollywood, where we're laying down our first track for the album. The next few weeks are going to be packed because after long-ass days on the set, I'll be in the studio from 10:00 p.m. until 2:00 a.m., longer if we can't get it right. Sleep? Who needs that.

Not that I'm sleeping well anyway.

I woke up spooning a pillow this morning—that's how desperately I miss Jordan's touch.

The guys are already in the recording booth when I get there. I storm past the audio engineer and producer, past Brix on the couch behind them, and don't even greet the guys when I reach them.

I throw on my headphones, scowl, and say, "Let's get this over with."

Everyone stares at me for a beat before Harley signals for the engineer to hit playback. I don't even know what I'm singing.

My brain is frazzled, I'm tired already, and this is only our first recording session. They really should've done this without me. They don't need me.

"Blake, you missed your cue," Harley says.

"Shit," I hiss. "Okay, go again."

"Are you okay?" Mason asks.

"Fan-fucking-tastic."

All four of them hang up their headphones.

It's the middle of the goddamn night, and we don't have time for this big-brother, concerned-friend thing.

"What's wrong?" Denver asks.

"This being queer thing isn't easy, is it?"

Harley turns to the glass window. "Brix? We're gonna need some coffee. For all of us."

"We don't need to talk about it," I say. "I mean, still get me coffee because I'm running on fumes, but we don't have to talk about how Jordan's ex-boyfriend got me kicked off the new Coby movie or how he's threatening Jordan with never working in Hollywood again if we're seeing each other." Fucking titsfor-brains, cockwombling twatface.

"That doesn't sound like a queer issue but an asshole issue," Ryder says.

"Wait, are you saying it wasn't your choice to give up Coby?" Harley asks. "I thought you'd decided to move on or something. I didn't realize—"

"They blindsided me. I had the script, we were in contract negotiations, and then bam. They signed someone else on the same night Ben threatened to ruin Jordan's career. I ..." I sigh. "I don't know what to do. Jordan's basically ignoring me, only doing our scenes together, in character. It feels like I haven't spoken to him in days, but we've been right next to each other.

I've never … No one has ever made me feel the way he does, and …"

They're all blinking at me.

"Shit, I'm getting all mushy and crap. Ignore me—"

"No," Harley says. "Bring on the mush. It sounds to me like you've fallen for him."

I have. I really have. I thought I was falling, but only a couple of days without him has made me irrationally emotional.

"Want us to beat up Ben?" Mason asks.

I laugh. "That won't bring more tabloid mania on us at all."

Harley purses his lips. "How powerful is Benjamin Randt, anyway?"

"Well, he got me fired from a franchise that was all about me. So, yeah, I'd say pretty powerful. I can't ask Jordan to give up Hollywood for me."

"He can't let his ex dictate his life, though, either," Ryder says.

I groan. "Ugh. I know. But I can't force him to risk everything for a relationship he still thinks is going to end. He says he's giving us a real shot, but I don't think there's been enough time for him to actually do it."

Brix enters with the coffee, and after a few sips, I start to calm down a little.

"Okay, let's get this song recorded." I turn my attention back to the sheet music in front of me and read over the lyrics and actually pay attention. "Wait …" I glance at Harley. "Is this what I think it is?"

"My coming out song? Yep. I figured it was fitting as our first single on the album, seeing as we will all be out. It's the perfect way—"

"To ruin our careers?" I half joke. I've already lost my movie franchise. If I lose Eleven as well … Then again, if Jordan turned up and asked me to leave Eleven, I'd probably do it.

Priorities change, and all I can think about in this moment is Jordan's and my future.

"It's possible," Harley says. "But we need to remember why

we're doing this album. Why we're getting back together. We want to make a difference in this industry, don't we?"

The rest of us nod.

I came back because I missed them all, but now that I know what it's like to be on this side of the line, I want to help make a difference to all the young queer and questioning people out there.

Harley talks about the music video we're gonna shoot for it, an all-seasons kind of thing. He wants to use some of the footage we shot in Montana—the goofing-off parts where we weren't singing—and he wants Brix to feature in it but in silhouette to still keep his identity somewhat secret.

Harley's animated and so damn happy it radiates from him, and I'm not jealous. Nope, not jealous at all.

Who am I kidding? I'm almost resentful at how jealous I am. Happy for Harley and Brix, but ... so fucking jealous.

I miss Jordan already.

CHAPTER 26
JORDAN

I DIDN'T REALIZE how hard it would be to keep my distance from Blake, and after only a couple of days, I know I can't walk away from him and what we have.

All those times I thought *this could be different,* deep down I knew they never could be. But with Blake … I don't even know how it's different. It just is.

I've been good at keeping my distance and making Ben think that he's won. It's been painful, and I admit, I caved last night and went to the hotel only to find the key no longer worked and Blake had checked out. It was frustrating because I miss Blake more than I thought I would, but it was lucky too.

I keep telling myself we only have to do this dance until filming wraps. Until then, I'm doing everything in my power to make sure I can keep both him and my career in film.

Sneaking around is too risky because after finding out Ben's the one leaking all the shit about Blake and me, I wouldn't put it past him to hire someone to follow me. And isn't that a kick in the teeth? I went from respecting him as a filmmaker, a person, and as a boyfriend to … this. Mistrust and paranoia about being followed.

Fuck Benjamin Randt.

I have a few ideas up my sleeve on how I can save my ass and keep seeing Blake, but I'm really hoping the assignment I gave Jojo works out. It's the least controversial, and it doesn't involve public displays of "This is none of your business, but I'm going to do an exclusive interview to tell my side of the story" type thing.

Instead of regular assistant duties, I've sent Jojo on a mission to gossip with other PAs and get dirt on dear old Ben. You don't act like he does and not make a few enemies in this town. I just have to find the right enemy.

If I can network with the right directors, the right producers, I don't have to lose anything. Because I realized something when Blake's contract with Coby Godspeed fell through: he still has options, and so do I.

I get a message from her that says: *Can't come to set today to wait on you hand and foot because Operation Make Cheating Assholes Pay is in effect. Going to brunch with a source. A PA friend of another PA. Real six degrees of separation shit. Side note, does Hollywood espionage get me a raise?*

I reply: *Get me what I want, and I'll give you a twenty percent raise.* She'd deserve it.

Blake looks miserable when he arrives to set, and when our eyes meet, I want to go up to him and kiss his worries away, but I don't.

I might be falling for Blake, but throwing my life's work away for him sounds like Disney movie crap that's unrealistic.

Blake was right when he said I've been closed off to the idea of forever because I know forever doesn't come easy. It takes work, not magic. So when we shoot our scenes today, I hold on to Blake a little bit tighter, kiss him that little bit harder, and I try to convince him that I'm still here. I'm still all in. And I silently promise we can be together soon.

When Ben calls for a ten-minute break, Blake leans in and whispers in my ear, "I miss you."

I glance around, and even though Ben's left the room, his lackeys haven't. I quickly squeeze Blake's hand before dropping it along with my voice. "I have a plan. You just need to miss me a little bit longer."

"What plan?"

Out of the corner of my eye, Jojo steps through the sound studio door and sends me a thumbs-up.

"You'll find out soon enough." I go to walk off when I pause. "Oh, and I miss you too. So fucking much."

It's the first time I've seen Blake smile all day, but then Ben steps back in the room, and I scowl at Blake.

"Don't look so happy, though. The asshole is back."

Blake's face falls, but the smallest of smiles remains.

I approach Jojo and drag her to the side of the sound stage where no one else is around. "What'd you find out?"

"I sent a list of names to your phone of producers, studio execs, and everyone who has pull in this industry who also happen to hate Ben. All you have to do is send them to your agent and get him to put some feelers out. Oh, and just so you know? It's a really long list."

That takes care of Ben being able to badmouth me all over town, but we still have to deal with the public fallout of Blake's and my "affair." That might need some extra thought. But for now, I can breathe easy for the first time in days.

Arianna pulls through for me, and as soon as she calls to tell me there are numerous directors and studios on that list willing to cast me in upcoming projects if for nothing more than to drive Benjamin Randt crazy, I drive over to Mason and Denver's house because I can't stay away from Blake anymore. Even if we still have stuff to work out, I need to see him. I don't care we were on set together just a few hours ago. I need to see Blake, not Madden.

I need his warmth and that fullness inside my chest I get

whenever I'm near him. Most of all, I need him to know that while I'm still scared shitless that I'll be heartbroken by him, I'm all in.

I belong to Blake in a way I've never belonged to anyone else.

I want to hold on to that feeling. Cherish it. Love it.

I want to love him forever. Or, at least, give us the chance to get there.

I've never done that before, and it'll be a first for me.

I took Blake's first time with a man. He took my first time with love.

Real, bone-deep, blind-trust kind of love.

Oh, shit, what am I doing? I pause at the gate outside Denver's Malibu mansion, but then I shake off my momentary freak-out and push forward.

Old habits die hard, but Blake is someone I truly want. I'll do anything to be with him, even open myself to being vulnerable.

I ring the buzzer and am immediately let through, but Denver answers the door when I reach it. "Is Blake here?"

Denver steps aside. I suck in a deep breath and prepare to do this big romantic speech, and then my feet practically trip over themselves when we enter the living room and every single Eleven member is here, with their partners, along with a dude who looks like a manager, a woman on his arm, and there's some other woman here with a child, and and and okay, this is all too overwhelming.

Then my gaze lands on Blake, who's on the floor, cross-legged, reading something on a sheet of paper and humming a tune.

"Oh," I say. "This is a bad time." I try to turn away, but Denver's there, arms folded, blocking my way.

"Jordan?" Blake croaks.

I slowly turn back. "'Sup." Kill. Me. Now.

"What are you doing here?"

My eyes dance around the room at the millions of people here. "I, uh, came to, umm, tell you something, but you're busy. Everyone's busy. You all look … busy."

Blake's lips turn upward. "Whatever you have to say, you can do it in front of everyone. We're basically family."

I blow out a loud breath, and then everything comes out in a rush. "I sent Jojo to do some digging, and basically, even if Ben threatens to get me fired from future projects, he can't do it when he doesn't have influence over half of Hollywood who he's already pissed off? And the other thing was I've been really thinking about that conversation we had where I said being half as famous was more fun for me? And I contemplated maybe trying to direct a movie instead of star in it? And I've gotten Arianna to put some feelers out there, and there's a studio interested in any project I want to bring to them? So I thought I'd do that. There's still the public issue of them thinking we cheated, but maybe we could just tell everyone we didn't? They probably won't believe us, but I can't live without you, and I want us to be together, and I'm rambling in front of all these people who are intimidating, and I've never done this before. I fear I will keep talking if someone doesn't stop me soon, and—"

Blake stands up and holds up his hand. "Breathe."

I take a deep breath.

"So, what I'm hearing is, you're refusing to choose between me and your movie career and are going to extreme lengths to make sure you get both?"

I point at him. "Yes. That. But, uh, obviously I needed to say it with a million more rambly words because I've never done this before. And I probably would have preferred to do it without everyone staring at me." I wave in the general direction of everyone but refuse to look at any of them.

Blake takes my hand. "Come with me."

"Wait," Harley protests. "We don't get to see how this pans out?"

"Nosey fuckers." Blake flips off the entire room.

The little girl in the corner with the woman gasps. "Uncle Blake said fuck."

"Kaylee," Ryder growls.

The woman laughs. "Please. You and Lyric have a swear jar. It's nothing she hasn't heard or said before. Besides, you let her watch his Coby movies where 'motherfucker' comes out his mouth every two minutes."

Kaylee jumps up. "Now you said it!"

Blake drags me out of the room and down the hall to a more formal area. "Did you mean it?"

Without the stifling audience, I can let out a breath and bring Blake against me as I whisper, "Every word."

"I want you to be sure."

"I've never been surer. More sure? The surest."

"I … don't know if any of those are words."

I shrug. "This is why we don't write scripts."

"True. Hey, were you also serious about the directing thing? Because no lie, I think you'd be great at it."

"Arianna gave me the idea. Transcend Studios were really interested in working together, and they suggested it. It kind of feels like the right move for me, but I've also decided that I'm going to take a break after this movie wraps and really figure out what direction I want to go."

"You're going to take a break? And do what?"

"Well, there's this music tour I want to follow around like a groupie."

Blake's face lights up. "You want to come on tour with us?"

"The last few days without you have been hard. I don't want to voluntarily miss you like that again."

"You know you'll have to, right? I mean eventually."

"Yeah. Eventually." I wrap my arms around his back tighter. "Until then, we have the rest of this movie, the tour, and then maybe I'll be looking for some hot and talented actors to fill my directorial debut with."

Blake's hands slide up my arms and then slide around the back of my neck. "Well, you just have it all figured out, don't you?"

"Yep. That okay with you?"

He moves his lips closer. "You're giving me everything I want and more."

"It's, umm, because … I kinda figured out, that, you know … I love you?"

Blake's eyes widen.

"Wait, no, I take it back. I don't."

He frowns. "You don't?"

"Okay, I do, but your reaction scared me."

He huffs a laugh. "I was taken off guard, is all. You've never said that to someone before."

I nod. "It's true. You're my first."

"Holy fuck."

"Is that a good holy fuck or a *Oh shit, I'm stuck with him now* kind of holy fuck?"

Blake shakes his head. "One day, those kinds of thoughts won't fill your head when I have something to say because you'll believe without even a single doubt that when I tell you I love you too, I mean it. I will always mean it. And I know you've probably got statistics and a million failed relationships running through your head at any given time, but I can be certain for the both of us. I love you, Jordan Brooks, and I'll gladly be stuck with you."

If possible, I fall for him a little more.

CHAPTER 27
BLAKE

WHEN WE WALK BACK into the living room, all eyes are on us.

I grin. "You all know my boyfriend, Jordan, right?"

Harley's ex-fiancée, who's now his manager's fiancée—it's not weird, not weird at all—coos. "Aww, that is so cute."

"What's in the water with this band?" Gideon asks.

Lyric opens his mouth. "Cu—" Then he glances at Ryder's daughter. "—Uhhhhhhmmmm … nothing."

Maggie, Kaylee's mother, covers Kaylee's ears. "Subtle. Really subtle. My poor daughter."

Little Kaylee pulls the most adorable confused expression ever. "I don't get it."

Maggie pats Kaylee's head. "How about we leave Daddy to do some business, and we'll go get ice cream."

Quickest sell ever. In a flurry of movement, they're out the door.

Everyone is still staring at us, waiting for a play-by-play, but I ignore them and drag Jordan over to the recliner chair that's free and push him down on it. Then I sit on his lap sideways and get back to work.

"Where were we?"

"Umm," Harley says. "Tour dates. But I have an idea. And you're all probably not going to like it."

We all groan because this is Harley. He knows this industry, he knows what he's doing, but he comes up with these ideas that throw everything we've planned into chaos, and we all know it's happening again.

"Do we take bets on this idea or let him tell us?" I ask.

"Put us out of our misery," Mason says.

"Gideon and I are anticipating a lot of interview requests after we drop this single and the video. Then with all of us *out* but none of us giving an actual statement … I thought we could do it all together."

We glance around at each other because yep, we don't like that idea. People are always going to say whatever they want, and I don't think interviews and tell-all exclusives will ever change their opinions.

But then I think about where I was a few months ago, completely unaware that the love of my life was about to turn my world upside down, and I would love to tell that story to anyone who wants to listen. Anyone who might be questioning or doesn't realize anything can happen if you're open to it.

Had I not accepted the role in *Faking It*, I might never have explored my true identity because the opportunity might not have ever presented itself. And the thought of missing out on what Jordan and I have makes me wrap my arms around his shoulders tighter.

"I'm in." I kiss the top of Jordan's head. "If that's okay with Jord."

He smiles up at me. "I'm prepared for the backlash."

"I'll make sure to point out we were both single when we started dating. People probably won't believe it, but I think we should at least tell our side even if it falls on deaf ears."

"We're in too," Mason says and squeezes Denver's hand.

All eyes fall to Ryder, who admittedly has a lot riding on this. He has the safety of his daughter to think about. Though, since he came out, Maggie and Kaylee have had security watching over them, and the media has been more insistent on getting photos of Lyric and Ryder than anyone else. This could add fuel to that fire, though.

Lyric squeezes Ryder's shoulder. "Just because they're doing it, that doesn't mean you have to. You coming out at all was a gift I never asked for but love all the same. You don't have to do more than that if you're worried about Kaylee."

Ryder reaches across his chest and lays his hand on top of Lyric's on his shoulder. "It's time. And doing it together is probably the best way to nip it in the bud. Instead of speculation, it will all be out then, and we'll have some idea on how it will affect the tour and album."

Gideon steps in. "I'll put feelers out and find the right show for this kind of thing."

"Think Oprah will come out of retirement like she did with Harry and Meghan?" I'm only half-joking.

Harley holds up his hands, mimicking weighing scales. "Royal family, queer boy band … Hmm, it's a toss-up."

"You know, Sean Rushton is rumored to be gay," Gideon says. "And his late-night talk show is the highest rated recently. He might be interested."

"He did my first-ever interview," Lyric says. "He was really sweet and eased me into it. I think he'd be supportive and ask the right questions while being respectful."

"Unless you wanted to go the prime-time type of interview, in which case we can look elsewhere," Gideon suggests.

I raise my hand. "I vote for late-night. It would be less stuffy and serious than something prime-time."

"I agree," Harley says. "We want it to be a big deal, but we don't want to make a big deal of it, if that makes sense."

"Normalize it," Denver agrees.

"Then we're in agreement?" Gideon asks. There are rounds of agreements all around. "I'll get on it."

He exits the room to make some phone calls.

"Okay, next thing." Harley turns to Jordan and me. "Does it look like your film will wrap on time? I want to shoot and edit the video as fast as possible so we can drop it the same time as the single. Then it will be interview, tour dates announced, and then full speed ahead to finish the album before we leave for the tour."

"We're on schedule. Well, the already altered schedule, but yes. We only have about a week left."

Jordan's hand tightens on my hip. "A week where we should probably still keep our distance on set. Let everything with Ben fall to shit when you do the interview."

I hate it, but I agree with him. "Yeah, I'd rather it happen where I didn't have to see him every day."

"What an asshole," Mason mutters.

"Yep," Jordan and I say in unison.

Only one more week of having to deal with him. At least until the press tour when the movie comes out.

We can make it one week.

We can't make it one week. Jordan and I are keeping it professional, as painful as it is, but it's like Ben can sense that we're together because he's scrutinizing us more and more each day. Or I'm being paranoid, one or the other. Maybe I'm not acting miserable enough. Last week, I was miserable, so I guess I was more believable than the forced longing looks I'm sending Jordan. Though the longing is real.

He stayed over the night he came to Denver and Mason's, but we agreed to play it cool. Only for one more week.

I already miss him, but in a weird way, I cherish the feeling. I've never actually missed anyone before. Not on this level. It's new, and I kind of hope it lingers enough for me to remember what it feels like to miss someone with my entire being. It somehow cements that my feelings for Jordan aren't temporary.

In between scenes where the crew is setting up for the next shot, Jordan disappears to his trailer, and it's way too tempting to follow him. I almost do it until I look around and spot Ben watching me.

So instead of heading for the trailers, I go get some food.

I'm in the middle of shoving a cookie in my mouth when I turn and almost run into Ben.

"Fuck." I spray chocolate chip cookie everywhere.

"I heard about the studio recasting Coby Godspeed."

"Mm, I bet you did."

Ben cocks his head. "It's a shame. You play dumb action hero really well."

Apparently, my eyes don't listen when I tell them not to roll back. "Plenty more roles in the sea ... or fish. Whatever that phrase is. I wouldn't know. I'm too dumb."

"Are there, though?"

"It's really sweet you're worried about my career, but I have it handled." *More than you'd know, asshole.*

"You might, but does Jordan?"

Okay, now he's pissing me off. He couldn't be any more transparent if he tried.

I grit my teeth and try to keep my cool because the last thing I need is more tabloid drama. I can see the headlines now: Blake Monroe Punches Director On Set.

"Listen," I say, proud my tone is calm. "I know what you're doing. For whatever reason, you don't want Jordan to be happy or successful. You think you made him, which also gives you the impression you're allowed to destroy him. I don't know why you have the need to make everyone feel inferior to your 'greatness'" —the air quotes make him flinch—"but it won't work with me. So go ahead and threaten all you want. Call around to your friends who do your bidding because they're scared they'll be next on your hit list, but remember that eventually, everyone in this industry will realize exactly what you're like. They might be quiet now out of fear, but nothing in this town stays a secret forever. All you need is one person to speak out against you, and they'll all fall like dominoes. Really think about who you're threatening right now."

With each word, Ben's face falls a little more and more.

"I'm not Jordan. I've had two successful careers in LA, and I'm not in the same position as he is where everything is on the line. If you hate me, come after me. Don't be a coward and pick the easy target, and don't emotionally manipulate your ex purely because your ego was crushed that he wasn't pining for you after you made the stupidest mistake by cheating on him."

Ben's gaze darts around at all the cast and crew that I'm now noticing are dead silent and frozen as they watch this altercation play out.

So I plaster on a Blake Monroe from Eleven smile, because fuck knows we had coaches to teach us how to smile properly way back when, and say with enough kindness to kill, "You're shit out of luck here because I'm not scared of what you can do, and when you take away the fear of bullies, they no longer hold any power."

Ben isn't as good at hiding how pissed off he is. "I could have you fired from this project, you know."

"From a movie that's got a couple of days of shooting left? I don't care how powerful you think you are in this industry, there is no way anyone from the studio would approve of that many reshoots. So how about you turn around, walk away, we finish this film, and then you can crawl back into whatever hole you came from." I go to step past him when I pause and lower my voice. "Oh, and leave me and Jordan alone."

I walk away, and a second later, a cookie flies past my head. I guess I should be thankful he has terrible aim. My feet stall, but I realize quickly he's not worth it, and as I storm off set and pass Jordan's assistant, Jojo, she lifts her phone and winks.

Later, after we're wrapped for the day, Jordan turns up on Denver's doorstep.

His phone is open to the viral video in his hand. The audio is shit, and it's unclear what we're saying, but by the look of awe on Jordan's face, what was said isn't important. "You didn't tell me."

I shrug and let him in, shutting the door behind us. "We got back to business, and I don't anticipate he'll be bothering either of us again anytime soon."

"This is crazy. The video has already been seen over three million times, and it only happened a couple of hours ago."

"What do the comments say?"

Jordan holds his head up high. "I wouldn't know. I didn't look. A smart person once told me not to."

"Okay, but really, what did they say? I know you, and I know you can't stay away."

"Fine. There are some that say you deserve it because of the whole cheating thing, but mostly, they say I dodged a bullet by getting away from all that toxic cookie-throwing energy Ben has. There have already been some old production assistants who've come forward and say how horrible he is to employees on set. It's about to all unravel."

"It's almost like it was planned for that to happen."

Jordan narrows his gaze. "Did you … *Was it* planned?"

"Ha. I wish. Nothing that brilliant is planned. It was only a matter of time, though. Your assistant—I mean, the anonymous source on set—might have got a jump start on it by uploading the video to the internet 'by mistake.' Oops."

"I don't entirely believe you."

"If I was as cunning as I'd like to think I am, I totally would have. All I did was stand up for you when he confronted me."

He wraps his arm around my back. "You did more than stand up for me. You fought for me. No one has ever done that for me before."

"I hope you can get used to it, because that's what it's going to be like with me. You have me in your corner. Always."

"Even when I'm wrong?"

"Jordan Brooks ever wrong? Is that even a thing that happens?"

Jordan laughs. "It's an anomaly, but it can happen."

"I'll be supportive of you even then. Even if that support means shoving my hand over your mouth to get you to stop talking. I'm kind and nice like that."

"I'll take it. Are you ready for this all to go public? We wrap in a couple of days, then you've got the single, the music video …"

"I'm ready for anything so long as I have you."

Jordan breathes in and closes his eyes. "You have no idea what words like that do to me."

"Yes, I do. It makes your chest full and your heart secure in the knowledge that you belong with me just as much as I belong with you." I lower my voice to a whisper. "I know because I feel it too."

There's no more talking after that. Only mouths and bodies giving in to each other over and over and over again. I drag him to the guesthouse and strip him naked. I lick and tease every inch of his body, and when I finally sink inside him and he murmurs the words "I love you," the fullness in my chest explodes, setting every nerve ending, every cell, every single part of my body on fire.

"I love you too."

CHAPTER 28
BLAKE

THE LAST FEW days on set are absolute hell. Time seems to slow down, and the remaining days feel like an eternity. Jordan and I no longer care about being seen together. We don't have massive public displays of affection or anything like that, but we arrive together, go home together, and I've been staying with him in his small apartment every night.

The last thing Jordan Brooks could be considered is humble, but his modest one-bedroom condo in West Hollywood shows that he hasn't adjusted to fame yet, and I find it cute. We need to get him an upgrade, but that can wait.

The moment Ben says the best words I've ever heard—"That's a wrap for *Faking It*"—Jordan and I are out the door before the wrap party even begins.

We hug the cast and the crew, but lucky for us, I have a scheduling conflict. I'm heading to another sound stage at the studio next door, where our Eleven music video is being made. The second it's edited, the single will drop, the *Encore* album and tour will be announced, and I'll be thrown back into the music world.

Jordan drives me in his Prius to the set and comes with me so he can watch. I told him he could stay at the wrap party if he wanted to, but he has no interest in spending time with Ben if he doesn't have to, and I'm on board with that. I've been waiting for his vengeance, for his wrath, but I get the impression he's too busy trying to do damage control for his own career to even think about ruining ours anymore.

The viral video has people speaking out against him, and he's already been dropped from his next project.

When we get to set, the others are all waiting on me.

"I know. I know. We're late. Let's do this. Where do you need me? Wardrobe?"

"Here." Harley throws me some clothes.

Because we're still very much keeping our reunion under wraps, it's a closed set with basically us, two production assistants, a director, and then limited camera crew.

While I get dressed, Harley shoves a tablet in my face. A music video starts, and it's all the single shots of the other guys and their storylines. There's some of the footage Jordan took back in Montana, and the whole theme is perfect.

It opens with Harley and Brix sitting on the cliffs in Rancho Palos Verdes. It's just their silhouettes, shot from behind while the sun sets and paints the sky.

Harley turns and starts singing his song—Brix's identity still a dark figure in the background—and even though the whole overarching theme is that love is love, it really is Harley's song. He's owning who he is for the first time in his life, and I couldn't be prouder of him.

It moves on to Mason and Denver having a food fight, laughing and being … them.

The song has a very chill vibe and actually reminds me a lot of Ed Sheeran's "Afterglow." It takes me back to the night in Montana where Jordan and I were in the hot tub and the guys were teasing us.

It evokes how much I wanted him then, how much I want him now, and how my feelings have grown in between.

"It's a perfect song," I murmur.

"Thanks," Harley says. "I'm paying an editing team an exorbitant amount to finish this off so we can drop it online as soon as it's ready. We just need to get some group videos of us all singing the chorus and then your stuff with your model." He nods toward a scantily clad male model in the corner. "Unless …" He looks at Jordan. "You wanted to do it with him? We could block out your identity like Brix if you want."

When Harley pitched this idea, we were still very much having to keep us a secret. Now it's not so much an issue.

"Sounds fun," Jordan says, "but I don't think you can afford me."

I lower my voice. "I'll pay you later."

"I'm in. Send the pretty boy home." This comes out with a practical growl, and I love it.

It's a long-ass night, and coming off a thirteen-hour day on set, we're both exhausted by the time it's all done and we're sent home to sleep.

My promise to pay him for being in a sappy love song music video will have to come later because the minute we step into Jordan's bedroom, we both crash out.

And Harley, the fucking magician—that sleep-deprived, workaholic magician—has the surprise release out into the world before we even wake by midday.

"You're famous!" Jordan says and shoves his phone in my face. He kneels next to the bed in only his boxer briefs, and as amazing as that sight is, I get stuck on his words.

"If you're only now realizing how famous I am, I'm really sorry to tell you that you fit the brainless-model stereotype."

Jordan ignores my snark. "Holy shit, this is everywhere."

"Eleven getting back together is huge news."

"It's not only that. The video already has ten million views, and it's only been up for a couple of hours. That has to be some kind of record." He taps away on his phone and quickly deflates. "Oh. Okay, no it's not. But it's still amazing. Just don't read the comments."

"Will you ever learn?"

"No."

"Let me guess, a whole lot of 'They should've stayed broken up,' a few homophobic slurs, death threats. Maybe something about sinning?"

"If it makes you feel any better, there's way more supportive comments than negative. Woah, eleven million views now just in the time we've been awake. This is crazy."

"Welcome to boy band mania." I lean up on my elbow and kiss him good morning. "Is it weird that I'm thankful but also overwhelmed? Any minute now, Harley's going to call with some crazy other idea, and it's going to be nonstop for the foreseeable future. I haven't gotten a break in ten years."

"You and me. Two weeks on some tropical island somewhere. I'll make sure to get my team to schedule all studio meetings for two weeks after the tour."

I was kind of hoping for longer than that, but I would never hold Jordan back from what he wants, and if he wants to get into directing, he needs to build relationships with other studios. He's already taking time out to follow me on tour, so two weeks is more than I could ever ask for. "Deal."

My phone buzzes on the nightstand, and I reach for it. "Oh, look at that. It's Harley." I answer it and put it on speaker. "What's up?"

"Pack a bag. We're going to New York."

I look at Jordan and give him my *I told you so* face.

I've been backstage at talk shows a million times before, so this is nothing new, but the butterflies and wariness in my gut are.

I thought we'd have more time to prepare for this interview, but in true Harley fashion, it's full speed ahead twenty-four hours a day. It's a whirlwind, but I have complete trust in him and what we're doing.

We're doing it right this time. We're being ourselves. We're being honest. And we're putting our happiness and truth first. It will probably cost us sales—we know that. But there are more important things than money.

Jordan, who came along for the ride to New York, wraps his arm around my shoulder. "You look nervous."

"It's the first time we're performing together in years."

"Didn't you do a tribute to your old manager a few months ago?"

"Okay, yes, but that was a spur-of-the-moment thing. This is … daunting." Even though this is supposed to be all about us, years of being in the business have me questioning *What if they don't like the new stuff?*

We've accounted for some dip in sales, but there has to be a bottom line. What if it tanks so badly, we can't even afford to go on this tour?

"Is it having to address your sexuality on national TV? Because yeah, that's daunting," Jordan says.

"That hadn't even crossed my mind. But *now* it has, so thanks for that."

"You guys will kill it out there." He kisses the side of my head, and I revel in the small gesture in a public place. I want to be able to kiss him whenever I want, and after this airs, I'll be able to. Within reason. I don't really have any desire to let paps sell photos of us doing it and get rich from them.

The other guys are close by. We're all ready to go onstage. Our earpieces are in, our clothes are uncomfortable but look amazing —according to Jordan—and we're just waiting for Sean Rushton to introduce us.

We're filming ahead of time. It will go performance, interview, tour information, and I have a feeling we'll be here all day and night. Gideon prepared us for the questions Sean's going to ask, and if he does cross any boundaries, it's in our contracts that we can make them edit them out. But I'm still nervous.

After three years of Eleven being apart, we're back.

Three years might not seem like much, but in Hollywood years, it's an entire marriage. Maybe two.

A production assistant tells us we can go onstage and take our places in front of our microphone stands. I haven't met Sean yet, but the set lights go up, and he's there behind his desk.

"Welcome back to the show," he says to the camera. His red hair and young looks remind me of when Conan O'Brien started out. "Boy band mania swept the world once again when these guys dropped an exclusive single yesterday."

The studio audience goes nuts, and I feel it—like a lightning rod to the gut. Adrenaline fills my veins, my heart thumps, and the thrill I always had performing with these guys alights.

Gone are the nerves; all that remains is the need to give the best performance of my life.

"It's official," Sean says. "Eleven are back. And here to sing their new single! Boys, take it away."

The lights illuminate us from above, each of us under an individual spotlight.

The music video plays on screens behind us. Harley opens the song, and we each sing our little verse or bridge or chorus. I'm usually relegated to backup vocals, which I'm happy to do, but even I get a little solo in this song. Harley insisted we do things fair and square this time around.

None of us are more famous, or the leader, or meant to disappear into the background. We're doing this whole thing as a team.

And as we close out the song, I realize we're all about to talk about our love lives. As a team.

The lights go down once again, and I suck in a sharp breath.

Sean cuts to a commercial break and invites us over to his stage, where they've got a three-seater couch and then two barstools at the back. Sean shakes each of our hands, and then Denver and Mason take the stools while the rest of us take the couch. Harley's closest to Sean because he'll do most of the talking. This is his coming out story more than it is ours.

I'm on the other end with Ryder in between us.

"Welcome back! We are here with the one, the only, Eleven!" Sean claps, while we all wave to an invisible audience behind the stage lights.

I'm glad they're blinding because I need them to be. I don't think I've ever been this nervous before. I've never spoken about my private life because I haven't been allowed to. Then, the last few years, I haven't had one. I've done nothing but work, basically.

Once the screaming dies down, Sean turns to us. "New single, new album, new tour … Everything is happening for you guys. Tell me, how did you manage to find enough time in your busy schedules to come back together?"

Good. He's easing us into it, then.

"The hardest one to tie down was Blake." Harley thumbs in my direction.

"Ah, yes, Mr. Movie Star," Sean says. "How did you juggle recording an album while filming?"

"A lot of late nights," I say easily. Or, as easily as I can manage. It comes out a bit croaky.

"*Faking It* will be out during summer, correct?"

"That's the plan." Here it comes.

"There were some rumors going around about you and a certain attractive co-star of yours …"

"Not everything you read is true, Sean. You should know that. But *those* rumors? Yeah, they're true."

The audience laughs. Positive reaction. That's good.

"Though, I'd like to clear something up," I say over the laughter and applause. "Jordan was one hundred percent single before anything happened between us. I was there for him through a hard time, and one thing led to another, and now … I couldn't be happier."

Sean leans back in his seat. "Okay, so let me get this straight."

He looks at the camera. "Or not so straight as it seems. Raise your hand if you are onstage and in a same-sex relationship."

All five of us raise our hands.

"Wait, Harley?" Sean asks even though he knows full well and this is not a surprise at all. He's a good actor.

"Hey, I've been queer a hell of a lot longer than any of these guys. Except maybe Ryder." Harley grins.

Someone in the audience screams, "Ryley forever!" referring to Harley and Ryder's ship name.

Ryder and Harley smile at each other.

"Are the Ryley rumors true too?" Sean asks animatedly.

Harley sighs. "We wish they were, but that would be like kissing my brother, and no thank you."

"Agreed," Ryder says. "I'm more than happy with my partner, Lyric."

"Ah. Lyric Jones. He's a friend of this show too and a rising music star."

"He is," Ryder says proudly.

Sean turns to Mason and Denver. "You two don't have the same qualms as Ryder and Harley about mixing band dynamics and love."

They hold hands.

"Not at all," Denver says.

"Though the transition from best friends to more was a little weird in the beginning, I have to admit," Mason says.

"Okay, I have to ask," Sean says. "Why now? Why are you all coming forward now?"

Harley recites his rehearsed speech but knows how to deliver it like he hasn't run over it a billion times. "The sad truth is, the music industry, film, television, you'd think it would be progressive, but one of the first things I was ever told when I was auditioning and trying to make it was 'Don't let anyone find out you're gay.' For years, we did what labels told us to do. We had advisors to make us marketable, coaches to teach us how to act."

Sean looks knowingly at Harley. "It's a tough business, and it's hard to believe in this day and age it's still like that."

"It is," Harley agrees. "When we split up, we were happy to be finally doing our own thing. Only, it didn't take long for me to realize I was still toeing that line. I was still acting how they told me to act. Pretending to be someone I'm not. When I proposed we all get back together, it was to do it on our terms. Do it our way. And live our truth the way we should have been allowed to from the beginning."

The crowd screams and applauds in support.

"What do you say to those who refuse to buy your album because of this?" Sean asks.

A growl comes from behind me. It's small, but I hear it. The mics probably pick up on it too, but Harley cuts off Mason's crabby response.

"I'm more interested in those who will pick it up because of it. There are so many young kids, teens, and even adults who struggle to come to terms with their sexuality. We wanted to do this so people out there can see they're not alone in this world. This isn't even so much about coming out in order to be happy because I've been very happy the past ten years. Sometimes closet doors hold you back, but sometimes they keep you safe." Harley looks right into the camera now. "So I want anyone watching this who feels like it's not safe to come out to know that you don't have to. You do what you need to do to be safe. But when you're ready, just know, you won't be alone." He turns back to Sean. "That's the message we want to send out into the world."

"And it's a wonderful message," Sean says and then smiles at the camera. "When we come back, the guys talk about their upcoming tour."

The crowd applauds, and the lights dim.

We did it.

We actually fucking did it.

CHAPTER 29
JORDAN

OKAY, so I've lived the life of a working actor for a few years now. I have a manager, an agent, and an assistant. I have no fucking idea how Blake does everything without at least an assistant to get him by.

After the interview, things only speed up, and it's been enlightening to watch.

When Blake throws himself into a project, he's all in, and the guys hit the interview circuit after baring their souls on national TV.

I've had a few meetings with studio execs, one of whom wants to develop a project to collaborate on after the tour.

The tour is only four months national, two months overseas, and minimal venues, and even though they were expecting a huge drop in ticket sales, some shows sold out within days of tickets being live. Most are at least eighty percent sold. They're definitely not the numbers Eleven is used to, having had sold-out nine-month-long tours previously, but I get the impression Harley was expecting an even bigger hit than they've taken. When Harley mentioned adding shows to the cities that were sold out, the four others glared at him. He threw up his hands and said,

"Okay, I got it. No overworking us like the other label did. I just thought I'd ask."

I understand where both sides are coming from. Watching from the sidelines is exhausting enough, but it's hard disappointing fans.

I told Blake if he wants to extend the tour, he can, but I've only allowed myself six months. Then I'll be back in LA working toward my new goals. Goals I never knew I wanted until I met Blake.

The idea of directing and stepping behind the camera appeals to me more than I ever thought it would. I always wanted to be an actor, but there's something to be said about stepping back and getting the recognition without the overabundance of attention.

I can't wait to start the next chapter in my life, and I'd love to do another project with Blake. Until then, I'm playing groupie to a boy band and following Eleven around the world.

And even though they warned me how crazy tours can get, no matter how much I thought I was prepared, it is nothing like the real deal.

From the sidelines, I get an amazing view between what the guys see onstage and how the audience reacts to them.

They only had a few weeks to rehearse after finishing off their album, but you wouldn't know it. They move in sync, their harmonies are still the best harmonies that have ever hit my ears —even if I'm tone-deaf—and you can tell by watching them that they're a team.

Lyric is their opening act, and it's amazing to see his latest single hitting the Billboard charts because of the exposure he's getting. Concert video of Ryder joining Lyric onstage for a duet has gone viral. Ryder's kid and her mother are still heavily surrounded by bodyguards, which Ryder hates, but it looks like it will be necessary for the foreseeable future.

Because Eleven are back. They're breaking down barriers and becoming queer icons around the entire world.

I've never felt prouder of another person before. I could watch

Blake perform all day. He really is the quietly charming one of the group, and he plays it up so well. Every now and then, during a show, he'll turn to where I'm standing offstage, and my heart tries to explode.

Lyric is usually at my side, still riding high from his own performance, and Brix is too mostly, though he disappears intermittently to check with his security team.

This is a once-in-a-lifetime opportunity, and there's no way I could ever forget it. This is the kind of thing you tell random people at the nursing home when you're old, senile, and have no idea what day it is or where you are. "I once toured with Eleven."

They'll reply, "Sure you did, old man. Whoever they are."

Then I'll complain about today's music and yell at the nurses to get off my lawn. I can't wait. Hey, Ash and Max say I never have long-term goals. Look at me now!

After another show in God knows where we are now, Blake comes off the stage, his blond hair soaked with sweat and his shirt drenched, and he kisses me hard.

He's always so alive and energetic after a gig. You'd think he'd be exhausted, but no, that comes the next day. I revel in these moments because the adrenaline filling his veins, the high, it leads to the best sex I've ever had.

Tonight, he's too impatient to wait until everyone is done showering in the dressing room, and we head back to the hotel for the night. Blake waves to the guys and drags me out the backstage door and into an awaiting custom Escalade without showering at all.

The partition between the driver and us is up, and as soon as we get on the road, Blake doesn't hesitate to get on his knees.

"I'm going to suck you off, but we're only a few minutes away from the hotel, so you need to come fast but not too hard. I need you to get it up again as soon as we get back to our room so you can fuck me."

"It might be impossible to promise that."

When Blake gets like this, he wrings me out with one orgasm. Then all I wish for is rest. Or sleep. Or death. A happy death.

He unzips my pants and frees my cock, while the car jostles over potholes and turns a corner. I have to hold on to his shoulders to keep him upright.

"If it's too much, I can always fuck you when we get back to the room." He doesn't let me respond before he sucks down my entire length to the back of his throat.

I throw my head against the seat. Not many men I've been with have wanted to—or could—fit all of me in their mouth. But Blake … I shudder at the pressure of his throat constricting around the head of my dick. Blake was determined to learn how.

My body breaks into an immediate sweat, trying to stave off orgasm. I'm trapped in a never-ending circle of wanting to tell Blake to go easy so I don't come and can still fuck him but then also wanting to unload down his throat.

I'm right on the cusp of my dick taking the decision out of my hands when the car pulls to a stop, and Blake slowly releases my cock with one long suck.

"Out of time. At least now you can fuck me."

The driver opens the car door, and I frantically tuck myself away. Thank God paparazzi aren't waiting outside the hotel like they have been at some places, or this shot would be everywhere.

Blake climbs out first, and I barely have my footing when he drags me through the hotel and up to our suite. "I need to shower first before you can get me all dirty. I'm sweaty in places you really don't want to put your mouth."

"Mm, after that little sample in the car, I'm not going to be able to hold out until you're out of the shower."

Blake tilts his head. "Fuck me in the shower?"

"You have the best ideas."

"I've heard relationships are all about compromising."

"Well, this is a great compromise."

We rush to the bathroom and strip down. Blake nips and kisses my skin, my neck, my chest.

Then he reaches for the lube in my toiletries bag on the bathroom counter while I turn on the giant walk-in shower.

This hotel has to know that people have sex in here when they make it big enough for eight people.

Blake throws the lube at me. "Oil up." He ducks his head under the spray and quickly washes himself with soap. I've never understood the advertisers who always put people in the shower to sell products until right this minute as I watch him lather up and touch himself.

Then, with a glimmer in his eye, he turns his back to me, leans over and rests his forearms against the wall, and shakes that delectable ass at me.

We were both tested, and now we don't bother with condoms. I prep him fast, and as I press my swollen head against his opening and he lets me in, I still can't get over how different it feels.

Not only because there's nothing between us, but because our bond has never been stronger.

Do I worry things will change once this tour is over and our lives take different directions? I wouldn't be me if I didn't have thoughts like that. But one thing I am sure of is that if things were ever to end between Blake and me, it wouldn't be because we didn't try.

I try with him every day because no one has ever made me feel this loved. This cherished. Or this wanted.

Blake wants me for more than my looks. More than my body.

He wants me for me, and I've never had that before.

I push in and out of him, harder and harder. The hot water beats down on my back, and I'm already way too close to coming. I slow my thrusts, and he protests.

"No!"

"Have. To," I say between hard breaths. "You need to come before I do."

"Screw that." He pushes back and starts fucking himself on

my dick. "I need you to fill me up. I need you to take me. And if you do come before me, I can finish in your mouth."

Blake keeps going, and I don't stop him. I can't, no matter how much I want to make sure he gets something out of this too.

"Jordan," Blake rasps, and I can't hold back. Before I know it's hit me, I'm already coming and shuddering inside him.

I still pump in and out of him until I'm empty, and then I drop my head to the middle of his shoulder blades. I don't want to pull out of him yet, but he has other ideas.

He presses himself closer to the wall so my cock slips from his ass, and then he turns around. "No passing out yet. You have a job to do." He grips my shoulder and pushes me down to my knees, but I'm still trying to catch my breath.

"Hang on," I say.

"It's okay. You don't have to do the work. Just suck on the tip because this will be all over so fast."

I wrap my lips around the head of his dick, and he jerks himself off into my mouth. It's hot and so damn sexy, it's impossible to take my eyes off his.

He bites his lip and breathes through his nose, and then when he comes, he throws his head back, exposing his long neck. I watch as he swallows in time with me, his Adam's apple moving up and down in sync with mine.

Blake wipes the corner of my mouth and then leans down and kisses the same spot. "You spilled a little."

I stand, wrapping my arms around him and maneuvering us back under the water. "I couldn't help it. You came hard."

"Is it me, or has sex on tour been ..." He purses his lips, trying to think of the right word.

"A compilation of fucking as hard and fast as we can—a *cum*pilation, if you will."

"Exactly. Is it hotel sex? Why's it so much more intense?"

"I think it has to do with your adrenaline levels. Have to say, I'm not complaining at all. In fact, when is your next tour?"

Blake doesn't smile, though. "Actually, I have to talk to the guys about that."

His sudden serious tone and melancholy is not like Blake at all. I get the bad feeling that Eleven's reunion tour might be their last encore.

CHAPTER 30
BLAKE

I LOVE TOURING, I love the guys, there's no denying that, but I didn't expect to miss acting as much as I have.

Going onstage every other night, singing, performing, and goofing around with the rest of Eleven has brought back enough nostalgia to last a lifetime.

But that's just it. With one tour, I already feel like we're back on that never-ending cycle of pumping out songs and performing them like trained monkeys.

I keep my mouth shut, though. At least for now.

Show after show, the high never fades, but the doubt in the back of my mind grows. And when the others mention dates we can try to fit in another album, another tour, when we haven't even finished this one yet, all I can bring myself to do is nod and smile.

Jordan tells me to talk to the guys, but I don't want a repeat of what happened last time. I don't want to go our separate ways and fall out of touch.

These guys are my brothers, and I worry my hesitance will cause drama. With all the Ben and Jordan issues still being played out in the media—who really cheated on who, is Jordan's and my relationship real or a rebound, am I really bisexual?—I've had enough drama for the next few years.

But as the tour winds down, I know I have to say something, because that's what this whole reunion has been about: doing things the way we want to, leading our own story, and having fun.

The tour was split, two months in the US, two months overseas, and then two months back in America and Canada.

It's the last week when I finally gather the courage to bring it up. We're on a plane on our way back to California for the last few shows, so we have time, and none of us can escape. I refuse to get off this plane angry.

"So ..." I start. Jordan squeezes my hand beside me. "What's the plan for after the tour for everyone?"

There's an awkward silence that falls between everyone.

"I, uh, signed the *Fandom* contract," Mason says.

"That's awesome." It's only a three-month gig, though, so that doesn't fill me with confidence that he doesn't want to get stuck into the next album right afterward.

I could maybe do a film in that time.

"You have the press tour for *Faking It*, don't you?" Harley asks me.

"Yeah. Then I'm hoping to shoot something else. Don't know what yet."

"My movie," Jordan says.

I'm dying to do that, whatever it will be, but if I only get to do one movie in between now and the next Eleven album, I'm going to be disappointed.

The other three are all quiet.

"Well, I'm recording a second album," Lyric says.

"I'm producing," Ryder adds.

Harley bites his lip, and I narrow my eyes at him.

"Why do I get the feeling you're holding something back?" I ask.

"I ... I have an idea."

The rest of us groan. Harley and his ideas.

"No, no. You might all like it. Maybe. I'm not sure yet." Harley glances at Mason. "This is not me wanting to abandon you, so please don't run away to Montana for me even suggesting it, okay?"

Mason flips him off.

Harley takes a deep breath. "Watching Lyric onstage this whole tour … I … umm …" He says the next part in a rushed voice, and I can barely catch it all. "I want to develop my record label more and maybe take a break from recording and touring. Not just with Eleven but my solo stuff too." Harley lets out a loud breath like it was hard for him to get that out.

Then, out of the corner of my eye, I see Denver relax like the weight of the world left his shoulders. "Oh, thank fuck. I had an idea myself. I've kind of taken on the role of Mason's manager, and I realized … It's probably stupid—"

"It's not stupid," Mason says.

"I want to start a management company," Denver blurts.

"That's amazing," I say. "Truly. And if I'm being honest, the reason I brought this whole thing up is I want to go back to acting. I'd love to do another album and tour, don't get me wrong. I love you guys, and this has been a perfect escape for me, but that's all music is to me anymore—an escape from my real job, which is making movies. I'd love to do a couple in between Eleven stuff. Unless you guys want to not do another Eleven album. I'm cool with that too."

"I don't want to say goodbye to Eleven," Harley says.

There are rounds of agreements on that.

"We all came back because we wanted to prove something, and we've done it," Harley continues. "We could walk away if we all wanted to, but this tour … it has been amazing. I'd want to do it again, but maybe in a few years?"

"How does another three sound?" Ryder asks. "A break will give me time with Kaylee, more time to produce, which I love. Mason finds the talent on his reality show, Denver manages them,

I produce them, and Harley puts them out on his label." He looks at me. "Oh, and Blake can …"

"I can cheer you all on while I watch from the sidelines. I'm serious when I say music isn't my entire life anymore. I love that it is for all of you, but I have a new life now." I look at Jordan. "One I'm really excited about."

Jordan leans in. "I told you to just talk to them."

"I think we were all a little scared to tell the truth," Harley says, overhearing. "But it sounds like we're on the same page. We'll always be a family. We'll keep recording and touring as long as the fans want us, but in between, let's take things for ourselves. We've given the last ten years to our fans. I want to enjoy being a label exec, enjoy living with my partner." He looks lovingly at Brix. "I want to take a break every now and then and enjoy life without thinking about work."

We all gasp in unison, like we'd planned it.

"Oh no, this is a dream, isn't it?" I say. "No way in hell those words came out of Harley Valentine's mouth."

"I'm more in fear of this plane going down," Mason says. "Surely Harley wanting to take a break is, like, end of the world type shit?"

"Zombie apocalypse when we land for sure," Denver adds.

Harley crosses his arms. "I hate you all."

"They have a point," Brix says. "After this tour, we're going on vacation, and I bet you a million dollars you can't go a single day without your phone or talking business."

"Challenge thrown, big guy. Also, you don't have a million dollars, so what do I get if you lose?"

"Me? For the rest of your life?"

"Well, that kind of feels like an unfair bet." Harley pouts.

"Are you saying I'm not worth a million dollars?"

Harley smirks. "I really want to be a smartass here, but no, I need to say this. You're worth a lot more than that."

Brix narrows his eyes. "At least a million and one dollar, right?"

"Exactly."

Everyone on the plane laughs, but Harley and Brix's bet reminds me of Jordan and myself and how this all began.

One simple bet changed my entire life, and I have Jordan to thank for it.

"Where are we going?" Jordan asks when he realizes I'm not heading toward his apartment or to Denver's.

It has been so fucking hard to keep this surprise a secret, especially since Jordan and I have been basically inseparable since the tour ended.

We spent two weeks in Cabo, enjoying each other over and over again and forgetting about the future, our work, or what else was going on, but now we're back.

We have meetings scheduled with writers, producers, and studios, and it's not long until *Faking It* comes out in theaters. We're going to be busier than we possibly ever have been, which is exactly why I've been covertly doing something that will mean we don't have to miss each other when we're working.

"Seriously, where are we going?" Jordan asks again.

"You're the most impatient person I know."

"You pronounced *important* wrong."

He's that too, which is what this is all about. I want to come home to him, spend my life with him, and I want to build a future with him.

There will be times we'll be apart, like when we're shooting on location, but at the end of the day, I want Jordan Brooks to be my home.

Eleven is my family, but Jordan is my everything.

When I pull into a quiet street and drive up the hilly road, landing at a gated house, Jordan frowns at me.

"Who's house is this?"

I use the clicker to open the gate and then grin at him.

"Did you … did you finally get yourself a place? I have to say, I'm kind of relieved. Being a boy band gazillionaire and having roommates was becoming weird."

I snort. "Not a gazillionaire. But you're half right."

"No, no, I think you living with Mason and Denver was becoming creepy. I was beginning to wonder when you were going to ask to swing with them. I had my answer all prepared."

"What answer would that be?" I hold up my hand. "And choose wisely, or I might take back your surprise."

"That you're the only man for me. Duh." He smiles innocently.

"Liar."

"Okay, I was going to make a joke about needing to wash my asshole first, but come to think of it, even the joke makes me feel weird. Which … is weird in general. Because I'm used to wanting an open relationship. It's how I've protected myself in the past. I never believed anyone could be just mine, so I reinforced that theory by encouraging people to go elsewhere. But with you …"

I reach over and squeeze his leg as I navigate the car up the long drive. "I don't want to be with anyone else."

"I don't want you to be either."

I park out front. "Good. Because I bought you something." I get out of the car and meet Jordan around at the hood.

He still looks confused, but he's slowly catching on. He glances between the house and me.

That's when I hold up the key.

"Me … You … bought …"

"Remember when you bet me ten million dollars that Marcus Talon would win another Super Bowl?"

"And then he won the very next one? Yeah, I remember rubbing it in your face."

"I'm paying up. I bought this house for me but also for you. It's ours. If you want it."

He looks up at the massive mansion again, the hard lines and box shape. "I haven't even seen inside yet, and I love it." He turns to me. "I love you."

"You'll move in with me?"

"Fuck yes. I have to call Ash, and—"

I take his hand. "Why don't you wait until you see inside first?"

While we were on tour with Eleven, I met Ash and Max briefly one night when they came to the hotel room before I needed to be at sound check, but I knew Jordan would want to see them for this.

So I flew them here.

As soon as we open the door, the two of them are there with smiles on their faces.

Jordan barely acknowledges them. "Are these marble floors? Check out the chandelier!"

Ash clears his throat.

"It comes with its very own Ash and Max?" Jordan yells and then rushes to hug them both. He looks back at me over his shoulder. "This is my favorite feature of the house."

"I thought you'd like it."

When they pull out of the hug, Max slaps Jordan's shoulder. "I never thought I'd see the day where you'd settle down with someone, but you have a winner with Blake. Ever since he picked us up from the airport, he has not shut up about how great you are. And if anyone can see past all your bullshit, they have to be a keeper."

Jordan holds his heart. "Aww, that was almost a compliment you gave me. Good try."

Ash rolls his eyes at both of them. "Go check out the rest of your new house, and then meet us on the terrace for drinks."

"We have a terrace?" Jordan exclaims.

Fuck, he's cute when he's excited.

I take him by the hand and show him everything else the house has. A gym, a music room for me to play in, a steam room, a hot tub outside with a pool, and then I show him our bedroom with floor-to-ceiling windows that overlook a long expanse of valley and LA in the distance.

"Is it too much?" I ask and am nervous about the answer.

"No. It's … everything." Jordan steps closer to me. "You give me everything, and I never knew I could feel this way. Like my heart wants to explode and break at the same time."

"Break?" I croak.

"At the idea that this could all go away. I want to hold on too tightly and am scared of losing it all."

"I know there'll be times where those old doubts will come back. I'd be lying if I said I didn't have doubts myself. Not because of you or who you are, but because of this industry. I want to do this right. And I want us to last."

"I want us forever," Jordan whispers.

And in that moment, he gives me everything as well.

EPILOGUE

BLAKE

THREE YEARS LATER

Waking up in your very own private hotel in the Virgin Islands is supposed to be relaxing. And okay, it might only be our very own for a month, and it's technically a working vacation, but still, getting woken up by Harley knocking on the door to my villa telling me to get my lazy ass out of bed and to work should not be allowed.

I roll over, and the other side of the bed is cold and empty. I sit up to get my bearings and spot Jordan at the small dining table in our villa. He has his reading glasses on—a new addition he hates because, in his words, he's never felt older—and is looking over something on his laptop. Probably another script a studio has sent him that they want him to direct.

Where Ben's career took a sharp nosedive after his bad behavior was exposed, Jordan's has only soared. His directorial debut was critically acclaimed, and it made him a big name instantly.

As for mine, I've had two major roles in blockbuster movies that surpassed Coby Godspeed in both box office earnings and my paycheck, but I'm still searching for that one golden role. I'm honing my craft and learning new things every day. I might not have been recognized by the Academy Awards yet, but I also have faith I'll get there eventually. Even if it takes seven nominations before I get the coveted win like Leonardo DiCaprio, I'm willing to put in the work.

With both Jordan and me solidly working, it's rare to be on vacation together, and we've spent a lot of the last three years on location away from each other, but we've never been stronger as a couple.

Our first time apart, we had some separation issues, some teething problems, but as we settled into our new normal between our careers and each other, we found a way that works for us.

It involves a lot of communication and naked video calls.

"This is supposed to be a vacation," I say to my very distracted boyfriend. His eyes are glued to the screen in front of him.

He doesn't even look away as he answers. "For me. Didn't you hear Harley? You have to get to work."

I slip out of bed and approach him, my cock hard and tenting my boxer briefs. Then I throw my leg over him and straddle his waist. He finally leans back and looks me in the eye.

"You need a proper break, or you'll burn out," I say.

"Says the guy who hasn't stopped working for three years."

"Okay, I admit we both need a break, but you forget that working with the guys from Eleven is relaxing for me. They don't put pressure on me—they're like my brothers. And when we work, it's actually fun for me."

"Reading scripts is fun for me too. Especially this one. You should read it. I recall us agreeing to do films together once upon a time."

We haven't found the right project to collaborate on yet. My agent regretfully advised me against Jordan's directorial debut, and Jordan didn't want the pressure of tanking a movie that could've been make-or-break for my entire career.

"What's the role?" I ask.

"It's right up your alley. It's about SEAL Team Six. I want you as the lead, and there's no way your agent will say no."

I groan.

"What?" Jordan frowns.

"I'm going to have to go back on the Coby diet, aren't I? All protein and muscle building."

Jordan's face morphs into a grin. "Is that a yes? You haven't even read the script."

"I trust you." I lean in and kiss him softly, but he pulls away far too soon.

"Are you sure you don't want to read the script? Remember what happened the last time you skimmed one?"

"Yeah, my life changed for the better. I have no regrets."

Jordan kisses me this time and runs his hand down my back to my ass. He grips tight and moans into my mouth, and then—

There's another knock on the door. "Hope you're decent!" Harley yells.

"We're not," I call out. "And I know you won't come in here because the thought of me or any of the Eleven guys having sex weirds you out."

"I won't go in there, but Brix will if I tell him to."

Shit. He has me there.

"Fine. I'll be down in five. Just let me get some clothes on."

"In five minutes and one second, my gorgeous man is coming in."

I climb off Jordan's lap, and he protests.

"How do they have a key to our villa?"

"Harley probably had keys made for all of our rooms so we don't slack off."

"So this is going to be a regular thing? Harley threatening to come in here while we're having sex?" Jordan asks.

"When we're having sex while I'm supposed to be working, yes."

"Weren't you the one who just said I should be relaxing? Sex is relaxing."

I poke him. "Sex with me is better than relaxing. It's on fire. It's the best. It's indescribable. It's not … relaxing."

Jordan laughs. "Well, after we've both blown our load, I have to say I'm pretty relaxed."

I nod. "I'll allow that. Okay, time to get dressed and write some songs." After I throw on some shorts and a T-shirt, I kiss Jordan goodbye and say, "At least go to the pool or the lagoon today. Get some sun."

He gasps. "And age my flawless skin?"

"Sunblock. Use it."

"I promise to go for a swim later. Will that make you happy?"

"Yes, but please also make it skinny-dipping and in the pool in front of the room we're writing in. Please."

"Anything for you."

I'm halfway to the door when it flings open, and Brix stands there all intimidating and huge.

"I'm ready."

He cocks his brow but doesn't say anything, and I follow him across the property to the main building of the hotel. The view is breathtaking. All white beaches and blue ocean.

As we enter, I pretend the other four aren't glaring at me. "Who's ready to get to work?"

On cue, the baby strapped to Ryder's chest in one of those sling things starts crying.

"Looks like Riff is against working today," I say.

Ryder pins me with a look. "He has been sleeping for the last hour. You know, when we were supposed to start?"

"Funny. I was sleeping too."

Ryder stands and starts rocking the baby. "Someone text Lyric to come get his baby."

"*His* baby?" Harley asks.

"Yes. When he cries, he's Lyric's. When he's adorable, he's mine. And when he has a dirty diaper, he's Maggie's."

When Ryder and Lyric announced they were having a baby with Maggie, the mother of Ryder's daughter, we were supportive, though their situation is unconventional. They figured they co-parent Kaylee so well together, and they all wanted another child, so it made sense to do it together. And with Lyric's second album breaking records and hitting the top of the charts, it's probably the best scenario having Maggie close. Ryder's been producing here and there for Harley's label, but his time is more split between Lyric's career and his kids.

I'm sure Mason and Denver will be next on the kid front. The last time all of us were in the same room was at their very private, very intimate wedding ceremony in Montana. Which then, of course, had photos leaked all over the tabloids. Somehow. Because that's how these things work. Some things never change.

I've seen each of the guys individually over the last three years. It's common for two or three of us to be seen together in the media when we catch up. One time we even managed four of us, but Ryder couldn't make it because he was on tour with Lyric.

Mason is back in the spotlight more than ever before with him judging *Fandom*. It's up to its fourth season now. Denver's still his manager, and they have started Denver's management company together. A lot of their employees represent clients who have signed with Harley's constantly growing record label.

Harley aimed for small but overshot it. By a lot. But that's the Harley Valentine effect. Overachiever that he is.

He really has found his perfect partner in Brix. Brix is there to remind Harley when he's overworking and to take a break, and Harley never fights him on it. He's probably the only person in the world who can tell Harley to slow down, and Harley listens. The amount of trust and love between them is palpable as it is infinite. Brix still runs Harley's security, but when the media caught on that they're together, he had to hire more guys. He's less of a bodyguard and more of a target now, but he's always by Harley's side.

All of us did as we promised, and we've never fallen out of touch again, so when it came time for us to assess a new album and schedule, we all agreed to meet here and see what we can come up with.

Even if this trip doesn't eventuate to a new album, I'm happy to just be here with them.

I wasn't lying when I said to Jordan that Eleven is my escape. They are my vacation.

We're all working toward something bigger, something better, but with Jordan's support and love, and my best friends close by, it's hard to think there is anything better out there.

Jordan is my everything. And whether we're recording, touring, or just hanging out, Eleven is forever.

THANK YOU

Thank you so much for reading *Encore*! The Eleven guys definitely sent me on a journey I was not expecting, and I'm sad to say goodbye to them. If you want more Eleven antics, you can sign up for my newsletter and receive a bonus scene with the boys on tour. We get to revisit each and every Eleven member and their men. *Warning: contains a boy band rivalry that only exists in Harley's head, public displays of adoration, and all the usual snark and love these boys have for each other.*

Get it here:

https://claims.prolificworks.com/free/hkfNqXbF

I need to give one last special thanks to my readers for their suggestions.

Thank you to Jeannie Cooper for suggesting the name Eleven for my boy band. When I hear that name now, I can't help thinking of my boys.

And to Samantha Blundell for giving Harley, Ryder, Denver, Mason and Blake their names.

I also have to thank my friend Todd for suggesting the nature in which Jordan and Ben's relationship crashed and burned (literally).

Want to stay up to date on everything Eden Finley? Join my reader group: https://www.facebook.com/groups/absolutelyeden/ Alternatively, you can join my mailing list: http://eepurl.com/bS1OFH

WHAT'S NEXT IN THE EDEN FINLEY UNIVERSE?

Eden Finley fans can look forward to so many new things in the future!

For those of you who read Pop Star, book one in the Famous series, you would have met Iris and Trav from the Mike Bravo team.

I'm currently working on the first book in the Mike Bravo series "Iris" and hope to have it released early 2022. Who's his love interest? Someone you haven't met before, but let's just say Iris meets his match.

My cowriter, Saxon James, and I are also finishing up our debut series CU Hockey. But never fear, we love writing together so much, I'm sure we'll find other projects to collaborate on. Maybe we already have … *winky face*

If you want to keep to date on any of our collaborations, you can join our joint group, Pucking Disasters:

https://www.facebook.com/groups/puckingdisasters

ALSO BY EDEN FINLEY

https://amzn.to/2zUlM16

https://www.edenfinley.com

FAKE BOYFRIEND SERIES

Fake Out

Trick Play

Deke

Blindsided

Hat Trick

Novellas:

Fake Boyfriend Breakaways: A short story collection

Final Play

CU HOCKEY SERIES

Co-written with Saxon James

Power Plays & Straight A's

Face Offs & Cheap Shots

Goal Lines & First Times

Line Mates & Study Dates

Puck Drills & Quick Thrills

VINO & VERITAS

Sarina Bowen's True North Series

Headstrong

STEELE BROTHERS

Unwritten Law

Unspoken Vow

ROYAL OBLIGATION

Unprincely (M/M/F)

FAMOUS SERIES

Pop Star

Spotlight

Fandom

Encore

Novellas:

Rockstar Hearts

SONGS THAT INSPIRED THE FAMOUS SERIES

POP STAR/ Harley:
"I Will Always Love You" Whitney Houston version.
Anything by Lewis Capaldi.

SPOTLIGHT/ Ryder & Lyric:
"Into the Unknown" Panic! At the Disco version.
"Take Me to Church" Hozier.
"It's Time" Imagine Dragons. (Really anything Imagine Dragons.)

FANDOM/ Denver & Mason
"Jealous" Labrinth.
"More than Words" Extreme.

ENCORE/ Blake:
"Afterglow" Ed Sheeran.
"Kiss Me" Ed Sheeran.
Anything else Ed Sheeran.

ACKNOWLEDGMENTS

I want to thank my long list of betas, especially Leslie Copeland from Les Court Services, Sandra from One Love editing for copy-edits, and a big thanks to Lori Parks for one last read through for those ninja typos that have the ability to sneak through many rounds of editing.

Lastly, a big thanks to Linda from Foreword PR & Marketing for helping get this book out.

www.ingramcontent.com/pod-product-compliance
Lightning Source LLC
Chambersburg PA
CBHW020749190726
48285CB00006B/1941